Robert Rush is th
works of fiction a

With thanks to
Toby Roxburgh
whose idea it was

Robert Rush

The Birthday Treat

Macdonald Futura Publishers

A Futura Book

First published in Great Britain by
Macdonald Futura Publishers Ltd

ISBN 0 7088 2104 9

Filmset, printed and bound in Great Britain by
Hazell Watson & Viney Ltd, Aylesbury, Bucks

Macdonald Futura Publishers Ltd
Paulton House
8 Shepherdess Walk
London N1 7LW

PROLOGUE

Their beautiful house was already sold and strangers were moving in. The few pieces of furniture they were able to take with them were being crated up by the shippers to be sent on ahead, though nobody knew for sure when they would see them again. Not until they had found a house in England and that could take forever! Her Mommy and Daddy were living in a motel while they made the final arrangements for departure and she, Lois, who did not want to go at all, was staying over with Grandma Carradine.

'Why do we have to go at all, Grandma?' she asked, scuffing her sneaker in the dry dirt of what had once been a fine garden.

'Now, Lois, you know why. Your Daddy's told you. I've told you . . .'

'Tell me again, Grandma. *Please!*'

The old lady, who seemed to shrink a little each year so that Lois sometimes thought that, by the time she got to be all grown up, Grandma would be like Alice – small enough to go down a rabbit's hole – sighed and set down her newspaper.

'Because people get stale, stuck always in one place, and people get homesick. Your mother's been here a long time. Naturally she hankers after her homeland, her own folks.'

'She doesn't have any folks,' Lois corrected her petulantly.

'I mean other English people. If you ask me, she never would have settled here if it hadn't been for your Daddy.'

'So it's all her fault,' Lois said, kicking a pebble hard across the browning, patchy lawn.

'It's nobody's fault, sweetheart. And don't you go thinking such things. Your Daddy wants it, too. He's been restless for the last two years or more and there are opportunities over there . . .'

'America is the land of opportunity,' Lois interrupted stubbornly.

Mrs Carradine reached out and took the sullen-looking child by the hand, drawing her close.

'Now listen here. Opportunity is what you make of it. The way you're going on, you're set to waste a chance most girls would grab with both hands. It's an adventure, sweetheart. You'll be able to see Europe and all the beautiful sights there. And best of all, by being cheery and doing your best you'll be able to make your Mommy and Daddy happy. After all, you are half English.'

'Well I don't want to be. I want to stay here with my friends and you and . . .'

'Heavens, child, what a pessimist you are. You'll soon make new friends . . .'

'I won't,' she said with gravity, her lower lip trembling. 'I just know I won't.'

'Sure you won't if you make up your mind not to.'

'And you . . . I'll miss you.'

'But you'll come visit me. I'll still be here.'

'Promise? Promise not to die?'

The old woman's laughter rang loud and clear through the neglected garden.

'Not until you give me permission. Now run along and amuse yourself. It's time for my nap.'

Grandma Carradine's house was spooky in the afternoons when she took her nap and Coral, the maid, liked to be left alone in the kitchen to listen to her radio and prepare vegetables for dinner. The house creaked in the afternoon heat, stretching its dry old timbers to hold a ghostly dialogue with itself. The shades were drawn in all the rooms, so that the antique furniture and faded imported rugs looked neglected, like they would when Grandma died and left them. But the house was preferable to the summer heat of the dried-up garden and so Lois braved it. She went from room to room, touching the elaborate and heavy furniture, setting the crystal pendants of an ornate clock tinkling like forgotten windchimes, peering at the fading photographs of Grandpa, whom she did not remember and must always be a ghost to her, and of her Daddy's younger self who also, in a puzzling way, was sort of dead.

Above everything in the world she loved her Daddy. The only good thing about selling up and leaving everything she knew and cared about, was that Daddy would be there with her all the time. The only thing she didn't understand was why Daddy had to go and marry an English person in the first place. She hated the English half of her blood, imagined it a different colour, which made her veins tingle and feel funny. Somewhere, she was certain of it, there was a doctor who could, probably for a whole lot of money, extract her English blood and give her a transfusion of good, red American blood that would make her all American. And then maybe she wouldn't have to go to England. Maybe then it would be illegal for them to take her.

Such schemes invariably occupied her lonely afternoons when, curled on her own bed, she tried to distract herself with a comic-book or by trying to pin up her floppy brown hair. These thoughts represented her optimistic moods and most often they gave way to a blacker view of the world and her future. This creaky old house had become Limbo to her. Heaven was the house on Marshall Drive, within spitting distance of the ocean, that she had known for most of her life. And where she was going was Hell: a place so black and terrible, so cold and wet and full of strange creatures that the prospect of going there, perhaps for ever, seemed to her worse than dying. She considered begging her parents to let her stay behind, in Limbo, with Grandma, even though it would break her heart to be separated from Daddy. Or, since she knew really that none of them would agree, of barricading herself in her room and refusing to go. Or going on hunger strike. Or running away. Or just dying of sheer misery.

She saw them, her mother, grandmother and aunt, all in picture hats with trailing vapours of black veiling, filing past her coffin. Her mother looked down angrily at her, while her grandmother dabbed at reddened eyes with a black lace handkerchief. Last of all came her Daddy, handsome in his mourning suit and dazzling white shirt. His face was terrible to behold. Beside himself with grief, he flung himself across her satin-lined casket, wailing in an unearthly way. Daddy scared her. She was rigid, cold, unable to reach her arms around his neck to comfort him. She tried to call out to him but her lips were embalmed and frozen. And when Daddy grabbed her up, gathering her into his arms, her body was stiffer than board, fragile as eggshells. As he screamed to her and hugged her, her body began to crack and flake, to split apart and fall like dust on to the satin bed of death. She tried to tell him:

Daddy. Don't, Daddy. You're killing me.

She jerked upright on the bed, sweating. The roller blind rattled up with a scary, rasping noise. The room was flooded with sharp light. She saw Coral silhouetted at the window.

'Oh,' she said, and let herself slump with relief.

'Milk and cookies in the library,' Coral said in her flat voice. 'Your Grandma said for you to come. And don't forget to wash up first.'

'I dreamed . . .' she began, but the impassive, preoccupied woman was already quitting the room.

Mostly, though, she dreamed of Hell, even on the nights when Mommy and Daddy came over for dinner and stayed to tuck her in and kiss her goodnight. The images of these dreams were so clear and sharp that she could have drawn them or related them like the details of a movie, if only her parents had not hushed and shushed her and told her not to think about them.

Sometimes it was like a moated castle which she had to enter even though she knew there were bad things inside. The drawbridge rattled and cranked up behind her, slammed shut. As the sound died away on the air she heard whispering and giggling, like the mice in Walt Disney's

Cinderella, but twist and turn and spin round as she might, she could never catch a glimpse of the whisperers.

Then she was walking up a long flight of stone steps, without a guard-rail. The steps spiralled upwards and she mounted them fearfully, pressed close to the damp stone wall, terrified of falling. What had been the castle below her was just a black well of nothingness into which she dared not look for fear of pitching down, falling.

Sometimes she reached the top of those steps, entered a maze of tapestry-hung corridors. She heard the sniggering, whispering voices there, the rustle of dainty clothes, but she never got to see the owners of those voices until she entered the room. The room was beyond a carved wooden door, and all the corridors, whichever direction they appeared to take, led her there. Beyond the door was a room and the room was a torture chamber. Seeing it, she flinched back from its metal horrors, screaming, but hands, unseen and cold, pushed her forward into the room. A body hung, upside down, from chains. Metal anklets bit into firm white flesh. The body swung as though with the last vestiges of life. In spite of her loathing and fear of it, she had to approach the body and when she drew close, horribly close, she saw that it was a female body, a girl's. Its full skirt hung down over its head but, worst of all, she recognized that it wore her panties. Shame made her swing round, away from this awful exposure and then she saw them. Six children, daintily, formally dressed in old-fashioned clothing crowded in the doorway. They were laughing at her and pointing with sniggering fingers. Their faces, though, were absolutely blank, like Raggedy-Ann dolls whose features had not been stitched in yet.

From this ever-changing dream she awoke sweating, the bedclothes knotted like manacles about her body and she would lie for what seemed like eternity, clutching her enormous Bugs Bunny and whispering to him that she wanted to stay, not to let them make her go to Hell.

In time, the children became the only certainty of her dreams. Often, Hell was no-place: a blank empty space in which the children floated, materializing and vanishing apparently at will; or a vast, shadowed, raftered room through which she wandered, lonely and afraid. Once, perhaps the first time she dreamed of that space, the ground suddenly ended in front of her. Her toes curled in panic over the edge of the floor and she saw, far below her, the blank, upturned faces of the children. They were waiting for her, begging her to come to them, and she knew that if she did she would die. The children seemed to be saying that they would catch her, but she knew that they would not. They were tempters and deceivers.

In time the children became sufficiently familiar for her to be able to sex them by their velvet and silk formal clothes. There were two girls and four boys. Sometimes they followed her. Sometimes her aimless path led her inevitably to where they stood.

In the worst dream of all, she wandered for the longest time along dark, twisting paths, unable to tell whether she was in or out of doors. A sudden sharp bend in the path brought her face to face with the waiting children. She had never been that close to them before. Appalled, she saw that they had developed features of a kind: narrow slits for eyes, toothless grinning mouths. The eyes and mouths were cut, incised in their blank flesh, and behind them flames danced. As the children approached her, one by one, the heat of these flames scorched her flesh. It was like they were trying to kiss or embrace her. And then, in the way of dreams, there was a stomach-lurching change of focus. She saw herself standing before their cruel gaze, with nothing on but her panties. As, in an agony, she watched herself trying to cover her vulnerable body, she saw her own head, gigantic, swollen, like a spherical wax candle, blazing.

From this dream she awoke screaming, fighting against her grandmother's frail arms.

'Hush, child, hush,' Grandma said. 'It was only a dream. A bad old dream. Grandma's here. Grandma's got you safe.'

Behind her, clutching the neck of a frumpy white nightgown, she saw Coral staring at her in tight-lipped disapproval. She lay down, teeth chattering, her head burning. Grandma's hand was cold on her forehead, cold like she was dead.

'She's got a fever, Coral. Best call the doctor and her parents. Hush now, darling. It's only the bad old fever.'

The doctor came and put her to sleep with a sharp prick in her arm. In that sleep, there were no dreams.

Her mother and father were with her a lot, and Grandma. Whenever she woke one of them was there, sitting close by her. They wiped her face with a cool towel and she told them:

'I don't want to go. Don't make me go, please.'

Once she woke when the room was dim and heard her parents arguing in low voices.

'We ought to talk it through with her.'

'No. She's just being stubborn, trying to frighten us into letting her have her own way.'

'It's a hell of a big step for a kid, Pearl.'

'I know that. But it won't make it any easier if we start pandering to her. We're going. She has to adjust to that.'

'But we ought to reassure her.'

'Okay. I give in – as usual.'

Her Daddy sat on the bed, holding her hand.

'How are you feeling, Princess?'

'My head hurts.'

'Keep still then.'

'Daddy, don't make me go to England. I'll be good. I'll do anything, only . . .'

'Shh. Steady now. Relax. Now you just try and tell me why you don't want to go.'

'I don't want to. I won't like it there.'

'See?' her mother said from the foot of the bed.

'Wait, Pearl. Is that all, baby? Is that your only reason?'

'No, Daddy.' She took a deep, shuddering breath. 'It's because something bad is going to happen to me there. I know it is. I know it, Daddy.'

'Nonsense,' her mother said, straightening the bedclothes. 'Here you could get mugged or shot – anything could happen. It's not like that in England. England's a safe place.'

'Something bad . . .' she wailed, twisting towards her father.

'Now listen to your mother. She knows. She was born there and she's telling you the truth. Didn't she ever tell you that England is the only place in the entire world they don't have a bogey-man?'

'No.' She stared at him trustingly. 'Is that true?'

'For honest, real, cross-my-heart-and-hope-to-die true.'

Her mother sat down on the other side of her then, smiling.

'Of course it's true, darling,' she said. 'And you'll be so happy there. I promise you. You'll love it.'

'It'll be your very own kingdom, Princess. You just wait and see.'

Her very own kingdom? No bogey-man at all? Her heart tripped with excitement. But what about the children, the mean, laughing, waiting-for-her children?

'What,' she said sleepily, hanging on to her father's hand, 'about the children? Are there children there?'

Her mother laughed softly and bent over her, hugging her as she lay.

'Of course there are, darling. Lots and lots of children. Nice children and they so much want to meet you and be friends with you.'

'Really? Not all of them.'

'Every last one,' Daddy promised.

31 OCTOBER

A squall of damp wind tugged at Pearl Carradine's lightweight coat as she turned back into the Crescent. She had spent ten minutes standing on the grass verge near the 'Private Road' sign, scanning the passing cars for her husband's dark blue Volvo. To the already endless-seeming list which almost constantly reeled through her head she added: winter clothes. Fourteen years in California had equipped them with no garments suitable for the English winters she, English by birth and upbringing, had increasingly remembered and missed. She pulled her coat tighter around her, reflecting for a moment that the list – an irritation in itself – had deflected her from the hard nub of anger that had lodged in her as Neil's lateness became a fact she could no longer conceal from her daughter. He *promised*, she thought, as the wind gusted again, buffeting her. It swept between two of the 'architect-designed, custom-built' houses that dotted, equidistant from each other, the Crescent. She looked at them, acknowledging for the first time that they were basically the same model, each tricked-out with the more obvious trappings of a 'style'. Number One was vaguely Georgian. Number Six, which faced it on her right, had acquired white plasterwork and black beams on the upper storey which prompted the Mercers to name it 'Elizabethan Lodge'. The windows were blank, unlit in all the houses, she realized. The dusk was deepening with massing rainclouds overhead. She shivered, not because of the wind, but because she suddenly perceived the place, their new home, as deserted and unwelcoming. This was not the England for which she had longed, felt homesick. This was . . .

She cut the thought off. She had to put a good face on things, for Lois's sake. It was quite bad enough that Neil had let their daughter down, that she had no friends to bring her presents, celebrate her birthday. Indeed, no presents at all until Neil got home, whenever that might be. Her anger flared again and drove her briskly, head down, across the road and on to the slope of their own driveway. Number Five had been described in the agents' glossy brochure as 'Spanish' and that, Pearl knew, was what had attracted Neil and Lois to it. It was the only piece of domestic architecture they had seen since coming to England that even remotely reminded them of America, their homeland, which they both missed, especially Lois. So, though she privately thought it hideous, she had allowed herself to be swept along by their enthusiasm. If it made them happy, compensated them a little for all they missed, then it was worth it to her. And she would get used to it, she vowed, just as they would settle and come to love England.

Pearl lifted her head, squared her shoulders. She would not let any of it get her down. Goddamn it, she would find a way of making this the most memorable birthday Lois had ever had. Even as she thought this her step faltered and her heart lurched. A slight movement at an upstairs window, and there she saw her daughter's face, a pale round floating behind the glass. The fading light struck the window in such a way that the bare twigs of a tree, planted in the centre of the Crescent, were reflected like a harsh black web across the face. For a horrible moment, her daughter's face seemed disfigured, misshapen, bloated; then, even as dread and panic flooded through her, it began to glow and its simple, cut-out features became clearly visible.

A sharp, slightly hysterical laugh escaped Pearl as she recognized the pumpkin lantern Lois had laboriously and grudgingly carved for Hallowe'en. In California, the house had always been filled with these lanterns, which were an essential part of Lois's birthday ritual, but here she had been forced to make do with only one. Even then, the pumpkin had had to be obtained, at vast expense, from

Harrods and Pearl was guiltily aware that she had been annoyed at Lois's lack of gratitude, her desultory carving, accompanied by endless questions about why the English did not make a big thing of Hallowe'en, 'like back home'.

Now Pearl felt a rush of warmth and sympathy for her daughter. She had carried the lantern from the lounge to her own room and lit the candle herself, no doubt feeling lonely and homesick. It seemed to Pearl a little private ceremony, touching in its simplicity, which made all the hassle of getting the pumpkin and making the thing worthwhile. She hurried to the front door and opened it, snapping on the hall light.

At once she heard Lois's eager footsteps in the uncarpeted upstairs hall.

'Daddy, Daddy,' she shouted, her voice full of that lightness and vibrancy Pearl had missed ever since they left America. Her daughter appeared at the top of the stairs, ran down the first four treads and then stopped, her face an ashen mask of disappointment.

'Oh.'

Stricken, Pearl shrugged off her coat, tears pricking her eyes.

'No, don't go back. I saw the lantern. It looks terrific. It was a really good idea to put it upstairs. Come on, darling, let's have a party.'

Slowly, very slowly, Lois turned on the stairs and came on down towards her mother with all the composed sedateness of a mature young lady.

Lois hated the dress. It was new and formal and ugly. It was an *English* dress. Navy-blue velvet with a stupid white collar and cuffs. She wore it with white knee-socks and black patent leather button-strap shoes. She'd bet she looked a hundred years old as she stared at her feet, tracking her mother into the kitchen.

This was the only completely furnished room in the house and the new bleached pine table in the dining area was set with three places, loaded with party fare. Lois stared at it from the doorway, her eyes settling on the ugly white cake that was its centrepiece. It was two cakes, really, placed side by side on a square silver board to make the figure twelve. Automatically, she counted the twelve candles, each one stuck in a little pink rosette. She thought it was dumb, ugly.

'You know, for a moment out there I thought the pumpkin lantern was *you*. Wasn't that stupid? I thought – it was just a trick of the light, of course – something had happened to your face. You see, I was expecting the lantern to be in the downstairs window . . .' Pearl turned to look at her daughter who was staring intently at the table, her bottom lip thrust out. 'It was really stupid of me because you're so pretty. How could I ever have thought . . .' Pearl came to Lois and, stopping a little, hugged her impulsively and warmly. 'I didn't mean . . . Happy birthday, darling.'

Lois knew that she was not pretty. She was interesting, intelligent-looking. She had good eyes and teeth, she knew. Back home she'd heard them all talking, Aunt Cynthia and Grandma, her mother. Grandma wouldn't even think her interesting if she could see her in this awful dress. She pulled away from her mother and went over to the table, standing so close to it that the sharp corner dug into her stomach.

'What's that?' she said, pointing to a wobbly green rabbit that made her feel slightly sick.

'It's a jelly. I got the mould specially. Isn't it sweet?'

'Why make it like that?'

'Because it's . . .fun. More interesting. I always had them when . . .'

'Why don't we have a bowl of Jello, like always?'

'Because we can't get Jello here.' Pearl heard and instantly regretted the sharpness in her voice. 'Come on, you sit here, at the head of the table. What do you think of the cake? It's a surprise.'

'I know.' Lois sat in the chair her mother pulled out for her.

'I hope it's okay. I got it from the bakery in Olton.'

'Why didn't you bake me one?'

'I will next year.'

Lois took the paper napkin from her place setting and, instead of opening it, began to tear pieces into her lap, making a lacy pattern. Pearl opened her mouth to reprove her then changed her mind. She reached across her daughter for the big glass pitcher.

'I made your favourite grape juice cocktail.'

'Thanks.'

'Now, where shall we begin?'

'I want to wait for Daddy.'

'Oh, Lois . . .'

Pearl suddenly felt exhausted, unable to keep up the pretence. But she knew she had to. She crossed the kitchen and took a cigarette from the open packet on top of the fridge. She'd been trying to cut down, meaning to give up.

'Well, why can't we? Nothing'll spoil.'

Lois's voice was querulous, whining. It scratched against Pearl's nerves. She drew heavily on her cigarette.

'Because he has obviously been delayed and there is no point in waiting. Besides, you must be starving. I know I am.' Pearl came back to the table and sat. Lois stared stubbornly down into her lap, at the now-shredded napkin. 'What would you like?'

'I'm not hungry.'

'Nonsense. Of course you are.'

Pearl picked up a box of matches she had set beside the cake and, without looking at her daughter, began to light the twelve tiny candles.

'There,' she said when they were all blazing, 'don't they look pretty?'

Lois slowly raised her eyes and looked at the cake.

'Sure.'

'Aren't you going to blow them out?'

'Mm.' She stood up, her chair scraping on the Spanish tiled floor and leaned towards the cake.

'Don't forget to make a wish.'

Lois, her face lit by the orange glow of the candles, turned her head towards her mother. The thick, neatly cut helmet of dark brown hair swung away from the right side of her face, swung dangerously near the candle flames.

'Your hair,' Pearl said. 'Be careful.'

'It's okay, Mom,' she said with that almost unnerving calm that she could sometimes display, and caught her hair back with her hand. Pursing her lips, she blew out all the candles with one breath then, straightening, she said in a soft, quiet voice:

'I wish that every boy and girl in the world will have a happy birthday.'

'Oh, darling . . .'

Pearl burst into tears.

Her very own radio/cassette recorder!

'Pearl, will you get off my goddamn back?'

The kitchen floor was littered with the fancy wrappings and the protective cardboard packaging Lois's present had come in. Heedless of the awful new dress, she sat among the debris, marvelling at this new possession. Daddy had shown her where the microphone was and how she could record her own voice.

'And what about you? Crying at the kid's birthday party? What kind of party is that?'

And there were cassettes, too. The new Elton John among them.

'You know how important this job is to me. To *us*. And Christ, Pearl, if you were to see those guys. I swear to God I feel sometimes like I'm the only person there who even heard of the twentieth century. And now we've got labour trouble over the goddamn US quota.'

Lois switched on the radio and spun the dial wildly. Snatches of music, booming English voices, hissing static, momentarily drowned out the raised voices of her parents. They were talking in the big room that wasn't fully furnished yet and their voices sounded hollow, amplified.

'I just can't handle it all by myself, Neil. I need your support. Anyway, you promised. It doesn't matter about me, but you promised *her*. It's her *birthday*. Don't you understand that?'

Lois retuned the radio.

'Wow,' she whispered. 'Real French.'

She concentrated, her eyes screwed up, trying to make sense of the too-fast French voice. She'd been good at French but she could not catch what this man was saying. Not much, anyway. Still, it was neat to have a radio that played real French. As the voice was replaced by music, she turned the dial again.

'If I don't make a go of this job, where the hell will we be? There's a lot for me to learn. Or unlearn is probably more accurate. I've *got* to get on top of it, Pearl.'

'I know, but do you have to sacrifice us while you're doing it?'

'Look, it's hard on all of us, but you seem to forget this was *your* idea. You wanted it. Not me. Not Lois. *You*. So you've damn well got to pull your weight.'

'I didn't force you to come here . . .'

'Like hell you . . .'

'I didn't.'

And now a blast from the past, a glorious golden oldie right from Radio One. The fabulous Beach Boys and 'Good Vibrations'.

Lois turned the volume up and up until the sound hurt her ears and began to distort. The plastic casing of the radio vibrated under her fingers. She snapped it off suddenly and set it aside.

'You're not trying. Neither of you. You don't want to be happy here and I am sick to death of taking the blame.'

'You don't give us a chance, hon. And you know why? You're not happy yourself.'

Lois stood up, clapped her hands over her ears until they sang, like the sound you get when you find a good old shell on the seashore and . . .

She had walked to the window, which was at the front of

the house and, looking out, her attention was suddenly caught by activity outside. The houses opposite were ablaze with lights. A station wagon was parked by the roadside and she saw children wearing masks and paper hats. For the first time in a long while she felt her pulse quicken with excitement. Her mother was wrong. They *did* have Hallowe'en. Those kids had been to a Hallowe'en party.

Kicking aside the rubbish on the floor, Lois ran to the side door. An old raincoat of her father's hung there. She reached it down and swung it like a witch's cloak about her shoulders. If only she had a mask or . . . But there was no time. She pulled the door open and dashed out into the cold and drizzly night.

Marge Beatty needed a gin and tonic: a big one. She must have been out of her mind when she offered to chauffeur the kids to that damn Hallowe'en party. And here they come, she thought, the devoted mothers of the Crescent, to claim their loud-voiced, bad-tempered little angels. Except Marion Young. Thinking of Marion made her think of Doug and she cheered up a little. She could always walk William to their door in the hope of seeing him. And that was all she could hope for, she thought, to see him. She twisted round, looking for William, who had piled out with the rest of the kids.

'Where's William?' she asked her daughter, Amanda, who sat quietly in the back seat, clutching her party trophies.

'Thanks ever so, Marge. I hope Andy behaved himself?' Ella Mercer leaned into the open window of the car.

Marge forced a smile. Ella's soft Scots accent always set her teeth on edge.

'Fine,' she said, glimpsing Sylvia Shillingworth approaching, with her lacquered Margaret Thatcher perm and studied smile.

'I was just thanking Marge,' Ella said, turning towards Sylvia.

'Yes, indeed. Bless you. I hope they haven't given you a splitting head?'

'I'll survive.'

'Hello, Amanda. Was it a nice party?'

'Yes, thank you, Mrs Shillingworth.'

It never ceased to amaze Marge that her daughter was so nice, so well-mannered. Where the hell did she get it from? Her father, of course, and Marge didn't want to think about him.

'I was looking for William. I thought I'd deliver him . . .'

Marge broke off as little Vanessa Hunter let out a squeal of fear. The children instantly drew together, closed ranks and fell silent as a figure rushed out of the darkness, from beneath the tree. Everybody turned to look at it as it whirled about the children, a great black cape swinging from its hunched shoulders.

'What the hell . . .' Marge said and began to open the door.

'Mummy,' Amanda whimpered in a tiny voice.

'Trick or treat. Trick or treat. Trick or treat.'

In a surprisingly gruff voice the figure shouted at the amazed and frightened kids. It continued to circle around them, the cape flapping, one accusatory arm stuck out in front of it as though to put the evil eye on them.

'It's all right,' Marge said automatically, and got out of the car. By the time she'd reached the pavement, Sylvia Shillingworth had identified the momentarily demonic figure.

'It's the little girl from Number Five,' Sylvia hissed. 'American, I think.'

'Stop that,' Marge shouted at her.

'You gotta give me a treat or accept a trick,' Lois shouted, breathless and still now, facing the astonished children.

'She's mad,' a boy said. 'Loony.'

'Oh now, William, you mustn't say things like that,' Ella said at once. 'It was just that you gave us such a scare, dear.'

'Trick or treat,' Lois yelled, stamping her foot hard enough to jar her kneecap.

'I think you'd better go home,' Sylvia said, 'before you catch a cold. Come along twins, Jane.'

She looked, Marge thought, exactly like a frigate in full sail as she swept past the suddenly bedraggled-looking kid and shepherded her own three off ahead of her.

'Thanks again, Marge.'

'Yes, we must all get inside before we take cold,' Ella agreed. 'Come along, Andy. And you come with me, too, Vanessa. I'll take you to your Mummy.'

'What's wrong with you? It's Hallowe'en. You gotta trick or treat.' Lois's voice rose into a shriek, cracked and tears threatened.

'You'd better go home,' Marge said coldly. 'It's not nice to frighten people. Come along, William.'

'It's all right,' William said, staring at Lois.

'I'm not leaving you here, William. Please get in the car.'

William hesitated a moment, glancing from Lois to Marge Beatty. Though he would never have admitted it, he suddenly did not want to be left alone with this crazy girl who glared at him. He walked past her, towards the car.

'You're mad,' he hissed, so quietly that only Lois heard.

'Trick or treat,' she sniffed, knuckling tears from her eyes.

Marge held the door open for William and then walked around the car.

'Go home,' she said over her shoulder.

The car roared away with unnecessary noise, circled the big tree and stopped outside Number Four. Lois did not move. She fought to control her tears. Her cheeks were burning. She saw the boy get out of the car and run up the drive. The woman shouted at him then, obviously angry, threw the car into reverse.

'I hate you,' Lois whispered. 'You're crazy, not me,' she told the curtained façade of Number Four.

The wind tugged at her father's raincoat which trailed on the muddy grass. She wanted to smash something. A rock through their windows. A rock through the windscreen of that woman's car. Anything. She looked around her in the sudden quiet, the dark, for a stone, but she could not see one. Then she saw her father in the pool of light flooding from the kitchen window and heard him call to her.

'Daddy, Daddy,' she shouted and ran towards him. 'Daddy, oh Daddy, take me home,' she sobbed as his strong, comforting arms closed with relief around her.

'I'm sorry,' Pearl said.

'So am I.'

'You're right. We've got to stop this. For Lois's sake.'

'And yours.' Neil touched her cheek.

'It will be all right,' Pearl said, resting her cheek against his hand.

'It's just the pressure. My job, the house, Lois . . .'

'She'll make friends.'

'She looked so damn cute in that dress and so . . . forlorn.'

'Now you know why I wept.'

'But no more. Promise?'

'Yes.'

Neil patted her cheek and stood up.

'Where are you going?'

'To have a talk with her. Besides, I've got a surprise for her.'

'Oh, Neil . . . What?'

'You freshen my drink and let Lois tell you when you go to tuck her in.'

'You make me feel ashamed.'

'Don't, honey.'

'No. It's true. You're a good father. I shouldn't have said . . .'

'Just fix the drink. I won't be a minute.'

She wanted to cry again, but this time with relief and happiness.

'Suddenly there was this demented child leaping around like a dervish and screeching, "Trick or treat. Trick or treat." '

Amanda, seated on her father's lap, flinched at Marge Beatty's piercing imitation of Lois Carradine's voice. John stroked the soft skin of her forearm and, putting his face close to hers, asked, 'Were you frightened?'

'Yes.' Amanda tilted her head back and regarded him with her very serious grey eyes.

'God knows what her parents must be thinking of,' Marge went on, pouring herself another drink. 'If you ask me, she's got a screw loose.'

'I hope she'll go away,' Amanda said, still looking at her father.

'No, love. You'll soon make friends with her. Shall I tell you something? I bet she was more scared than you.'

'Not her,' Marge said, rattling the toning row of lilac, purple and mauve plastic bangles on her right wrist. 'She's a little monster.'

John Beatty saw the flicker of fear in his child's eyes. All her young life she'd been plagued by nightmares, crippling terrors.

'It's all right,' he told her. 'She's just a little girl.'

Marge snorted. 'You didn't see her.'

'I feel as though I did. That's enough, Marge. Anyway, it's time this little lady went up the wooden hill.' He stood, swinging his doll-like daughter in the crook of his arm.

'Oh, can you see to her?' Marge said, her lips pouted a little, as though deliberately to remind him how attractive she was, how much he desired her. 'I promised I'd look in on poor Marion. Just for half an hour. She gets so low.'

'So that's why you got all dressed up,' John said before he could stop himself.

'This?' Marge held out her arms and looked down at

herself with feigned surprise. The gesture caused the soft wool of her tight purple trousersuit to tighten invitingly over her breasts. 'Only your lectures on the practice of economy prevented me throwing it out last winter,' she said.

John knew for a fact that the suit was only months old, bought in a seasonal sale from the boutique where Marge worked part-time, but he wasn't prepared to say so, not in front of Amanda. He wondered, not for the first time, why Marge persisted in these little lies, the pretence that men never remembered women's clothing when they dressed with no other thought in mind but to attract them.

'It's time Douglas did something to cheer Marion up,' he said, moving towards the door.

'Oh, don't be so mean. Men can't. They don't know anything about post-natal depression. You've never had it,' she said, following him to the door.

'Neither have you,' he pointed out quietly.

'That was just good luck. Honestly, you're so bloody selfish. Don't you ever have anything to do with men when you grow up, Amanda. Mummy'll see you in the morning.'

As John carried Amanda up the stairs, she looked at him gravely and asked, 'Is she a monster, Daddy?'

'No, darling. Just a little girl.'

'Promise?'

'I promise.'

'But Mummy said . . .'

'Mummy exaggerates. Now you forget all about her, okay?'

'She frightened me. I won't ever like her. I wish she was a monster out of a space ship, and it would come back and just take her away.'

'Hi, sweetheart. Can I come in?'

'Oh, Daddy, don't be silly. You don't have to knock.'

'A gentleman always knocks on a lady's door.'

Lois sat up and switched off the softly playing radio.

She was wearing pyjamas bought in California and suddenly looked very young and vulnerable. Neil sat on the edge of her bed and took her hand.

'All better now?'

'I guess.' She pouted a little.

'Want to talk about it some more?'

'It's just that they're so *weird*.' Her voice rose. Neil recognized indignation and bewilderment in it.

'You'll teach 'em,' he said. 'I bet you this time next year this street'll have the biggest and best damn Hallowe'en party ever.'

'How can I teach them?'

'By making friends with them. You can do that.'

'They won't let me.'

'Sure they will. When you start into school it'll be easy. You'll be an ambassador bringing the grand old American traditions of Hallowe'en to the natives. And you'll be a year older and happier and wiser. I promise.' He leaned forward and kissed her forehead. Lois smiled and put her arms around his neck, snuggling. Neil slipped his hand into his pocket and pulled out a small gold box. 'Happy birthday, sweetheart.'

'What? But Daddy, I already . . .'

He smiled to see the flush of pleasure on her cheeks, the wonder in her eyes as she took the box and held it on her knees. Not for the first time, he was amazed and pleased by the natural resilience of children.

'Oh, Daddy. It's beautiful.'

Out of the box she pulled a gold link chain, from which hung a solid oval locket, inscribed: *For Lois from her proud and loving father*.

'It's the best, the most beautiful . . .' She could not go on. She hugged him as tight as she could. As long as she could go on hugging him, everything would be all right. He patted her back gently.

'Just be happy,' he whispered.

*

Lois did not try to go to sleep. Her father had said that she should think about what she wanted to put in the locket: a photograph, a lock of hair . . . She fingered it where it lay on her chest and was almost happy. But she thought more and more about what he'd said about being an ambassador, getting to know the kids. It made her feel funny in her stomach, but she knew she could do it. It was a challenge. She thought about it and she thought, and eventually, as always happened, she had a really good idea.

Careful to make no noise, she put on the bedside lamp and got out of bed. In a cupboard in the corner of her new room were boxes containing her possessions, still waiting to be unpacked. Her mother had made her label them carefully and now she was glad of it. It only took a couple of minutes to find what she was looking for: her Birthday Book. She sat cross-legged on her bed and looked at it. It was an oblong blue book with spaces to write down the birth dates of all the people you knew and wanted to remember. At the top of each page it told you what astrological sign they were born under and from that you could check out what kind of person they were by looking at the notes in front. She had never used the book much, but now she would. With it, she would get to be an ambassador like her Daddy said. The kids would like her once they knew about the book and that she wanted to remember their birthdays specially.

Lois laid the book aside and turned to the cassette recorder. She inserted a blank tape and set the controls for 'record'. Then she lay down, the machine balanced on her chest, and began to speak very softly into the microphone.

'My twelfth birthday. Daddy gave me a locket and this radio/cassette recorder. I am going to be an ambassador and teach these English kids about Hallowe'en and write down their birthdays in my astrological birthday book.' She paused, frowning with concentration. 'I made a wish today because I was miserable, but it wasn't a real wish. It doesn't count 'cos I said it out loud so Mom could hear. She cried. Anyway, even if it was I'd take it right back.

I'm going to make a new wish. This is my proper, true and honest Birthday Wish. I wish that all those kids who were so dumb and horrible to me tonight will have birthdays as bad and miserable as mine was, except for Daddy talking with me and giving me the locket. I wish that their birthdays will be horrible. As horrible as mine. Or better yet, worse.'

Lois thought for a minute or two and then switched off the machine. She placed it on the floor beside her bed and turned over, yawning.

24 DECEMBER

Somehow, they had made it through to Christmas. Thank God.

The Hunters at Number Three were having a party and Pearl, as she relaxed and soaked in a hot tub before dressing, let her mind wander back across the last two months or so. The house was more or less straight now. The carpets were laid, the new furniture delivered and positioned. The few special pieces they had sent on from America had arrived undamaged and, although they looked out of place, at odds with the new stuff, they gave Neil and Lois a lot of pleasure. The central heating had broken down in mid-November and Lois had caught a bad chill that she seemed unable to shake off with her usual healthy ease. Neil was more settled in his job, was actually getting excited about a new programme schedule he was working on for the Fourth Channel. She still didn't see enough of him, though he tried to keep his weekends entirely free. Even so, the burden of the house and of Lois fell squarely on her. It was horrible, she knew, to think of her daughter as a burden but, just for this once, she decided to push her guilt firmly away. Besides, it was true. It wasn't Lois's fault, of course, but lately Pearl had occasionally found herself longing for the life they had left behind, not because she missed California, but because there Lois had been occupied, fully-stretched, out from under her feet.

First there had been the problem of a school. She and Neil simply could not agree where to send her. For reasons that went too deep for analysis, were a sort of gut-reaction instinct, Pearl wanted her daughter to have a traditional English education and St Hilda's had seemed perfect to her. Lois had hated the uniform and Neil deplored the absence of boys. Besides, he wanted Lois to fit in, to make friends among their neighbours' children – and they all went to Olton School. Finally, finance had settled the question. They simply could not afford St Hilda's.

Then they had discovered that Olton School had no exact equivalent of the sixth grade and that, after studying Lois's less than brilliant academic record, they planned to put her back a year. This would give Lois a chance to get used to English methods and the syllabus. That would never have happened at St Hilda's, Pearl was sure of it. Lois had raged and whined, of course, and it was okay for Neil to be sympathetic and gentle with her, but he didn't have to put up with it all day long, every day. Lois had really perfected the trick of reserving her best side for her father. On top of all of which she had caught this lingering cold, which had made it impossible to send her to the damned school anyway. Which meant that Pearl was caged up with her . . .

She drew a deep breath, held it, counted to ten and slowly let it out. She would not get all worked up about it tonight. She intended to enjoy the Hunters' party, get to know some new people, consolidate the few acquaintance-ships she had managed to make. Next month Lois would be going to school, downgraded and resentful, forced into association with children younger than her, but at last Pearl would have some time to herself. If she really worked at it, she was certain she could break down the wall of cool British reserve and have the women of the Crescent dropping in and out of her house, she of theirs, just as she had in California. And maybe Neil was right. Lois would soon form her own social ties. Perhaps it was a good thing for her to be placed with younger children, since all those living in the Crescent were younger than her and there were no other children near enough for her to conveniently befriend. Maybe they should have settled in Olton or even London, but she had so wanted to live within sight of green English fields, the countryside again. Indeed, despite the damp, muddy November, the cold, bleached December, she had already grown fond of the view from the big lounge window. There was nothing but fields and big old trees which, in summer, would be soft with dark green leaves, and Farmer Applegreen's old barn. What a gorgeously apt and English name that was, Pearl thought. Oh yes, there were compensations and things were getting better all the time. She closed her eyes and waved her hands under the water to create sensual little ripples that caressed her breasts. She anticipated the spring, the marvellous new green growth. Neil would love it. Lois would be happily settled in school and they would hold a barbecue in the back garden, which she planned to fill with all the old-fashioned flowers of her childhood. And all their new friends would come, the friends they were going to make tonight.

'You look happy.'

Though startled, for she had not heard Neil come in, Pearl did not show it. She opened her eyes and smiled up at him. He was wearing a short brown robe which made him look boyish and very handsome.

'I was thinking of spring, making plans,' she told him.

'Good.'

He turned away from her, slipped off the robe.

'You'll like the spring. Everything's going to be all right.'

'I know it.'

'Darling?'

'Mmm?'

'Don't take a shower.' He turned towards her, puzzled. She sat up, the soapy water running from her firm breasts. 'Get in with me. There's lots of room.'

Neil laughed, that excited, anticipatory gurgling laugh that she associated with making love.

'You know I hate tubs.'

'I bet I can overcome your prejudices.'

He laughed again, his eyes sparkling. 'If you're sure there's room.'

'Masses.' She drew her knees up and he stepped into the water, knelt and reached for her.

'What time do we have to be there?' he whispered.

'They won't mind if we're half an hour late.'

She stretched her slippery legs around his thighs and drew him close to her, feeling his sex stir and harden beneath the water, brushing her.

The children were to have their own party in the playroom. Ben Hunter had bought a second Christmas tree to stand in the corner. Vanessa had removed her dolls and her precious dressing-up box to the safety of her own bedroom. Yvonne had wrapped small, gimcrack gifts for all the children and piled them under the tree. The room looked festive enough with its loops of red and green paper chains and its trestle table of traditional party fare; yet Yvonne, making her last check that everything was right and ready, felt the sense of loss which dogged her life more keenly in this room than anywhere else. It had been a nursery, planned to adapt into a playroom as the children grew. Ben had repainted it almost at once and all the paraphernalia of a baby's life, especially the cot, had been whisked away. Yvonne had never found the courage to ask him if he had sold it or stored it. She would have liked it burned or hacked to pieces with the wood-axe.

She moved diagonally across the room, her taffeta skirt whispering in the evening silence. Vanessa was downstairs, watching television. Ben was shaving and dressing. Most of the time the feeling lay dormant, flared up only as a nagging sense of there being something she had forgotten, something she must do, something she had mislaid. Her doctor and Ben said this was a natural, a good way to deal with it, but it made her feel guilty. A child, after all, was not like an earring or a library book, to be mislaid, to slip the mind.

She reached the door and turned to face the room, seeing it starkly as it had been that morning. A flat sunless light falling through the partially opened curtains. The frieze of hopping rabbits around the walls. The white and blue packets of disposable nappies. The blue plastic baby bath.

The gently moving mobiles that had turned the ceiling into a fairyland of colour and movement. And her baby dead in his cot. Such a plump, strong baby. Planned and attended, waited for, made in love and mutual pleasure. He had such a down of dark hair on his head, was going to be so like his father. She had reached down and found him cold in his cot.

She turned away from the memory, which had the clarity and timelessness of a nightmare, and pressed her forehead against the dark green painted door. It had been baby blue that morning when it seemed that she would never get it open, when her child lay a literal dead weight in her arms and even her screams could not wake him.

She did not understand. She would never understand. Nobody could explain it. They had quoted the statistics at her, explained that mothers always blamed themselves, that the vague and yet cruelly accurately named 'cot death' was a phenomenon they did not yet understand themselves. There was nothing she could have done. She must forget about it. The best course of all would be to become pregnant again. She was healthy, had uncomplicated pregnancies, comparatively easy labours, normal children. Then why, why, *why*?

Without realizing it, Yvonne had begun to bang her forehead against the door. She stopped herself at once, stepped back from the wall. She had thought that she was safely through that period, that impulse to give way to the madness of grief. She had to hang on, for Vanessa's sake. She pulled open the door and hurried along the corridor to the stairs. Some of the tension left her as soon as she was out of that room. She hardly ever went there. Mrs Clegg, who came twice a week from Olton, always cleaned it. Vanessa was a tidy child. And now she wished that she had insisted on holding the children's party somewhere else, even if it did mean moving furniture and entail the possible expense of having a carpet cleaned.

The sound of canned laughter on the television set greeted her as she reached the hall. As always, as the nightmare receded, she was filled with anxiety for her daughter, her surviving child. In the seconds that it took to cross the hall to the archway which gave on to the big living room, she saw her daughter slumped, slack-mouthed and not breathing . . . Vanessa's laughter sounded, warm and alive, over the tinny rattle of the television speaker. Yvonne leaned against the wall of the archway. The lights on the big Christmas tree threw spots and glints of colour on her daughter's loose, golden hair. Her thin shoulders shook with laughter and, seeing her, Yvonne was able to get a grip on herself. She pushed away from the wall, took a deep breath and turned back into the hall without speaking to Vanessa. Perhaps the hardest thing of all was constantly preventing herself from smothering Vanessa with love and care, imprisoning her away from the inexplicable dangers of the world.

'Hello. You all right?'

She felt the blood rush to her cheeks as Ben came down the stairs. She did not meet his eyes.

'Fine. Just going to check in the kitchen.'

She fled from him – there was no other word for it – because she did not want him to know, did not want his evening spoiled by her loss; but once inside the kitchen, warm and smelling of Christmas spices, she stood lost, blank, not knowing what to do, what it was that had slipped her mind, evaded her. She began to move aimlessly about the room, looking for something.

Lois had not wasted the weeks between Hallowe'en and Christmas. Nor had she forgotten her birthday vow – in fact it had become her main source of amusement, her solitary preoccupation. She was seldom bored except in the company of her mother, whose presence and attempts to occupy her time seemed like an interruption in the honing and shaping of The Plan.

Always an observant child, she had become acutely so, feasting on her mother's brief contacts with their new neighbours, hoarding every scrap of information which passed between her parents when they thought she was not listening. Above all, she had used her eyes, watching from the windows of the house, from the fields behind it, the comings and goings, the social interactions of those children whom she was determined to make her friends. So, although she had had only the most fleeting and unsatisfactory contact with them, she already knew quite a lot about them.

She knew that the twins at Number One were called Jason and Julian and were more best friends with each other than with any of the other kids. They had a dumb baby sister called Jane who did not interest Lois at all. Mrs Shillingworth, their starchy and almost comically English mother, was 'very proud' of her children and Lois wondered why.

Amanda Beatty who lived next door was such a nice little girl. Everybody said so. And she had bad dreams, sometimes woke screaming in the night. That interested Lois, and the way everybody spoke of Amanda as though they felt sorry for her. That was because of her awful mother, though nobody ever said so. But Lois knew. She knew a lot of things about Marge Beatty, things so secret she did not confide them even to her tape-recorded diary. She couldn't think about Mrs Beatty without a giggle of laughter rising in her which made her mouth smirk in a knowing and special way. Her own mother had noticed that smile once, when Daddy was telling her about a conversation he had had with Mr Beatty, but Lois had been able to pass it off, pretending she had been thinking about something else. After that she practised thinking about Mrs Beatty and keeping her face straight, the bubble of laughter controlled.

Vanessa Hunter was one of the two children to whom she had actually spoken. Their mothers and they had collided in the doctor's surgery in Olton when her cough was real bad. Under any other circumstances, Lois would have dismissed her as a dumb kid, too young and dull to merit her attention, but as it was she had high hopes of Vanessa. She had much more confidence than Amanda and her rather small eyes, which prevented her from being *really* pretty, had shown a flicker of interest, curiosity on which Lois knew she could build. Vanessa liked dressing up and playing with dolls and went to dance class every Saturday morning with Amanda and Jane Shillingworth. Lois had expressed a cautious interest in joining them, when she was better. That made her want to laugh, too.

She regretted that she had not spoken with William Young for he, of all the children, interested her most. It was he who had stared at her that night and called her crazy-mad. For this reason alone William would have specially interested her, but there was more to William than that. Twice they had encountered each other, once when Lois was mooching in the garden and again when she was returning from the fields behind the Crescent. On both occasions he had shied away from her, his steps veering literally in a new direction, as though at all costs he must avoid her. Yet as he did so he gave her sideways glances and once had stood at his own front door, his key poised, looking back at her over his shoulder. That was the perfect opportunity for Lois to say something, smile or wave, but she had not been able to. She did not understand her own reticence, but felt obscurely that its cause lay in William himself. Then he seemed older then the others, more mature. On the few occasions when, weather permitting, the children had played outside, Lois had been excited to observe that it was William who organized their games. His naturally assumed authority attracted her. She definitely wanted to get to know William.

Beside him, the Mercer boys, Andy and Luke, seemed very small fry indeed. The younger had made no impression on Lois at all, but Andy had openly offered her friendship in his own clumsy way. They had had quite a long talk, really, through the chainlink fence which separated their back yards, with Luke's solemn eyes moving dumbly from her face to his brother's. Andy had asked about America, about surfing and the Golden Gate Bridge. Lois had learned that he was into models and inventing things. Then, blurting it out, red-faced, he asked her what colour pants she wore, only he'd said 'knickers' and she didn't understand. When she did, she had burst out laughing and he'd run off. She knew that he was scared she'd tell her mother but, of course, she had not. And at the first opportunity, perhaps, she suddenly thought, at the party that very night, she intended that he should know that she was no tell-tale tittle-tattle. Then he would be grateful to her.

All this information she had confided to her cassette-diary, updating it whenever some new tidbit came her way. She had listened to it and listened to it, getting used to the deep tones, the rather gruff timbre of her own voice, until each detail was embedded in her mind. Now she was anxious to add to that information, to be able to talk to her machine about them as her true and proper friends. But those scraps of knowledge made her feel secure and confident. She would not walk unarmed, as it were, into that party tonight, but with the advantage over them. It never occurred to her that they might have made similar gleanings about her, except for Andy, and she counted on his embarrassment to seal his lips. But they had wondered about her, especially William, and Lois would not disappoint them.

She looked at herself critically in the long mirror which was fixed to the wall of her room. She saw a tall, bud-breasted girl with a closed and interesting face. Her brown hair shone. It was longer now, cut into a short fringe but tapering off into a sleek swathe on to the collar of her bright orange shirt. Over this she wore rust-coloured cord dungarees. She'd had to appeal to Daddy for the right to wear them to the party. Mom had wanted her to wear that awful party dress. Daddy had backed her up, of course, possibly because he understood that in these clothes she looked herself, looked different from the other kids. She'd just bet that Amanda and Vanessa would be covered in frills and ribbons, their hair artificially curled. Not that she cared.

She grimaced, inspecting her 'good' teeth and pensively fingering the chain of her precious locket. Doing so, she caught sight of her watch. Where were they? They were going to be late.

She ran to the door and went out, yelling for her parents, excited and suddenly afraid of missing all the fun. In her excitement she forgot the house rule of always knocking before entering her parents' bedroom.

'Daddy, Mommy . . .'

They turned towards her, startled, a little embarrassed. Daddy had one long leg in his pants and no shirt on, just his underwear. Her mother, in bra and waist-slip, was brushing her hair before the dressing table mirror. There was a smell of intimacy, of something shared and private, in the room that, momentarily, dismayed Lois and made her feel shut out.

'Don't you knock any more, young lady?'

'Sorry. Only we're going to be late and you aren't even dressed yet.' She wanted to ask what they had been doing but something, some instinct, kept the words inside her.

'Well, we'll be ready a lot quicker if you leave us be,' her father said, wobbling on one leg to get his pants on. He looked funny but Lois didn't want to laugh.

'I don't want to be the last there. I don't want to *miss* anything.'

'You won't,' Pearl said with authority. 'Just wait downstairs for us.'

She looked automatically at her father, zipping his pants, and he nodded at her brusquely. She backed out, closing the door, but that didn't prevent her hearing:

'Don't be hard on her. She's excited.'

'I'm not. It's just . . .'

'I know what you're going to say and it's not true. She hasn't spoiled anything. I'm still here. With you. Alone.'

She couldn't make out her mother's soft reply and she didn't want to. She knew what they'd been doing and it wasn't fair. It was ugly and something she didn't want to think about. They had no right to make her late so that she had to walk into some strange room with all their eyes on her, with them already friends and not wanting to make space for her, let her in. It wasn't *fair*. She thumped down the stairs and went into the lounge and threw herself on the big couch. For two pins she'd just not go to their dumb party. She wanted to tear all the lights and tinsel off the Christmas tree because there was no way she was ever going to have a good time and it was all their *fault*.

Then, as suddenly as it had come, her anger burst and vanished. Her book. The Birthday Book. She'd almost forgotten it. She tore back upstairs and into her room and clasped the book to her, a quiver of anticipation and excitement running through her. And by the time she had checked her book and the special pen she could clip inside it and smoothed her hair and told herself that it was better to look interesting than to be pretty, her parents were ready and waiting for her in the downstairs hall.

'Have a nice time now.'

Her Daddy's words and especially the impulsive little hug he gave her – a gesture noted by the vague-looking Mrs Hunter who had conducted them upstairs, much to Lois's satisfaction – calmed her nerves. Yvonne Hunter's hand trembled visibly on the playroom doorknob before she turned it and stood back to let Lois pass first into the room.

'Children . . .' she said breathily, but there was no need to call them to order. They fell silent the moment Lois appeared: silent and staring at her. 'Yes . . . well . . . This is Lois Carradine from Number Five. Now, let me introduce you . . .'

'It's okay,' Lois said, beaming up at her. 'I know all their names. *Your* names,' she corrected herself, turning towards the assembled children. 'Hi, Vanessa,' she said, fixing the girl's too-small eyes with her own. 'We've met already. Just like me and Andy.' Colouring, the boy ducked his head away from her.

'Oh well I'll leave you then,' Yvonne Hunter said and seemed anxious to get out of the room, to get back to the grown-ups' party, Lois supposed.

'And you're Amanda and the twins are Jason and Julian, but I can't tell which is which.'

'How do you know?' It was, inevitably, William who spoke, challenging her.

'That's for me to know and you to guess at.'

He turned away from her, back to the spread of food. As though this was some sort of cue for the others, they all turned away, grouped themselves, picked up conversations, just as if she had never entered the room. One of the twins laughed loudly at something William said. For a split second only, Lois wanted to run, felt the sharp prick of tears behind her eyes, but she got hold of herself and felt more determined than ever. Loudly, so that she would be heard over their chatter, she said:

'Vanessa? Please may I have some of that trifle? It looks real good.'

'Help yourself,' Vanessa replied, with a shrug of disinterest.

'Oh, right. I didn't know you were so informal here. The British are supposed to be very formal people, so I just thought . . . Back home we'd naturally expect our hostess to serve us.' She knew even as she walked towards the table, the twins moving aside to make room for her, that she had hit just the right, condescending adult tone to impress and unnerve them. Vanessa's cheeks burned.

'Why do you talk so funny?'

She treated Jane Shillingworth to a sticky smile.

'I don't talk funny, Jane. I just talk like an American. Just like you talk like a little English girl should.'

'How does she know my name?' Jane asked her brothers, who told her to shut up.

Lois tucked the Birthday Book under her arm and, somewhat awkwardly, helped herself to trifle.

'If you're American, what are you doing here?' either Jason or Julian asked her.

'Because my Daddy works here. Besides, my Mom's English.'

'Mom!' William sniggered, but no one else seemed to think it was funny.

Vanessa stood beside her and offered a paper napkin.

'Thank you.'

She moved away from them then, towards a cushioned window seat. She was scared of dropping the book or, worse, of spilling the trifle. Carefully, she put the book down and then sat, not at all disturbed by the fact that they were all watching her again. She took a spoonful of trifle.

'What's that book?' Vanessa came towards her, trailing Amanda.

'She probably thought we'd be so boring that she'd better bring something to read,' William said and drew uncertain gusts of laughter from the twins and Andrew Mercer.

Lois ignored him. 'It's my birthday book.'

'You mean you got it for your birthday?' Amanda asked in a very small voice.

'No. It's a book for writing in . . .'

'Homework,' William sneered and nudged the nearest twin.

'You write down your friends' birthdays in it so you'll remember to send them cards and stuff.'

'Oh.' Vanessa stared at the book, nonplussed.

'It tells you what sign a person's born under, too,' Lois added.

'Sign? What's she on about?' one of the twins asked.

'Your astrological sign,' Lois told him sweetly.

'The stars,' William said. 'Horoscopes. You know. A load of old rubbish.'

'My Mum reads them every morning,' one twin volunteered.

'Yeah. Then moans because they never come true,' his brother added.

'Why did you . . . I mean why bring your birthday book

with you?' Amanda asked, venturing closer but staring at the book rather than Lois.

'Well, I just thought . . .'

'Probably wanted to tell your future,' William said. 'Where's your crystal ball?'

'Oh shut up, William,' Vanessa shouted, rounding on him. 'You're not funny and anyway it's my party and if you don't like it you don't have to stay.'

If she hadn't been so pleased, Lois would have felt sorry for the boy. He did not blush as most children would have done, but his already handsome face paled until he looked sick.

'It's not really about telling the future at all. Just what kind of a person you are. Here, I'll show you.' Lois picked up the book and opened it. 'You see here, Aquarius? That's the sign of the water-bearer. That means you are likely to be quick-thinking but stubborn, sensitive and creative. Here, you can look for yourself.'

Amanda took the book gingerly and Vanessa immediately sat down beside her, looping her loose hair behind her ear and reading with her. Lois stood up and carried her paper plate and plastic spoon back to the table. Carefully, pretending to be absorbed in the task, she selected a mince pie.

'Why did you bring it, then? You never said.'

These were the first civil words William had directed straight at her and Lois took her time before answering. He was as tall as her and he had the courage to meet her eyes.

'I thought I might make some new friends among you guys, that's all.'

'You guys!' one of the twins snorted.

'Which one of you is Jason?' Lois asked.

'They don't know themselves half the time,' Andy said. 'Don't take any notice of them.'

'Who wants his name in the birthday book, then?' the nearest twin teased him.

'Piss off, Julian,' Andy shouted and pushed him.

Lois laughed.

'What's funny?' Jason demanded, leaping to his brother's defence.

'He is. "Piss off".' She managed to keep the laughter going, though it wasn't really funny.

'Lois,' Vanessa called. 'How do you tell which sign you're born under?'

'Here, I'll show you.'

She went back to the girls and explained to them about checking the dates printed under each sign.

'When's your birthday?' she asked Amanda.

'July the seventh.'

'Okay. Here we go. That means you're Cancer.'

'Ugh,' one of the boys said with disgust, and the others laughed.

'The sign of the crab.'

'Crabby Amanda,' Andy said in a sing-song voice, causing more laughter.

'Here, read it for yourself,' Lois said, thrusting the book at Amanda.

'What am I?' Vanessa asked, bouncing on the window seat. 'You can read while I look, Mandy. Oh hurry up.'

Amanda read slowly and thoughtfully, then let the impatient Vanessa snatch the book.

'Recognize yourself?' Lois asked, licking crumbs from her fingers. Amanda shrugged.

'Aren't you going to write it down?' she asked.

'Well, I . . .' Lois caught her breath and held it for a moment. 'I'd love to only . . . Well, it's for my friends and folks. I mean, I don't know . . . Do you want to be my friend?'

Vanessa looked up from the book at Lois, then to Amanda.

'Go on, Mandy,' she said, nudging her friend.

'All right. If you want.'

Lois felt the attention of the boys burning into her back.

'Terrific. Okay. Let's write it in.' She took the book from Vanessa. 'How about you?'

'Yes, please.'

'Oh this is great, really. You know, I'd really like to be friends with all of you.' She turned deliberately to the boys, her face smiling and expectant.

'Yeah. All right. Why not?' Andy said and swaggered towards her.

Then they were all gathered around her, shouting out their birth dates, demanding to know what sign they were. Lois felt completely happy, triumphant even.

'Just a minute.' William caught Jason roughly by the shoulder and pulled him aside so that he could face Lois. She looked up at him, her heart thudding suddenly. 'If you want to be friends with all of us you've got to do something. Show you're worthy.'

She looked at Vanessa, an appeal for help, but the girl stared down at the floor. Lois sensed a ripple of interest pass among the boys.

'What?' she said, trying to keep her voice calm.

'You've got to do a dare,' William announced, but he did not sound very certain.

'That's stupid. Kids' stuff.'

'You only say that because you're scared,' William said.

'Yes.' Julian backed him up.

'I am not.'

'You are.'

'Okay.' She stood up, pushing the book into Amanda's lap. 'You name it, I'll do it.'

'Right.'

Marion Young sat alone, her untouched drink in her limp hand. She looked, Ben Hunter thought, as though she had been washed up there, abandoned. Immediately in front of him, Gerry Shillingworth was explaining the intricacies of international credit financing to Neil Carradine, John Beatty and his loyally smiling wife. At the far end of the room Pearl, Ella Mercer and Yvonne were in a huddle over the buffet. Between the two groups, ostentatious in their separateness, were Marge Beatty and Doug Young. The latter, looking sleek and young in a green velvet suit that was almost indecently tight, was bending confidentially over Marge, who laughed up at him, fully aware that he was ogling her cleavage. Not, Ben wryly admitted, that it was not something worthy to behold. The more he looked the more he envied Doug and resented his role of host, the nagging reproach of poor abandoned Marion. He edged around the Shillingworth group and approached Doug.

'Anyone drinking wine here?' he asked, proffering the bottle he held.

'I'm strictly a gin lady, Ben, as you ought to know by now.'

'I'm fine,' Doug said, straightening.

'I was just thinking . . .' Ben signalled with a discreet nod of his head. 'Marion looks a bit out of things.'

'I know.' Marge's long fingers snaked around his wrist. 'Do go and see if you can cheer her up, Ben, there's a love. She's sick to death of me, I know.'

'Marge has been marvellous. Really keeps an eye on her while I'm at work. As for me . . .' He shook his head and pantomimed a sigh of grieved exasperation which made Marge want to laugh out loud.

'She always liked you, Ben.'

He backed off, smiling, nodding, but he did not go over to Marion. Angry with himself, the whole situation, he motioned Yvonne aside.

'For God's sake do something about Marion.'

'What?' She looked over to where the young woman sat, round-shouldered, her face devoid of make-up. 'I don't know what to say to her. Ask Doug . . .'

'He's too busy admiring Marge's tits.'

'Ben!'

'It's true.'

'What's wrong with you?'

'Nothing. I'm just sick to death of the ghost of Christmas past sitting there.'

'I don't . . . I feel so . . .'

'Bloody hell,' he exploded. 'I would have thought you of all people would have been able to understand, to help her.'

Yvonne's face paled beneath her make-up. That lost, terrified look came back into her eyes and he longed, would have given anything, to have been able to snatch the words back. He reached out to her dumbly, but she stepped aside.

'She's got her baby. I don't have any sympathy for her,' Yvonne hissed and pushed past him, her skirts rustling, and went through the arch towards the kitchen.

Ella Mercer who, while apparently listening to Pearl, had caught the gist of the Hunters' angry exchange, said, 'I was just thinking, Ben, that maybe I should go and have a word with poor wee Marion over there. She looks so down, poor soul. If you'll excuse me, dear.'

'Of course,' Pearl said. She moved closer to Ben and asked, 'What's wrong with her?'

'Baby-blues, so I'm told. Though if you ask me . . .' He glanced towards Doug who was again stooped over Marge Beatty, whispering something smilingly into her ear. 'Excuse me,' Ben said gruffly, embarrassed. 'I must help Yvonne in the kitchen.'

Pearl, who had greater than average curiosity about people, began to feel strained by the overlapping tensions in the room. This was rather more than she had bargained for. She had thought there would be more people, people from outside the Crescent. Only Marge Beatty and the handsome young man leaning over her seemed to be enjoying themselves. She tried to catch Neil's eyes but before she could do so, Nigel Mercer appeared through the archway.

'Ah, Mrs Carradine. Nigel Mercer. Ella's told me a lot about you. Sorry if I've seemed unneighbourly, but you know how it is at this time of year. The job. The boys. We never seem to have time for anything. Sign of middle-age, they tell me. Anyway, how are you? Settling in nicely?'

'Yes, thank you. And please call me Pearl.'

'Oh. You're English. I could've sworn Ella said you were Ya . . . er . . . American.'

'My husband is. I was born in Leicestershire.'

'Ah. Expect your husband finds it a bit different over here, eh?'

'Yes, he does, I think.'

'Finds us a bit slow, a bit behind the times, I shouldn't wonder. Americans always do, you know.'

'Oh no, I . . .'

She was mercifully distracted by Ella busying her way towards them.

'Honestly. I don't know. She's drugged up to the eyeballs and not a thought for the poor baby. I said to her, is there anything I can do for you, Marion, and she said she supposed I could go and see if the baby's all right. Really, I don't know. She's just dumped it upstairs in Vanessa's room. I won't be a jiffy.'

'Oh would you look in on the children while you're up there?' Pearl said.

'Oh don't aggravate yourself about them, Pearl. As soon as they get bored or want somthing, they'll be down here. Let sleeping dogs lie is what I always say.'

Ella swept away, leaving Pearl feeling faintly foolish.

'I worry,' she told Nigel. 'This is bound to be a bit of a social ordeal for my daughter. She doesn't really know anyone.'

'You take Ella's advice,' he said, grasping her elbow and steering her down the room. 'My two'll soon make her feel at home. You come and introduce me to this American whizz-kid hubby of yours.'

The Hunters' house was Dutch in style and the large window of the playroom was set halfway down the long back slope of the roof. The children were clustered around the window, all except Lois, who was kneeling on the window seat, her hands on the sill.

'Go on then,' William urged her. 'You said you'd do anything, anything we said.'

'I know.'

Cold, damp air hit her face. The dare was that she should climb out and walk along the window ledge. William said that anyone could do it. The window consisted of three sections: a wide, fixed central panel, with two tall, hinged panes at either side. She was to climb out and inch her way along the sill and enter through the other window.

'It's easy,' William said, his breath brushing her cheek. 'You can hold on to the tiles. They come right down over the window. There's nothing to it unless you're scared, of course.'

Lois stood on the window seat and pushed her upper body out into the black night and looked up. The tiles were as he said. There were no stars, no moon, no lights across the fields. She pulled her head back into the room. If she didn't do it they would never be her friends. William wanted her not to do it. Even Vanessa looked as though she wanted her to chicken out. She turned around and sat on the edge of the open window. It felt so cold. She reached up with her hands and felt the overlapping, abrasive tiles. They hurt her fingers as she pulled herself up. She just didn't have to think about it. She stuck her bottom out into space, lifting one foot on to the ledge, then the other. Her heart was racing and she stood perfectly still, trying to steady her breathing. If she took a big step to the left, she could move her left hand along and then close her feet together. It would only take about three steps. Two if they were big enough. Better try it. She shifted her weight onto her right foot and slid the other along the narrow ledge, rebalanced, and took her hand off the tiles. For a moment she felt dizzy, became aware of the nothing at her back, the empty space. She grabbed the tiles again and by sheer reflex brought her feet together again.

The window slammed shut, startling her.

*

Ella Mercer stooped over the baby, careful not to disturb him. He was fast asleep, his dimpled fist knuckled into his cheek. He snuffled a little, reminding her of Andrew when he was just a baby and the warm, special feel of him against her breast. She could not resist. With the back of her finger she touched his downy little head, his temple. You great lairy thing, she castigated herself as she smiled down at him. Well, he was all right, anyway. That was all that mattered. She straightened up and, by the dim nightlight, fluffed out her fading hair, looking at herself in Vanessa's mirror. She wouldn't mind another baby. It wasn't too late. Quietly, she let herself out of the room. It was the silence that made her pause, cock an ear towards the playroom at the far end of the corridor. She knew well enough that when children were quiet there was invariably trouble afoot. Setting her lips, she marched down the corridor and threw open the door.

'You're mighty quiet for Christmas revellers.'

They looked guilty but there was no other evidence of naughtiness. Her Andy was kneeling on the window seat, tweaking the thick green curtains together.

'Making yourself cozy, then?' she asked.

'That's right, Mum,' Andrew replied.

'We were trying to make out the stars . . .' Jason explained.

'Only there aren't any,' Julian finished for him.

'And like you said, Mrs Mercer, we thought it would be more cozy with the curtains drawn.'

She scanned their faces, alert for any sign of trouble or distress.

'When I was your age,' she told them, 'we used to play games not go star-gazing.' Then she spotted the absence of the Carradine girl. 'Where's young Lois?' she asked, her voice hardening with suspicion.

'She's . . .' Amanda began, but William stepped confidently towards Ella.

'She's just gone to the loo, Mrs Mercer. Then she's going

to write down all our names in her birthday book and tell us what signs we were born under.'

'Bathroom, William, I presume you mean? Well, that all sounds very nice. Enjoy yourselves.'

She closed the door firmly behind her and hurried back downstairs, where she made a point of reassuring Pearl Carradine that all was well with the children.

The backs of her legs were shaking like her knees wanted to snap and send her falling down, down . . . Only it wouldn't be like that. She imagined her legs falling away from her, grisly below-the-knee-stumps dancing and bouncing on the rough tiles below. She imagined the legs of her dungarees flapping empty in the wind, her half-legless body dangling from the roof tiles. Her arms ached. Her shoulders, her fingers ached. She did not think she would be able to hold on. She almost wanted to let go. She closed her eyes and tilted her head back, breathing through her nose. She almost did let go when a spatter of raindrops hit her upturned face. She was going to get all wet. It didn't matter. You didn't take cold, you didn't feel wet when you were dead. Her breath escaped her in a sob of panic. Oh God, she did not want to die. Don't look down. Shift along a little more. Get as close as possible to the window that opened. Bastards! Why did they have to draw the drapes, shutting her out? Though maybe that was better than their faces, their horrible, ugly, mean, vicious, spotty, dumb faces, leering at her. She made the move, concentrating her whole terrified mind on it. Her legs shook even more. Her arms were being pulled, inch by inch, out of their sockets. She saw herself go shooting out into space, armless, screaming, sucked into the black hole of the night. She saw her own helpless body drifting and tumbling over and over like she'd seen some poor guy do on *Star Trek* once.

Dear God, please don't let me fall.

She thought she was going to wet herself, mess herself,

even. She mustn't think about it. She mustn't spook herself. It was all in the mind. Daddy said that. *Daddy*. Daddy used to say that when she was real small and got scared of things. Oh, if she should never see her Daddy again! Daddy would kill them if she fell. He would shoot them. She just knew he would and she felt proud. It would serve them right. And then she thought that if she died they'd make another baby. They'd replace her. And that made her want to fall, because she hated them.

The fingers of her right hand slipped a little. She worked them back into place, concentrating on the pricking pain of the cement tiles, rough on her fingers.

She was not going to fall. She was going to stay alive to show those kids how much she hated them. They were not going to break her down. They were not going to scare her off. She was going to show them. If she had to stand out here all night, until her Daddy came up to rescue her . . . She wished her watch had a luminous dial. She wanted to know how long she'd been out here. She wished she was not so damn scared, so tempted to peek over her shoulder into the endless spinning black that sucked and pulled at her . . .

The wind gusted, blowing rain against her shivering body.

Oh dear God please don't let me fall. Daddy. Daddy. Oh Daddy, please come and stop my legs shaking. Please, Daddy, because I can't, can't, can't . . .

It was like one of those dreams when you are just falling. For no reason. None at all. And you wake up with a bump, scared out of your skull. The bump of impact, the desired landing, squashed and broken like a no-person on the earth so hard and so very far below.

Daddy!

'I could slip over to the house,' Marge said. 'Pretend I'd left the cooker on or something.'

'Too dodgy. Somebody would be bound to notice.'

'At least admit you're tempted,' she said, her lips parted, her eyes shining.

'I'm practically coming just looking at you,' Doug said.

'Hi. Mind if I butt in? You've been monopolizing this beautiful young lady too long. And I can't say I blame you in the least.'

'And I was always told Americans weren't gallant. Tell me, Neil, do you come from the Deep South?'

'No, ma'am. California born and bred.'

'Well . . . California, here I come,' she laughed and tucked her arm through Neil's. 'You don't know Doug Young. Neil Carradine.'

'Pleased to meet you.'

'Oh she'll settle in in no time at all,' Sylvia Shillingworth told Pearl. 'It's a super school and please, if you do have any problems, do pop over and have a word. I'm parent governor, you know. And that's what I'm there for – to liaise, to listen, to act as a bridge between parents and staff. You will join the PTA, won't you?'

'Oh certainly.'

'You know, Sylvia,' Yvonne Hunter put in, 'I was only saying to Ben the other day that our kids mix so much better than we did. I mean, look at us. Gaggles of women and all the men in huddles, talking shop . . .'

'Except those around the honey-pot.'

'Oh, Sylvia, really!'

'Sorry. I'm very fond of Marge, but she does bring out the cat in one. But you were saying?'

'That when I was Vanessa's age we never played with boys, but our children, well, they all seem to mix in together.'

'That, my dear, is because we had the good sense to send our children to mixed-sex schools. I honestly think that's the best thing that ever happened to education. When I think of all those dreary years locked up with a lot of pimply girls . . .'

'Neil agrees with you . . .'

'Good for him. And, fond of you both though I am, I

shall go and tell him so. This party is too much like boarding school. I intend to fraternize with the boys.'

Pearl watched her go and thought that it was not such a bad party after all. As Neil always said, once the alcohol level reached that certain, sociable point . . . She began to tell Yvonne about the barbecue she planned to hold in the spring.

William stared at the minute hand of his watch, solemnly counting off the seconds.

'Oh, *please*, William.' Amanda's eyes were full of tears. She kept crossing and uncrossing her legs. She wanted to go. She felt awful.

'It wasn't my fault Andy's stupid mother came nosing in.'

'She's not stupid. Don't you say that or I'll . . .'

'Or you'll what?'

'Oh stop it, stop it,' Vanessa shouted. 'I don't care what you say, William. I'm going to let her in.'

Jason grabbed at her but she eluded him, ran to and climbed up on the window seat, pulling the curtain aside.

'It's okay,' William said to Jason, with affected boredom. 'Time's up anyway.'

Vanessa screamed.

'What is it?'

'Shut up or you'll have the bloody parents up here.'

'She's gone,' Vanessa wailed. 'We've killed her.'

William felt his heart rise up into his throat, felt the blood drain from his face until his skin felt cold and tight.

'*You* killed her.' Amanda began to cry.

'Shut up,' he said and ran to the window, tearing back the other curtain. They could see her legs and chest. 'See?' His hands trembled so much he could hardly get the window open and when he did he could not find the courage to speak.

'She must have walked all the way back again,' Julian said, a hint of admiration in his voice.

'Yeah. That means she's done it twice. That's good,' Jason agreed.

They watched. They saw her legs falter and then slip through the window. They saw her ashen face as she sat down again on the window ledge. They saw raindrops shining on her hair. They saw her legs trembling. She ducked her head in through the window. Her hand shook as she reached out to steady herself against the wall.

'Hey, you guys, it's freezing out there,' she said. She felt light-headed. It didn't sound like her voice at all, but some part of her applauded the way she spoke. She swayed a little and at last felt the floor under her feet. Her legs would not hold her. She sat down and clasped her arms around herself to make her trembling look like the shivers.

'Will one of you shut the window? I'm chilled.'

She did not need to make her teeth chatter.

'I will.' William reached behind her and closed the window.

'I thought you were dead,' Amanda said and threw her arms around Lois's neck. The others crowded around, shocked but smiling, all talking at once.

'I really think we ought be going,' John Beatty said.

'Why? It's Christmas. Even you college-types don't work at Christmas,' Gerry Shillingworth boomed.

'If you ask me they're always on bloody holiday anyway,' Nigel Mercer said and they all laughed, except John, who was tired of the jokes, of the same old conversations, of his wife's blatant flirting with Doug and now Carradine.

'I was only thinking of Amanda . . .' he said lamely.

'Oh God, I'd forgotten. The annual small-hour trek into the bedroom to fill the stockings and then the little buggers wake up at crack of dawn. Perhaps you're right, old son. Perhaps we should call it a night.'

'They've been awfully good, the children,' Pearl said. She wanted to go, too. She wanted to go before Neil made her properly angry, before there was any real danger of everything being spoiled.

Marion Young stood up abruptly. 'I want to go home, Doug.'

She did not speak very loudly but the effect of her speaking at all was to silence all other conversation. They had forgotten her. Marge's laughter hung in the silence, taunting.

'In a minute, love,' Doug answered, without even glancing at her.

'No, now. I can't stand another . . .' She burst into loud and ugly sobs.

Lois had them now. She sat on the window seat, her ordeal temporarily forgotten, her face flushed with triumph and excitement.

'Okay, okay. Now you, William.'

'August the third. I'm a Leo.'

'Leo the Lion,' Lois murmured as she carefully inscribed his name and date of birth in her book. 'That means you are of a sunny disposition unless thwarted, and then you're real moody, it says here.' She looked at him steadily, her eyes narrowed a little. 'It also says you're a born leader, but I guess you're right – it's just a lot of old rubbish.' She snapped the book shut and stood up, not allowing herself to relish the pain and anger in his eyes. 'Okay, gang, that's everybody taken care of.'

'Except you,' Vanessa said.

'I don't need to write down my *own* birthday, Van.'

'No. I mean *we* don't know when yours is.'

'October thirty-first. Hallowe'en. Back home they used to say I was a witch.' She pulled a terrible face and bounced at them, her fingers clawing the air. When the laughter died down she waved her hands to get their attention. 'Okay. Now I want you all to make a solemn promise. Every one of us will make a real big occasion of each other's birthdays, all right? We won't forget. We'll all celebrate and have a real good time. Agreed?'

They all agreed, their faces shining with excitement. Lois had worked a kind of magic for them. From Christmas to Christmas was usually a bleak stretch of time but now, suddenly, the coming year was full of prospects, dotted and broken up by their birthdays, in which they would all share, which they had already begun to anticipate.

'Lois.' William stood by her side, plucking at her sleeve.

'Yes?'

'I'm sorry. I didn't mean to keep you out there so long. Honest. It wasn't *my* fault. Mrs Mercer came in. We *had* to draw the curtains. Anyway, I'm sorry.'

She looked at him, her face without expression, closed. His lower lip trembled. She sensed that with one word she could make him cry. The knowledge thrilled and slightly shocked her. Not yet, she thought. Hold on, hold back.

'It's okay, William. I wasn't really scared or anything. And you needn't be, either. I'm not going to snitch or anything, even though it was your idea.'

'I think you're jolly brave and a good sport,' he said gruffly, blushing a little.

'Just so long as we're friends.'

'Shake on it.'

She took his hand and then burst into peals of laughter because he was so solemn and so unbelievably English. And when she explained why she was laughing, imitated his tone and manner, they all joined in, even William.

'Well, did you have a good time, sweetheart?'

'Yes, thank you, Daddy. Why was that lady crying?'

'She wasn't feeling too good, I guess. Don't worry your head about it. It's one hell of a way to close out a party, though,' Neil added to Pearl.

'Poor girl. In a way, I felt quite grateful to her, except that I was so sorry for her.'

'Marge sure coped with her, though, didn't she?'

Pearl did not want to discuss Marge Beatty. She had glimpsed the humiliation on Marion Young's face when Marge went to her, soothing and comforting.

'Bed, young lady,' she said to Lois. 'Or Santa Claus will have called it a night without delivering.'

'Oh, Mom, you know I don't believe in all that dumb stuff.'

'So give your poor old Dad a break, huh?'

She ran into his open arms. 'You're not old, Daddy. I love you.'

'I love you, too, sweetheart. But bed now, okay?'

'Can I ask you something?'

'Now, Lois, that's enough.'

'Just one *question*, please?'

'Neil, don't let her . . .'

'Oh come on, Pearl. It's Christmas. What is it, honey?'

'If anything were to happen to me . . . Like supposing I fell off of a real high place or something and died . . . What would you do?'

'Baby, wherever do you get these crazy ideas from?'

'That's enough, Lois. You're over-excited and just being silly. Come on. Bed.'

Pearl pulled her from Neil's loose grasp. She did not resist or complain.

'I'd be brokenhearted, sweetheart. Good night, now.'

'Good night, Daddy.'

In the hall, Pearl gave her a little push. 'Go on now. I'll be up in a minute. And don't forget to hang up your stocking.'

'Okay.'

Pearl came back into the lounge.

'That kid.' Neil shook his head. 'What brought that on?'

'I don't know. You shouldn't take any notice of her. I expect some of the other kids were talking like that. You know how competitive they are. "What would your Mummy do if you got run over by a bus?" Vying with each other. That's all.'

'Still, she got on all right, didn't she?'

'According to Yvonne Hunter she was the life and soul of the party.'

'That's my girl.'

Lois was too tired to record her diary that night. She put the Birthday Book under her pillow and slept with her hand on it. Before she drifted into sleep she recited their birth dates slowly, smilingly to herself. She had already committed them to memory. March tenth. August third. May thirtieth. That was two for the price of one.

That night she dreamed that she was falling, falling, turning over and over in the limitless air. After a while, though, it wasn't scary. She did not land with a sickening jerk into wakefulness. She began to fly. A flickering light, a radiance glowed beneath her as she flew, completely confident, through the darkness. She swooped down, weightless, drawing nearer and nearer to the source of this light until she saw an enormous candle-lit birthday cake.

Lois smiled in her sleep.

JANUARY/FEBRUARY

In January, before the children had to go back to school, it snowed for three days. A soft and persistent snowing which filled the children with, in turn, dread and excitement. Would it lie? Would it be deep enough? When could they go out to play? An optimist, Andrew Mercer, more hindered than helped by his younger brother, built a sled from odd bits of lumber stored at the back of the garage where his father had a seldom-used workbench. The fourth day was crisp and clear, with temperatures just below freezing. Wrapped in warm scarves and woolly hats, wearing wellington boots, the children took it in noisy turns to be dragged across the fields, beyond the barn to where the ground rose, providing them with a sufficient gradient to sled.

Lois stood on the top of the hill, her eyes squinted against the white dazzle. The Crescent seemed very far away, miniature. From here she could see the Applegreen farm, even the distant skyline of Olton. The hedge with the stile in it which separated the fields from an unmade road that gave Farmer Applegreen access to his various acres, snaked like a thick black line across the white. That and their tracks, the smooth indentations of the sled runners criss-crossed by a chaos of footprints, were all that blemished the gigantic white frosting. Her eyes followed their tracks to the foot of the hill. Halfway up, where there was a noticeable lessening of the gradient, a sort of levelling off, Vanessa and Amanda were climbing on to the sled. William had dubbed the run below this point the Nursery Slope. Andy and the twins had already made the whole run, their faces red with nervous excitement. She watched William give the girls a push-start. Vanessa's squeals were piercing. Shading her eyes, she could see how tightly Amanda clung to her, her face hidden against Vanessa's back. William, climbing towards her, paused to speak to Luke who was making an enormous snowball, which he planned to roll down the hill to make it bigger and bigger until it was the biggest in the world. Lois thought he was scared to go even on the Nursery Slope. When William resumed his climb, she turned away, gazing indifferently towards the barn.

'You can go next, if you like,' William panted.

'It's okay. I'll take my turn.'

'Suit yourself.'

He shrugged and watched the girls begin the agonizingly slow ascent, pulling the sled behind them. The twins and Andy were scampering about the halfway point, pelting each other with snowballs.

'I suppose you've never seen snow before.'

'I have, too. In the mountains. My Daddy took me.'

'Oh. What's wrong with you, anyway?'

'Nothing.'

'You're not much fun.'

'You mean I'm not doing some stupid dare.'

William did not want to be reminded of that, not ever. The possibility that Lois might break her word, tell her parents, had clouded his Christmas. He turned away and saw that Vanessa and Amanda, having reached the top of the first slope, had abandoned the sled and were watching the snowball fight.

'Hey,' he shouted. 'Vanessa, Mandy. Bring the sled up here.' They ignored him. Amanda began to stockpile snowballs for Jason. 'Hey, you two, come on. You have to bring the sled back after your go.'

'We have,' Vanessa shouted back.

'No, you haven't. I want it up here.'

'This is where we started from.'

'What's that got to do with it? Bring it here.'

'No.'

'Jason, Julian, tell them they've got to . . .'

'I'll get it.'

Lois ran past him, flying and leaping down the steepest part of the slope. William watched with his mouth open.

'You've got to abide by the rules,' Lois told the other girls, picking up the sled's rope. 'You have to bring it back, not just to where you start from. You're mean and selfish, Vanessa Hunter. Just 'cos you're scared to go all the way down. And you,' she told Amanda, who crouched in the snow.

'What rules? We don't have to do what *you* say,' Vanessa replied. 'Do we, Mandy?'

'You do if you want to be in the gang. What's the point of having a gang, else?'

'What gang? Who wants to be in a boring old gang anyway?'

'You do, because if you don't you won't have anyone to play with.'

'She can play with me,' Amanda said. 'Like we did before you started bossing everybody.'

Lois glared at them, incensed by their sudden solidarity, their selfishness.

'Okay,' she said. 'But you don't get to have any more rides.'

'Who cares?' flounced Vanessa as Lois walked away, bending her legs against the slope.

'You go,' William said. 'You brought it up.'

'No. It's okay. You can bring it back for me,' she smiled. 'I'll give you a start.'

'Right.'

Eagerly, William positioned himself on the sled, the rope held tight.

'Ready?'

He nodded.

'Okay.' Lois bent to the back of the board seat and pushed. 'One, two, three.'

She watched him, gather momentum, slip away from her, gaining dizzying speed, crest the plateau and descend again. At the very last moment, he jerked hard on the rope, sending the sled into a spectacular skid which threw him off into the soft snow. Immediately, Andy and the twins began to hurl snowballs at him. Amanda and Vanessa, standing shoulder to shoulder, giggled inanely. Lois turned her back on them, not wanting to be a part of their foolishness. She didn't care if William brought the sled back or not.

But he did, stamping and brushing snow from his anorak.

'Here you are, Lois. Your turn now.'

'You know what's wrong?' she asked him, ignoring the sled.

'No.'

'It's because we don't have a headquarters. We can't be a real gang, all sticking together, unless we've got a place of our own.'

'So?'

'I know a place we could have.'

'Come on. Hurry up, Lois,' Andy shouted. 'I want my turn.'

'Where?' William's eyes were alight with interest.

'Tell you when I get back,' she said, and stretched herself along the sled, her head pointing down the slope. 'I don't need a push-off,' she told him, digging the toes of her yellow boots into the snow.

None of them had gone down head first. They all saw what she was doing and stopped to watch. All of them, in their different ways, were impressed, as she shot down the first slope, bumped a little through the halfway point, and glided down to the bottom. She stayed on, gripping the top of the runners tightly, until the sled came to a natural stop in the soft snow. She stood up quickly, as though nothing had happened, and began to climb back.

'Show off,' Vanessa said as she reached the halfway point.

'That was great,' Andy said. 'I'll take it now.' He wrested the rope from her fingers.

'You do it, then,' Lois told Vanessa calmly, and continued on up the slope.

'You said we couldn't have any more rides.'

'You said I couldn't make the rules,' she retorted.

'Where?' William demanded to know, drawing her aside as soon as she reached the brow of the hill.

'The barn,' she said casually.

'No. We can't.'

Lois looked at him as though she did not know the meaning of 'can't'.

'It's a terrific idea, but the barn's out of bounds.'

'What's that?'

'We can't go there.'

'Oh. Off-limits. Well, who says?'

'My father. Mrs Beatty. All the grown-ups. You ask anyone if you don't believe me.'

'My parents don't.'

'Well . . . Did you ask them?'

Lois shrugged.

'It's dangerous. You could get hurt playing there. They all said. When we first moved here, Mr Applegreen said we could play in the fields but not the barn.'

'No, he didn't.'

'How do you know?'

'Because I asked. I asked him before Christmas. So there.'

William considered this, then, 'Even if he doesn't mind, our parents would never agree.'

'Bet you I can fix it.'

'No. I mean, how?'

'Never mind how. Do you agree?'

'What about?'

Lois held up her gloved hand, ticking her points off against her fingers.

'First, to go there now and take a look at the barn, to see what you think. Then, if I can fix it with the grown-ups, you agree that it will be our headquarters and that it will be my gang.' William looked down at his feet, shuffled them in the loose snow. 'You can be my deputy, if you like.'

'All right. But you won't be able to fix it. And I don't think we should go there now. If they found out, well, they'd never agree because we'd broken the rules.'

Lois smiled, but without warmth, disparagingly.

'I do believe you're scared, William Young. Okay. Suit yourself. But *I'm* going.'

They all went, Lois marching ahead, William reluctantly following. The others, of course, wanted to know where they were going and William, thinking they would support him, told them what Lois had said. The twins thought it was a great idea and Andy said it was worth a try.

'I don't want to be in a gang,' Amanda said.

'Good. Nobody wants you,' William said.

The boys grouped together, discussing the possibilities. Vanessa saw the unmistakable sign of tears on Amanda's face.

'It'll be all right,' she told her. 'It might be fun. If we don't, what'll happen to the birthdays? It would be awful – just think of it – if when your birthday came round . . .'

'You're only saying that because yours is first,' Amanda sulked.

'That's not true. Well, I'm going, anyway.'

So the two small girls brought up the rear, disconsolately. Only Luke, puffing and panting, straining his whole body to push the giant snowball up the hill, remained absorbed in his own obsessive act of creation.

Lois leaned against the barn, one leg cocked against the old wall. She had told the truth. Her American boldness and directness had taken Mr Applegreen by surprise when, one December afternoon, he had met her and asked her what she was doing on his land. He was nice, Mr Applegreen. She had told him who she was and where she lived and could she play in the barn? He didn't use it for anything, did he? And she would be very, very careful.

She wouldn't damage anything. And if, just by accident, she *did* break anything, her Daddy would pay. By mentioning this in her open, eager way, she had implanted the unquestioned idea in the farmer's mind that her parents knew of her intentions and had given their blessing. Reading this in his slow, kindly face, Lois had added, 'Daddy was planning to ask you himself only he's been so busy, settling into a new job and all.'

'All right, little lady. But just you mind you behave yourself and don't go doing anything silly. We don't want you hurting yourself, do we?'

And she knew she could get the parents to change their minds. It would be easy. And she *had* to have the barn. It was necessary to The Plan. She'd worked it all out. Once they had a headquarters, a real, private place of their own, they would be a real gang. They would have to obey the rules. *Her* rules.

'Well?' Jason said. 'Is this it?'

'Aren't we going in?' Julian demanded.

'First,' Lois said, pushing away from the wall and facing them, hands in pockets, 'you've got to understand. We've all got to agree that this is the best place for our headquarters, so if anyone has any other suggestions, let's hear 'em. No? Okay. So, if we all agree then you've got to leave the parents to me, okay? When I want you to ask them, or do something, I'll tell you. Until then you're not to mention anything about this. It's our secret. Got that?'

They murmured that they had.

'Can we go in now?' Andy asked.

'Not yet. Right, then when we've got it, you have got to agree that I am the boss around here. It will be my gang.'

'Why?' Jason asked.

'Yes, why you?'

'Because . . .' Lois paused, looking intently at William. He tried to avoid her eyes but could not.

'Because it was Lois's idea and if she persuades our parents . . . They'd never listen to us.'

'And because I'm the eldest,' Lois added, pleased with

him. 'And I did your dare.' She raked them all with her eyes, challenging them. There was no dissent. Lois walked to the big double doors and pulled the nearest one open just wide enough for them to file through.

'Now remember. We've got to respect this place, treat it right. So no dashing about exploring. You don't know it like I do. Besides, it gets pretty dark in there.'

'Have you been here before, then?' Jason asked.

'Lots. Okay. In you go.'

One by one they filed through, Lois shouting after them to wait for her, not to go exploring. Only Amanda remained.

'Come on,' Lois said.

Amanda shook her head slightly, backed off.

'What's the matter? You really don't want to be in the gang?'

'It's not that . . .'

'What then?'

'Spiders,' the girl whispered, and shivered.

'Spiders? I don't get it.'

'Won't there be . . . spiders in there?'

'Oh . . .' Lois understood. 'Well, if there are, they'll be asleep now. They hibernate in winter. Didn't you know that?'

Amanda shook her head again, still hanging back. Lois eased herself around the door.

'I'll tell you what . . . If there are any, I've never seen one, I swear. Cross my heart and hope to die. But if there is, I'll kill it for you, okay?'

Amanda lifted her wide, troubled eyes. They were naked with the desire, the need to trust.

'Promise?'

'I promise. And if I should break that promise, I hope all my hair falls out and I'm struck dumb. Okay?'

Slowly, Amanda walked towards the barn. Lois put her arm around her shoulders and led her in.

The barn was wood, built on brick foundations. A false ceiling, in effect a second floor or loft, spread above their heads for three-quarters of its length. This second floor was held up by stout wooden pillars and reached by means of a wide, fixed wooden ladder. The remaining quarter rose sheer to the beamed and raftered roof. There were a few greying bales of straw against the end wall and they, plus a few forgotten, rusted items of machinery – a scythe, a chain harrow, parts of a ploughshare – were all it contained.

Lois led them up the ladder. There was quite a lot of loose hay piled at the back and a heap of tarpaulins on the second floor. With a flourish, Lois showed them the heavy trapdoor which opened in the floor.

'What's it for?' Julian asked, crouched on the lip, peering down.

'I don't know. But we can fix up a swing or something. You could do that, couldn't you, Andy?'

'I suppose.'

'It's dark,' Vanessa said.

'We'll bring torches. No naked lights. No candles or matches. I promised Farmer Applegreen and that's got to be a rule, okay?'

'We haven't agreed yet,' William reminded her.

'Okay. But if we do. Now, what do you say? We could fix it up, bring things here, make a real den of it.'

'Yes,' Julian said.

'Definitely,' Jason agreed.

Julian bent and, grunting, hauled the trapdoor up, fastening the bolt. He stood on it, bouncing a little, to test it.

'Stop that,' Lois commanded. 'It might not be safe.'

'Chicken,' Julian grinned.

'No. If one of us got hurt here it would be off-limits straight away. So we've got to be real careful, sensible. Always.'

Julian stepped off the trapdoor and stood close by his brother.

'Vanessa?' Lois prompted.

'Could we make it nice? Like a house? Get furniture and things?'

'Sure.'

'All right then.'

'Andy?'

'Yes.'

'Amanda?'

'I don't mind.' She looked around her, scared, wanting to get out.

'We agree,' the twins said.

'It's terrific,' Julian added.

'Great.' Jason.

'Seems I'm out-voted,' William said.

'Doesn't matter. You have to say.'

'All right. I'm game.'

'Fantastic,' Lois yelled. 'Welcome to our headquarters, gang.'

'Not yet,' William reminded her. 'We haven't got permission yet.'

'Right. And until we do, none of us is to come here. And you're not to say a word to your parents about it. Have you got that?'

Several voices answered 'yes'. It was cold. They were getting bored. Amanda could not stop worrying about what might be lurking in the deep shadows.

'Does that include you?' William asked.

'Maybe. Anyway, it's up to you. If you won't leave it to me, I guarantee you can forget all about it. Okay, now go down the ladder one at a time. It's old and might not bear all of you.'

Amanda went first, feeling gingerly for each rung.

'When can we come again?' Andy asked Lois.

'Soon as I've fixed it. It's too cold to do much here yet, anyway.'

The sun was low and hazy when they emerged from the barn.

'Race you to that tree over there,' Lois shouted, and set off at a run. In her head, she chanted to the rhythm of her pounding feet: A *real* gang. A *place* of our own. A *real* gang. *My* gang.

Jason beat her.

The snow melted and the school term began before Lois had a chance to raise the question of the barn. She told her diary:

'School is *awful*, the pits. All the kids in my class are so small, except for one girl and she is a freak. She is *not* normal. Nobody gets to have a good time. Most of the time there is nothing to do and the teachers pick on me. They don't know how to spell anything over here and all they ever ask is dates. English history dates. I *hate* English history. I wish I was back in California, with Miss Sylvester and the gang. Only if I were I'd be in Senior High now, with Bobbie and Frank and Diane. And I bet all the teachers there would be really good and nice, like Miss Sylvester. Just think of it – Senior High. It's not fair. William knows a lot. He is a straight "A" student, but none of the kids appreciate that. They just like to goof around, but in a dumb way. They don't ever do anything neat.'

Because she was accustomed to a different syllabus, a different approach to the business of learning, Lois was judged to be 'behind' and was given special homework. She had to swot up dates and events, laboriously copy out the spelling of words like 'color' and 'center' and write over and over sentences like: 'The sidewalk is a pavement. The trunk of a car is the boot, the hood is a bonnet' until her patience became stretched and she became angry. When she weighed it all up, there was only one good thing about school: it cemented her relations with the gang. Because of them, because of The Plan, she had neither wish nor impulse to make more friends. She demonstrated this to the children of the Crescent by absolutely refusing to take her Birthday Book into school and so they saw themselves as privileged, talked about the book to other children and remained separate, a playground group who naturally sought each other out and sat together in their various classes. And as it happened even the special homework came in useful.

It was a dull evening in February, cold and dry. Lois had finished her French, the one subject in which she was ahead, and was staring dully out of her bedroom window, lacking the energy or interest to tackle the basic history they deemed that she needed. Suddenly she saw Mrs Beatty come tripping out of her house, a thick winter coat clutched around her, and hurry on foot towards the main road at the bottom of the Crescent. Scarcely pausing to think, Lois gathered up her Xeroxed history papers and took down her duffel coat. Into the pocket she slipped a plastic flashlight.

'Mom? Mom? I'm just going over to William's house. He's real good at history and I can't understand this stuff.' Seeing her mother's frown, she added, 'He said he'd help me. Honest.'

'All right, dear,' Pearl said, relieved that she did not have to feel inadequate at her own lack of knowledge. 'But don't be a nuisance now.'

'I won't.'

Lois vaulted the low box hedge that separated William's front garden from hers, dashed across the crazy paving Doug Young had laid to save work, and leaned against the doorbell. It always took Marion an age to answer the door. When she did so, she looked pale and distracted, the baby humped awkwardly in the crook of her arm, mewling.

'Hi, Mrs Young. Can I see William, please? I need some help with my history.'

'Oh . . .' Marion stared vaguely over Lois's head, into the deserted, darkening Crescent.

'Could you have him come to the door, please?'

'William? He's doing his homework.'

'I won't interrupt. I promise I'll only be a minute.'

Suddenly, as though she had reached a major, a monumental decision, Marion Young stood back from the door.

'You can go up,' she said. 'You know where his room is.'

'Thanks, Mrs Young.'

Lois took the stairs two at a time, rapped her fist perfunctorily on William's door and burst in.

'What do *you* want?'

William was seated at his desk, an anglepoise lamp shedding a cone of light on a book, his face truculent.

'I gotta be real quick. Is your Dad home?'

'No. Why?'

'It doesn't matter. Hey, listen, do something for me?'

'What?'

'Cover for me. If anyone asks, say you helped me with my history. And think up some reason why I haven't memorized it all for tomorrow.' She hurried back to the door.

'Hang on. What's all this about?'

'I'll tell you tomorrow.'

'Where are you going?' William half rose from his chair, puzzled.

'To fix the barn for us. See you.'

She crept down the stairs, biting her bottom lip, but all the downstairs doors were shut and she could hear music and garbled voices from the television set. She went out of the front door, closing it quietly, and sprinted to the back of the house where there was easy access to the fields. She was so elated that it felt like no effort at all to run all the way to the dark bulk of the barn. The continuing frosts had made the ground solid and her feet seemed to be attached to springs. She arrived breathless and panting, but exhilarated. The big door creaked as she pulled it open and she paused, listening. The place had its usual, empty, silence. She took out her flashlight and swept it around. Nothing. She climbed up to the loft and, using the flashlight again, found herself a place to hide, in the far, dark corner, behind the pile of musty-smelling hay. She sat down, her back resting against the wall, tweaking the hood of her duffel coat over her head. Already she could hear the laboured approach of a car engine, bouncing along the track Farmer Applegreen maintained for his tractors and machinery. It grew louder and then silent. Lois hugged herself with excitement and pleasurable anticipation.

'At least it would have been warm in the car,' Marge Beatty grumbled.

'That car cramps my style,' Doug Young told her. 'And it's been so long . . .'

Marge's warm, throaty laugh faded into the rustle of clothing, heavy breathing, the moist sighs of a kiss.

'Besides, you'll soon warm up,' Doug told her.

'Is that a promise, or do you just rely on my innate abilities?'

'Come on.'

A flashlight pierced the shadows of the barn, climbed the ladder jerkily as Doug hauled himself up. Marge followed behind, grimacing. Her head and shoulders above the lip of the upper floor, she paused. Doug was crouched over an old hurricane lamp, the torch resting on the floor beside him.

'Are you going to help me up, or do I have to scramble about on my hands and knees?'

'Wait. Just let me get this thing going. Besides, you can manage.'

'Oh come on, Doug.'

The flame took uncertainly, fluttered and then settled as Doug replaced the glass casing. When he stood up, his overcoat hanging loosely open, his shadow, resembling that of a giant bat, danced across the exposed roof. He went back to Marge and, taking her hands, guided her up into the loft.

'I don't know why you bother with that damn lamp,' she said, freeing herself.

'I like to see you,' he said, and then laughed.

'What's funny?'

'You – in a tracksuit.'

'Oh very amusing. It's okay for you. You don't have to make excuses to get out of the house.'

'But keep-fit classes . . . Really!'

'How else can I dress suitably for tramping across fields and climbing filthy old ladders? I suppose you think I should do it in high heels and a suspender belt.'

'It's an appealing idea. Come here.'

He removed her coat and tossed it on the pile of tarpaulins standing against the wall. Marge shivered, rubbing her arms.

'Anyway, it's true. There are classes. Claire really goes. Mind you, with her figure . . .'

Smiling, not really listening to her, Doug hooked his finger in the white plastic ring tab at the throat of her tracksuit top and pulled it down. He gazed with admiration and excitement at the shock of her nudity underneath. She smiled at him, knowing he would be pleased, excited. He squatted down, parting the unzipped fronts of the tracksuit, cupping her breasts.

'God you're . . .' he breathed, his throat suddenly dry with wanting. His hands moved to the elasticated waistband of her trousers. 'Under here, too?' He almost seemed to be begging, his eyes glittering up at her. 'Nothing?' His hands roamed, kneaded her buttocks, seeking the telltale line of her underwear.

'There's a sure way to find out,' Marge said, her voice thick and teasing.

His hands trembled so much they seemed to flutter against her belly as he gripped the top of her trousers and pulled them down, marvelling. He grasped her buttocks, pulling her towards him, and buried his face between the inviting roundness of her slightly parted thighs. A strangled moan escaped him.

'Easy,' she protested, slightly off balance, steadying herself against his shoulder.

She clung on to him, swaying, her hair tumbling forward about her face. In response to his tongue, his nibbling, searching lips, she began to buck against him, her breathing sharp and deep.

'No . . . Stop. Doug . . . please, love . . .'

He pulled away from her, holding her hips.

'Let me lie down, please.'

'Wait.'

He slipped his arm around her waist, held her while she stood first on one foot, then the other, while he pulled the tracksuit over her feet.

'Quickly,' she urged, tugging him towards the tarpaulins. She sat down, leaned back, braced on her elbows, and raised her legs. Doug knelt at once, taking the weight of her legs over his shoulders, and pressed his face again into her damp and urgent softness. She began to moan then, to cry out. Her breath hissed out between her bared teeth and was caught again in sob-like gulps. She shouted disconnected words, meaningless, just sounds, and then became silent, holding her breath until everything exploded in a shout that rose and fell away, declined to a murmur, like the arc of a graph etched on the cold air of the barn.

He was breathing rapidly. His knees cracked as he stood up, pulling off his overcoat. Her legs hung limp and open to the floor.

'You liked that? It's so bloody good to hear you. Marion never . . . She holds it all in. Marge? Marge?'

'Yes.' She sounded exhausted. She struggled up, shaking her sweat-damp hair out of her face. Her eyes, caught by the lamplight, had a glazed and hungry look. He pushed down his trousers and stood between her splayed legs. She reached for him, under the tails of his shirt, stroking him. He trembled at her touch, his breath gurgling in his throat.

'Please, darling . . .'

She pulled down his briefs and bent her head towards him.

He talked all the time, making more sense than she had done, his fingers twined in her hair.

'Steady . . . steady . . . Oh Christ, I . . . No . . . no . . . wait . . . please . . . I can't . . .'

She laughed, a sound that mocked and excited him.

'Oh that was good, so good.' He stooped, kissing her ravenously, his hands moving at random over her body.

'Now,' she whispered. 'Please, Doug. Now.'

She slipped back on the tarpaulins and he caught her legs, raising them. She looped them behind him and let him pull her forward until their flesh grazed, wet and urgent. Stretching, she reached down between them, found him and guided him, groaning, into her.

Lois had imagined how it would be many times, ever since she had first learned that Mrs Beatty and Mr Young met here in the barn. *Her* barn. She had not known who he was then and it had amused her to recognize him days later in the Crescent, his arm around his own wife's shoulders. Three times in all she'd seen them. The first time by accident, returning from a solitary walk. Marge Beatty had been alone then, looking nervously around her before slipping into the barn. And then he had come, striding across the fields from the opposite direction. Another time they had been coming out of the barn, looking guilty and tired, hurrying across to the stile where his car was parked, tight-up under the hedge. During that time before Christmas of listening and learning, her vague ideas of why they should meet so had crystallized. Her ears had heard what her mother, what the other women did not say: she had caught the tone of disapproval that made their pleasant words dangerous. And once it had become an element in The Plan, she had begun to imagine how it would be. She had imagined them kissing a lot, like in the movies, holding each other very tight and even, with a slight shudder of apprehension and shame, that Mrs Beatty would be bare on top. But never this. Never anything like this. The noises they made scared her and when, more in panic than curiosity, she had dared to peep out at them, she had had to make her own sense of what they were doing because they were against the wall to her left, Mr Young's back to her. Making that sense had caused her to feel dirty, distrust her own imagination. But it could not be anything else. She wasn't dumb. She knew how her Daddy was made and, no matter now much she tried to ignore it, she could not escape the fact that they were eating each other. It made her feel sick to her stomach, but it also made her shudder and feel itchy and hot in a really creepy way.

After that she just sat back against the wall with her eyes shut, pressing her knees rhythmically together, listening to them. She had always hated Mrs Beatty. At will she could recall the haughty, slightly disgusted way she had looked at her that night, last Hallowe'en. The cold tone of her voice, shutting Lois out forever into some no-place, could still be summoned to mortify her ears. Worst of all, the way Mrs Beatty had ordered her home, speaking carelessly over her shoulder as though Lois did not matter, could not impinge on her life. Well, she'd just see about that. Especially now, now that she knew how ugly and bad they were together, how dirty . . .

It was purely a reflex action that made her take out and switch on the torch she carried, thrusting its white beam on to them like a searchlight as she staggered up from her corner and blundered towards them.

Mrs Beatty was twisted round on the tarpaulins, her face looking naked because her hair was thrown back from it. She had one long leg up on the tarpaulins and the other trailing to the floor like she was dead or something. And he . . . He was half-kneeling on the tarpaulins, half-lying on Mrs Beatty. Acting like a great ugly, dirty baby, with her breast in his mouth. He was grunting and drooling and his behind, peeking out from under his rucked-up shirt, was pumping and flexing like it had some horrible kind of life of its own.

Then Mrs Beatty turned her face towards her and she saw Marge's eyes grow so wide it looked like they would spill out over her face. Lois wished they would, wished that she would be blind and ugly with her jelly-eyes running like a lot of grey and white goo all down her face. But the fear, the naked, undisguisable horror in those eyes, made almost blank by the relentless flashlight, steadied Lois. She took a deep breath and narrowed her own eyes.

Nobody spoke for the longest time, even though Mrs Beatty was shaking her head and her lips were moving, shaping silent words. She beat with her clenched fist on Doug's back. She tugged at his hair. For a while, Lois did not understand, and then she realized that Mrs Beatty could not stop him. She wanted to shrill with laughter as she imagined him going on like that forever, pumping his rear end up and down like some mechanical, demented puppet.

'Doug. Doug. For Christ's sake . . . Doug.'

Marge Beatty's voice was shrill and terrible, scratching the air with panic. He turned his head then. Lois would never forget it. His eyes stunned by the beam of her torch that showed up the beads of sweat on his brow. The slack and stupid way his mouth fell open, a thread of saliva attaching it to Mrs Beatty's glistening nipple. For a moment Lois could even see the silver stoppings in his teeth. Then something really weird happened. His face, which had been drained of all colour, became all red and screwed up. He was making funny whimpering noises, biting his full bottom lip, which William had inherited. His rear end was still, quivering with a kind of tension and Mrs Beatty looked like she was going to cry.

'Doug . . . For Christ's sake . . .'

She was pushing him away, pushing him off her. She was swearing at him and hating him and he did not seem able to understand. He rolled away from her, panting, like he was dying, and Marge Beatty struggled to sit up, pulling her tracksuit around her as though she was ashamed for Lois to see her big breasts.

'What do you . . . Doug. For God's sake . . . Who are you?' she shouted into the light of Lois's torch.

He seemed to pull himself together then, though he still looked like someone coming out of a trance. Mrs Beatty was tugging her leg out from under him and shouting incoherently. Lois saw his thing, all wet and red and horrible.

'For God's sake cover yourself up,' Marge shouted. 'Give me my trousers.'

It was really funny then, him trying to hold his trousers up and hobbling to reach her pants. He got all tangled up with his underwear and it was just the funniest thing Lois had ever seen. She let the laughter out and heard it grow as they stared at her with appalled faces.

'You . . .' Marge hissed, recognizing her.

'What?' Doug looked confused.

'It's her, that little bitch, the Carradine kid . . . You vicious little cow, spying . . .'

Lois roared some more. There were spots of red anger on Mrs Beatty's cheeks, but it wasn't scary because she was struggling to pull on the bottom half of her tracksuit.

'I'll kill her,' Marge screamed. 'She's mad.'

'Steady on.' Doug put his hand on her shoulder, but she shrugged him off.

'Get your fucking trousers on,' she yelled. 'Standing there . . . with her . . .'

His trousers were still around his knees and he bent quickly to pull them up. Lois let her laughter subside.

'All right, you . . .' Marge Beatty, fully dressed now, started towards her.

'Steady on, Marge.'

'Piss off. You leave the little cow to me.'

'Think, for Christ's sake.' He caught her arm, whirling her towards him.

'How dare she? Are you just going to stand there and let her . . .' She swung towards Lois again. 'How long have you been there? Why didn't you . . .?'

'Marge. Calm down.' He had to shout very loud and it startled Mrs Beatty, making her look at him, white-faced and uncertain.

'She plays with Amanda,' she said in a stricken voice. 'That monster . . . goes to school with my daughter . . .' Her voice quivered with tears.

'That's just what I mean. William, too. So think, for Christ's sake. Don't go bawling her out . . .'

'She's disgusting, mad . . .'

'Marge!'

He held her upper arm bruisingly tight, pulling her close, protectively against him. He looked over at Lois who, instinctively, lowered the flashlight a little.

'What were you . . . doing there, Lois?'

'Nothing.'

'You were watching us, spying, you little bitch. I'll damn well make sure you . . .'

'Marge,' he shouted again and shook her arm. For a moment it looked like he hated her and might slap her. Lois wished he would. She put her hand up to her face to conceal her smile. Doug saw the gesture and took heart from it. He thought she was crying.

'Don't be upset,' he said, forcing his voice to be steady. 'You scared us.'

'Upset . . .' Marge screamed, but he shoved her roughly back against the tarpaulins and she seemed to collapse. She sat down, her head dropping forward, her hands clenched together.

'Were you there when we came in?' he asked.

'Yes.'

'Of course she was there,' Marge Beatty moaned. 'She came here to spy on us. What do you want?' Her head jerked up, her eyes blazing at Lois. Doug stepped in front of her.

'Is that true, Lois?'

'No, sir. I was here and I didn't know what to do . . . I just got scared . . . I didn't . . .' She swallowed hard, making a noise as though stifling tears. 'We want the barn, that's all. To play in.' She took a small step towards him. 'I spoke with Mr Applegreen and he said it was okay. I've been here lots. I didn't *know* you came here.' Her voice rose, trembling with the injustice of all Marge had said of her. 'Only all the others, William and all,' she added quickly and saw the flicker of pain cross his face, 'they said their parents wouldn't let them come here. So I was seeing if it was really safe and everything so we could all ask you . . .'

'You don't believe a word of that?' Marge Beatty stood at his elbow. 'I know her. She's . . .'

'Shut up, Marge. Leave this to me.'

She turned away in exasperation, picked up her creased and crumpled overcoat.

'If you thought the barn was unsafe . . .' Doug began.

'*I* didn't. They said, William and the others. That's what *you* said, and Mrs Beatty and all the others. I knew it was safe 'cos I talked with Mr Applegreen and anyway I know from coming here. I just wanted to make sure. I didn't know you were gonna come here and . . . and . . .'

'All right, Lois. All right. Nobody's blaming you.'

'Hah!' Marge snorted, tossing her hair back.

'She is,' Lois said. 'And I think I'd like to go now. I have to go home.'

'Go home and *what*?' Marge demanded, not looking at her but presenting her sharp, drawn profile as though she would not deign to notice Lois, ever.

'All right, Lois.'

Lois walked slowly towards the ladder, keeping a wary eye on Marge Beatty. Pocketing her flashlight, she lowered herself carefully over the side.

'Lois?' Doug Young came towards her and squatted down so that their faces were nearly on a level.

'Yes?'

'You won't . . .' He put his hand into his jacket pocket and pulled out a wallet. 'I'm sorry this happened. Can I count on you not to mention what . . .' He pulled out a crisp, brown, ten pound note and held it towards her.

Lois stared at the paper money then shook her head.

'I don't want . . . Honest . . . I couldn't.'

'Yes, you can. Come on.' He thrust the note towards her.

'I don't want it,' she repeated, her face creasing with anger. 'But you could maybe fix it for us about the barn.

That'd be neat. If you said William could come I bet all the other kids' parents would . . .'

'All right, Lois.' His voice sounded cold and resigned, wasted. He pushed the note into his pocket and stood up, his face set.

Lois felt her way carefully down the ladder.

The next morning, on the school bus, Lois told William that he should ask his father that night about them all using the barn to play in.

'Why me? What about the others?'

'Just do it, William. I bet you it'll be all right.' He still looked doubtful and in danger of becoming stubborn. 'Trust me, William,' she told him.

Pearl did not understand why Marge sounded so resentful and seemed so ill-at-ease. After all, it was her idea that the children should be allowed to play in the old barn. An uncharacteristic idea, admittedly, but welcome, and her own. So why was she behaving – Pearl thought for the right expression – as though it were some kind of punishment or something?

They were all, except Marion Young, gathered in Marge's living room. A watery but hopeful sunlight fell on to the parquet. Marge was handing round cups of real, enticingly aromatic coffee. Sylvia Shillingworth had confided to Pearl that she thought Marge was reluctantly turning over a new leaf, that probably John had put his foot down, and not before time.

'All right,' Marge said, raising her voice. 'You all know why I asked you here.' She ignored the murmurs and nods of agreement. 'This barn business. Well, it's up to us now. I went over there yesterday, as I promised you individually I would, and saw Mr Applegreen. We went around the barn together. It's perfectly sound structurally, and he is willing to move out some old tools and stuff. He insists upon certain rules, of course. No matches or naked flames of any kind. That sort of thing. But it is up to us, if we all agree that is, to make sure our children understand that they must respect the place and use it with some caution.'

'Like an adventure playground,' Ella said. 'Marvellous places, but a child has to understand that it is potentially dangerous.'

'But if it's dangerous . . .' Yvonne cut in. 'I don't see how . . .'

'*Potentially* is not the same as actually dangerous, Yvonne. Ella is quite right. Properly organized, the barn could be a stimulating challenge to our children.'

'I'd like to say something,' Pearl announced, aware still of being the newcomer. 'I think it's a marvellous idea, but if any of us have any doubts, I don't think we should proceed. I mean if one child or family are not allowed to play there, for whatever reason, then I don't think the rest of us should go ahead. It wouldn't be fair on the ones left out.'

'Absolutely. Hear-hear,' Sylvia agreed.

'Well? Have you all discussed it?' Marge asked listlessly.

'Just a minute, Marge. Without wishing to appear rude, don't you think one of the men, or a professional, should look the place over? I mean, you're scarcely . . .'

'I can tell a rotten floor when I see one, or a rickety ladder,' Marge snapped. 'For the agreed rental, Applegreen's willing to check and do any running repairs. That's how confident he is.'

'I'm sure, dear. But you're not a professional surveyor, nor is Mr Applegreen who, after all, does have a vested interest.'

'And neither's Gerry or Nigel,' Ella said. 'I for one am not prepared to pay out extra for a survey. No, Marge's word is good enough for me.'

'You could always go and have a look for yourself, Sylvia,' Pearl suggested.

'Yes. I'll come with you,' Yvonne said anxiously.

'You mean we've got to have another meeting?' Marge said, her voice drooping with boredom.

'No, Marge. Since you find it so burdensome, we can agree now with the proviso that if Yvonne and I should not be completely satisfied, we have the right to withdraw. I can manage to walk over this afternoon, Yvonne, if that suits you?'

'Fine.'

'So are you in favour?' Marge asked, playing with the handle of her coffee-cup.

They were. Their husbands' views were trotted out, the importance to children of having a place of their own was discussed and endorsed. They were so glad that their children were friends, anxious that they should remain so. Laughing, Ella pointed out the advantages of not having them storming in and out of each other's houses all the time. Marge did not contribute. She fidgeted and stared longingly at the gin bottle across the room.

The meeting broke up when it became obvious that Marge was not going to offer to make more coffee.

'Oh, just a minute,' Sylvia said as they moved towards the hall. Marge shot her a look made up entirely of daggers. 'What about the Youngs? Since we agreed with Pearl's all in or all out proposal, we must . . .'

'They've already agreed,' Marge said. 'I discussed it with Marion yesterday.'

'Oh, good.'

'I'll feel easier if William's involved,' Yvonne said. 'He's such a sensible boy.'

'I think you'll find the twins are rather reliable, too,' Sylvia said, hurt.

'And Lois is getting so mature . . . I can't help noticing. I'll make sure she keeps an eye on them all.' Pearl wished she had not spoken when she saw the expression – part pain, part barely suppressed fury – on Marge Beatty's face. She smiled wanly at Marge and hurried away to have a scratch lunch with Ella.

9/10 MARCH

Lois got off the school bus at the entrance to Mr Applegreen's drive. She stood by the propped-open, rickety old gate and waved to Vanessa and Amanda as the bus drew away. The house and attendant farm buildings were about a quarter of a mile away. Hitching her big canvas bag on to her shoulder, Lois set out. It had rained for days and the potholes in the uneven, muddy road were filled with yellow water which reflected the high, scudding clouds. Lois walked on the verge, on a narrow strip of grass and embedded hard-core that divided the road from a soggy-looking ploughed field. She walked quickly, slightly awed by the sense of cold, washed space around her, glancing up and down at the clouds and their clear reflection. It made her feel a little dizzy, as though the world had turned upside down.

The farmyard itself was muddy and smelled of damp manure. Lois glanced around her and then called for Mr Applegreen. There was no reply and she could not see him anywhere. She walked towards the milking parlour, hearing the contented hum of machinery. Standing in the doorway, she saw Joe, who worked for Mr Applegreen, sluicing down the concrete walkways.

'Hi, Joe.'

He straightened up, looking at her with his small, sharp eyes. A smile dawned on his soft, heavy face, and his eyes moved up and down as though unable to settle on hers. Mr Applegreen said Joe was a bit simple but a good worker. Lois liked him because Joe liked her. He set aside his big broom and came slowly towards her, his wellington boots slopping in the water.

'Where's Mr Applegreen?' she asked.

'He's just gone round the back.' Joe jerked his head in the direction of some ramshackle old sheds.

'Thank you.'

'You can wait for him here,' Joe said, plucking at her coat sleeve. 'Keep me company.'

'I'd love to, Joe, but . . .'

'He won't be long.'

'I'm running an errand for my mother and I've got to be real quick.' The disappointment on his face touched her. 'I'll stop by soon, Sunday maybe, and visit with you.'

'Not on Sunday,' he said dully.

'Oh well, next week some time, okay? 'Bye, Joe.'

She resisted the slow, restraining grasp of his hand and went towards the sheds. At the corner she looked back and waved. He looked at her sadly, moistening his lips.

'Mr Applegreen.'

He was standing just beyond the sheds, contemplating a pen of bedraggled-looking chickens.

'Hello, my duck. What brings you here?'

'Is Mom's chicken ready yet? I thought I'd just stop by and save her a journey.'

A look of consternation settled on his face.

'Why, no. She said Saturday.'

'Oh, that's okay.'

'I was just going to do 'em, see.'

'Oh. Were you really? Can I watch?'

'No. You wouldn't like that.'

'I would too.'

'No. Isn't a thing girls'd like.'

'I bet I would. I'm really interested. Oh please, Mr Applegreen.'

'Well . . . as long as you don't go upsetting yourself.'

'I won't. Tell me how you do it?'

'There's nothing to it. Just wring their necks and then bleed 'em.'

'How many do you have to do?'

'Four all told. A nice plump cockerel for your mother and three hens. Now, you come with me.'

He led her into one of the sheds and switched on a dusty lightbulb hanging from the ceiling by a primitive-looking twist of wires.

'I got the old boy penned up, see? Been fattening him, though he's starved today to get him ready, like.'

Lois looked at the cockerel fussing in a slatted wooden pen. He poked his head out between the slats and twisted his head inquisitively.

'Do the hens first,' Lois said.

'I still got to catch 'em.'

'I'll wait here.' She hunkered down near the cockerel and regarded him.

Shaking his head, Applegreen went out again. He'd never known a child like it. She had such a way with her. Lois stared at the cockerel's beady brown eyes, at his smart, gleaming feathers, until she heard the alarmed squawk of chickens outside. She stood up then and carried her bag to an old saw-horse in the corner. Resting the bag on it she swiftly undid the fastening straps and took out a half-pint Thermos flask which she pushed into the deep pocket of her duffel coat.

'Now you're sure?' Mr Applegreen asked.

The hen swung upside down from his strong fingers laced between its scaly legs. The clipped brown wings were spread and the long neck craned this way and that, panicked.

'Sure. I have to write an essay on something really unusual for Monday. This'll be just great.'

'Nothing unusual in topping a chicken,' Applegreen said. 'Well, set yourself over there.'

He carried the struggling bird to an old, battered chair and sat down, the hen splayed across his knees. With dexterity born of long practice, he fixed a loop of twine around the chicken's legs.

'Some fellows do 'em hanging from the beam, but the string can break. It's better this way,' he explained.

Lois watched in fascination as his fingers settled around the bird's neck, feeling beneath the feathers.

'All you got to do is stretch 'em,' he said, 'and give a little twist to the wrist. Like this.'

With both hands on the bird's neck, he pulled sharply with his right and gave a deft twist. Lois held her breath, expecting to hear a snap, but there was nothing. It was all over so quickly, she felt cheated.

'Is that it?'

He stood up and looped the string over a nail hammered into a beam which supported the shed roof. The chicken began to flap and dance, its wings beating loudly.

'It doesn't look dead,' Lois said, drawing closer.

'That's just nerves. I've seen hens run around the yard when they've had their heads chopped off. She's dead all right. Now . . .'

From one of his many capacious pockets, Applegreen drew an old horn penknife and flicked open a small, lethally sharp blade. With his left hand he pulled on the flapping chicken's neck again, to hold it steady.

'Got to cut the jugular, see, to bleed 'em. Else the meat be all pink.'

Feeling with his thumb, he located the spot and, with one swift stroke of the blade, opened the vein. Blood welled out, bright and thick-looking.

'Oh wow,' Lois said and watched the last flutterings of the bleeding bird. 'Are you gonna do the others?'

'Aye.'

He wiped the blade of his knife on his trousers and shut it with a sharp click. Then he strolled out of the shed. Lois did not waste a moment. She pulled the flask from her pocket, unscrewed the plastic cup and then the black stopper. The chicken was still fluttering, spraying the steady stream of blood on to the floor. Standing well back, Lois pushed the lip of the Thermos against the chicken's neck. A few drops dribbled over the silver lip of the flask, but the chicken swung away. She caught hold of the neck, feeling its feathery warmth with interest, and held it steady against the flask. The red stream flooded in with a dribbling noise. Lois smiled as she watched it, her eyes shining, completely absorbed in her task.

'Whatever are you at, girl?'

Lois's head snapped up. A flush of crimson spread across her surprised cheeks.

'I . . . I didn't think you'd mind,' she said.

'Get away from there, go on.' He gestured her away with a live hen, flapping and squawking in his hand. 'Whatever made you do a thing like that?'

Lois clutched the Thermos to her chest possessively.

'It's for school,' she blurted. 'I didn't think you'd mind.'

'For school?' He looked at her as though she was out of her mind, crazy. 'What would schools want with . . .'

'A test we have to do, for science,' Lois said quickly, moving towards her bag and fishing the stopper from her pocket. 'We have to test all sorts of liquids with litmus paper. As many as we can.' She corked the flask. 'And when I saw the chicken bleeding I just thought it would be something different, to test the blood. I like to be different,' she added defensively, facing him.

'Well, I don't know. Don't seem right to me. Young girls messing with blood and stuff.'

'You get to cut up rats and frogs when you're older. I expect I'll do that. William's got to, because he's going to be a vet.'

Applegreen shook his head. No wonder the world was going to pot if schools taught kids to do things like that. The chicken flapped violently, distracting his attention from Lois. She thrust the Thermos hastily into her bag and began fastening it. Applegreen went to his chair and sat down, pulling the bird across his lap.

'I'd better be going now,' Lois said. 'Thank you for letting me . . .'

'Yes. You'd best be off. Tell your Mam cock'll be ready by nine.'

'I sure will. And thanks again.' She swung the canvas bag gaily on to her shoulder. 'You're not mad at me, are you? I didn't mean to . . .'

' 'Course not.' Mad at himself more like, for having let her watch in the first place. She never would've thought of the blood if . . . 'You run on home now and be sure to wash that Thermos out properly afore you uses it again.'

'I will. Good night.'

It was the look on her face, he thought. Holding the bird steady and catching the blood. Wasn't natural. The look on her face. His hands moved on the chicken's neck. He gripped tight, jerked savagely. No matter what, it wasn't right.

Lois stood, her arms stretched out, draped in a tent of bright green, shiny material. She flapped her arms, making the folds of material flutter like ghoulish bat wings. She crooked her fingers, fashioning claws with which to rent the air. In a deep, scratchy voice, she hissed:

'Blood of chicken,
Blood of hen.
Drink it down,
A curse on men.'

'For heaven's sake hold still, Lois,' Pearl said, snatching at the hem of the dress.

'Very nice,' her father commented. 'What'll you do if the wind changes?'

'Oh, Daddy!'

'Keep still. There.' Pearl sat back on her heels and surveyed her daughter. 'Put your arms down. Lois?'

'You said to keep still.'

'Don't be smart. That's better. Yes, it looks okay.'

'Can I try the mask and the hat?' The dress flying about her, Lois ran to the table where a large, black, pointed hat rested.

'No. I told you. It's not stuck yet,' Pearl said, scrambling up and pursuing her.

The hat was made of cardboard and Pearl had only just glued the brim to the crown.

'Just a little try, Mommy. Please?'

'It'll only come apart. You can try it all on tomorrow.'

'I've got to *wear* it tomorrow.'

'I know that. Now go upstairs and take the dress off. I need to fix that hem.'

Pouting out her bottom lip, Lois began to haul the dress over her head. Pearl slapped her bare arm impatiently, causing Neil to look up from the wodge of papers balanced on his crossed knees.

'Ow,' Lois protested.

'I said upstairs, miss. Now do as you're told.'

'Ok*ay*.'

Sullen, dragging her feet, Lois went into the hall.

'And bring it down to me when you've changed.'

'Yes, Mom.'

Pearl heaved a sigh and began gathering up scraps of cloth and cardboard.

'She's growing up,' she said.

'You could've fooled me. Sounds just like an over-excited kid getting ready for a party.'

'I meant physically. Haven't you noticed?'

'Not particularly.'

'I shall have to get her a bra soon.'

'Great.'

'What? What do you mean?'

'I mean, I don't want a daughter with no tits. I think that could seriously disadvantage her. What's bugging you?'

Pearl tried a shaky smile, ran her fingers through her hair and sat down opposite him. 'I worry.'

'Because she's . . . developing?'

'Because it's a difficult time for a girl, because she's not mature in *that* way.'

'Honey, why don't you talk with her?'

'I have. I will some more.'

'So, stop worrying.'

'She'll start soon, the Curse.'

'You've told her? She knows what to expect?'

'Of course.'

'Well, then?'

'I don't want to make her over-conscious of her body. I don't want her to be ashamed or anything, but she must learn . . . She ought to be more conscious that she's not a kid any more, not physically.'

'You don't think nature will take care of that for her? Listen, she'll be all right.'

'She would've taken that dress off right in front of you,' Pearl said, shaking her head.

'Well, I should hope so. I'm her father, for God's sake. I used to bathe her, remember? What do you think I am, some kind of . . .'

'Shh. Here she comes.' Pearl stood up, smoothing her skirt.

Neil glared at her back as Lois came into the room, wearing striped pyjamas and carrying the green dress.

'It's a real neat dress, Mom. Thanks.'

'You're welcome,' Pearl smiled, and took the dress. 'Now, don't you think half an hour's homework before bed?'

'I guess. Can I have a piece of pie first? I'm starving.'

'All right. In the fridge. And don't make a mess. Use a plate.' Pearl sat down, shaking the green dress out over her knees and leaning towards her work box. 'Oh Lois,' she called suddenly.

'Yeah?' She hung her head around the door, hair swinging.

'I just remembered. I saw your lunchbox in the kitchen but not your flask.'

'Oh, I forgot to tell you. I left it in school. I'm sorry.' Lois withdrew her head, pattered off to the kitchen.

'Well, you'll just have to take a cold drink on Monday,' Pearl shouted. 'Honestly, I don't know.' She shook her head.

'They say forgetfulness is a sure sign of emergent sexuality,' Neil told her and, in spite of herself, Pearl laughed.

'Ugh!' Jason exclaimed, pulling a face. 'Yuk!'

'It's just what we need,' Julian told him, reaching into the refrigerator and lifting out the liver.

There were two pounds of it, mauvish-brown and gleaming, piled slice upon thick, slippery slice in a shallow dish. He carried it carefully to the draining board.

'Come on, quick. Where's the bottle?'

'Here.' Jason handed him a small, screw-top jar.

'Is Mum still on the phone?'

'Yes. Get on with it.'

'I can't do it all by myself.'

'I'm not doing it. It makes me feel sick.'

'Just hold the jar.'

'All right.'

Jason unscrewed the lid and held the jar against the dish. The tip of his tongue protruding between his lips, Julian tilted the dish towards the jar. The liver slipped.

'Ugh!'

'Shut up.' Julian put his hand on the cold liver, pressing down, and tilted again. Thin, watery-brown blood flowed unsteadily into the jar. Jason did not look. 'What was that?' Julian froze.

'What?'

'The phone. Wasn't that her hanging up?'

'I didn't hear anything.'

'It goes "ting".'

'Just get on with it.'

'Hold steady then.' He lifted the dish, his hand still holding the liver, and tilted it further. More blood ran into the jar. 'That's it. Quick.'

Jason put the jar down and walked away.

'Come here, nutcase. Put the lid on. Put this back in the fridge.'

'You do it.'

'I've got to rinse my hand. Quick, Jason, before she gets off the phone.'

Wrinkling his nose, Jason screwed the cap on the jar and

gingerly lifted the dish of liver. Just as he was closing the fridge door, Sylvia Shillingworth came bustling in.

'And what do you think you're doing?'

'Nothing,' the twins said in automatic unison.

Julian turned the tap off and stepped sideways, concealing the jar from his mother with his upper body.

'Have you touched anything in the fridge?' Sylvia pulled the door open.

'No, Mum. Just looking.'

Julian seized the jar and slipped it into his pocket. He prayed the lid was on tight.

'Well, don't. You had an enormous breakfast. I fully intend to give you *some* lunch, but nothing heavy because I know you'll eat yourselves silly at Vanessa's party.'

Julian dried his hands on the kitchen towel.

'If you're hungry,' Sylvia said, relenting because she loved her children and could never stop being proud to have borne them, 'you can have an apple.'

'Thanks, Mum.'

'Now do find something to do and get out of my kitchen.'

She smiled, watching them jostle each other through the door.

'Have you got it?' Jason hissed.

'Yes. Come on.'

They ran out into the Crescent and took the narrow footpath which ran between Numbers Three and Four. When they reached the fields, they slowed to a walk and Julian pulled the bottle from his pocket.

'Good job you screwed the lid on tight.'

'It would've been funny if I hadn't,' Jason laughed.

'You wouldn't have thought so when I thumped you.'

'Let's see.' Jason took the jar, held it up to the light. 'Looks like muddy water,' he said.

'Why do you think she wants it?' Julian asked.

'I don't know.'

'Let's not give it to her unless she tells,' Julian proposed, taking the bottle back again.

'No. Better not.'

Julian frowned at his brother who ran ahead, taking stylish shots at an imaginary football.

'You scared of Lois?' Julian asked.

'No. 'Course not.'

'Why not ask her then?'

'Because I don't want to know. That's why.'

'Yes, you do.'

'No, I don't. You're the nosy one, not me.'

'Which twin's the nosy one?' Julian shouted, sing-song, and they began running together, laughing and making up crazy parodies of the questions they were always being asked. 'Which Twin?' was one of their favourite and most private games.

They let themselves into the barn, pushing one of the doors open to let in the light. Jason ran to the rope they had fixed from the trapdoor: a rope with knotted foot and hand holds. Jason leapt at it and began to swing back and forth, whistling tunelessly. Apart from the rope they had not done much to the barn, yet. There was an old mattress upstairs and a low, child-sized table and two miniature chairs Mr Hunter had given them.

'How long do you think she'll be?' Julian asked.

'I don't know.'

'What time is it?'

'What happened to your watch?'

'Nothing.'

Julian put the jar down safely by the wall and began to climb the ladder.

'Have you ever thought,' he said as his brother swung towards him, 'how funny it was the way the parents just gave in over the barn?'

'No.'

'Seriously.'

'Mrs Beatty fixed it. *She* thought it was a good idea.'

'It wasn't her. It was Lois. She said she'd fix it.'

'Yes. But we don't know that she did. Mrs Beatty . . .'

'We know all right,' Julian argued, frowning. 'We just don't know how.'

Jason dropped down from the rope. The twins looked at each other, instinctive understanding passing from one to the other. It had always been like that, moments when there was no need for words, when things too complex for language could be clearly shared. Jason shivered.

'Hey, who goes there?'

Lois was silhouetted in the open doorway. Jason turned towards her.

'Monkey-nuts,' he said.

'Oh, Jason. That was last week's password. "Witches's Sabbath", right? Phew, am I puffed!' She was carrying a bulging bag of shopping. 'Did you get it?' she asked.

'It's over there,' Julian answered, jumping down from the ladder. 'What have you got?'

'Huh?'

'In that bag,' Jason explained.

'Oh, just a chicken for my Mom. Where is it?'

Julian retrieved the glass jar and handed it to her. She peered at it, a gloating smile on her face.

'What is it?'

'Blood.'

'What sort, dummy?'

'Liver,' Jason said and made a retching noise in his throat which made Lois laugh.

'Terrific.'

'What's it for?' Julian asked, as she tucked the jar into her shopping bag.

'Surprise.'

'Tell us.'

'No. You'd only go and blab and then there'd be no fun at all. I've got to go now. Thanks a lot, and I'll see you later, at Vanessa's.'

'Wait. We'll come with you,' Jason said.

'We're bored,' Julian added, swinging the door shut behind them.

*

'Daddy says I don't look a bit like a witch. He says I look too pretty.'

Marge turned her head to regard her party-clad daughter. She was lying listless on the bed, something she seemed to spend a lot of time doing lately.

'But I told you, darling. You're a white witch, one who only does good magic. You don't want to be all in black, and old and ugly, do you?'

'No.'

'Of course not. Go and wait downstairs now, darling. Mummy wants to rest.'

Amanda closed the door quietly. Marge sighed and looked at the ceiling. It had been over three weeks now and there was a dull ache in her, a longing which threatened to explode, get out of control. After that night in the barn, Doug had said they had better cool it. She hadn't thought that he would be able to keep it up, for he was as hungry as she. There was someone else. There had to be. There was no way Doug could go for three weeks . . . She wasn't jealous, just desperate. Stifled by domesticity, the lack of excitement. In the last few days she had begun to look at men in the street. It made her squirm to acknowledge it. Look at them in such a way as to make them think . . . A boy had come into the boutique, waiting while his girl tried on a pile of dresses. A boy, little more than a kid, and she had wanted him. She had even considered ways of . . . and he had seen and recognized, had smiled at her in a way which would have outraged most women, which did outrage Marge, now. But at the time . . . Marge squeezed her eyes tight shut against tears of frustration and bitterness, of self-pity.

This time, Yvonne had put her foot down. The party was to be held downstairs, in the big sitting room, where she and Ben had carried the dining table. Ella had agreed to help her and to contribute some Devil's Food Cake, that being considered appropriate to the theme Vanessa had chosen: Witches and Warlocks. Yvonne had cut down an old black, crushed-velvet dress of her own and allowed Vanessa to paint her fingernails bright green, to wear black lipstick and a month's supply of green eye-shadow.

Finally, she had plaited her daughter's hair in four wired pigtails which stuck out like writhing snakes from her head. Vanessa, in short, looked horrendous, but very happy. Ella had even pretended not to recognize her and to be terrified of this evil apparition.

The boys had not entered very enthusiastically into the dressing-up aspect of the party. Indeed, the Shillingworths looked rather comic in their thick blue dressing gowns, to which a few stars and paper moons had been precariously stuck. William's only concession to costume was a false nose and glasses, worn with an incongruous straw boater, while little Luke Mercer was inexplicably wearing a baggy silver space suit. The boys' prize, Yvonne decided, watching them as they played a raucous game of musical chairs, would have to go to Andy, who was swathed in a too-long black kimono and sported a drooping greasepaint moustache.

The girls were more difficult, especially since little Jane had had to remain at home with a cough and a suspected temperature. The choice was restricted to Lois, who wore a hideous, lumpen green mask over the upper part of her face and walked around crook-backed and cackling, and Amanda. Marge Beatty had really excelled herself there, Yvonne admitted. Amanda looked like a cross between the Sugar Plum Fairy and a slipper satined Puritan maid. Full marks for interpretation and prettiness, but she supposed Lois should really have it, for sheer guts and gusto.

As the game came to an end, with William an outright winner, Yvonne moved forward, clapping her hands for attention.

'Now for the prizes for the best costume. After long and careful deliberation the judges have reached a unanimous verdict. The boys' prize goes to Andy Mercer.' Yvonne led the applause as Andy, hitching up the trailing skirt of the kimono, came forward, blushing. 'And now for the girls' prize. A very difficult decision, but after much thought and debate, the winner is . . . Lois Carradine.'

Lois swept forward, her green dress billowing, and acknowledged the applause with a wobbly curtsey.

'Thank you very much, Mrs Hunter,' she said, taking the prize, 'but I really think Amanda should have got it.'

'Not at all, Lois. You deserved it. Now come along, everybody. Tea is served.'

As soon as the children were seated around the table, Yvonne left Ella to cope and went into the kitchen to put the finishing touches to the cake. She had iced it entirely in green except for the white *Happy Birthday Vanessa* piped across the top. Personally, she thought it looked disgusting but when she carried it, the candles already lit, into the room the children were thrilled.

'A green cake,' Lois exclaimed. 'That's really neat, Vanessa.'

The twins pulled faces and said it looked like sick, but Ella shushed them sternly. Vanessa, her face flushed with excitement, bent over the candles and blew them out.

'Did you make a wish?' Lois demanded.

'Yes.'

'What was it?' Andy asked.

'Don't be stupid. She can't tell or it won't ever come true.'

'I'd tell,' Andy said.

'Which just proves you're stupid,' Lois retorted.

'That'll do, Lois,' Ella said firmly. 'We don't like rude children here. Now, pass your plates everyone.'

Behind the mask, Lois's eyes flashed with anger, but she said no more. As soon as all the children were served with cake, Yvonne and Ella retired to the kitchen and made themselves a pot of strong tea. As they were pouring second cups, Lois appeared.

'I have to go now, Mrs Hunter. Thank you for a lovely party.'

'So soon?' Yvonne said, surprised.

'I volunteered to go on over to the barn and check on things there.'

'Oh. Yes. You will be careful, won't you? I mean, with everyone being so excited . . .'

'Sure. And thanks again.' Lois ran out, clutching her awkwardly balanced hat.

'I'm not sure I should have agreed to let them go to the barn.'

'Oh, Yvonne. You'll fret yourself into an early grave,' Ella cautioned her. 'They'll have a grand time and come to no harm. You mark my words.'

'I hope so,' Yvonne said, and tried to put the nagging worry out of her mind.

In the dusk, they looked bizarre and incongruous, crossing the field towards the barn. Amanda's silver slippers had been exchanged for heavy brown school shoes and she wore a plaid cape over her costume. William had abandoned all pretence of dressing up and walked a little apart, his hands stuck into his pockets. Most of the decorations had fallen off the twins' dressing gowns, making them look like two strays from *Peter Pan*. Only Andy seemed to be in really high spirits. He kept running ahead of the others then, turning round, snatched open his kimono to show the girls his underpants. At first they had giggled, flushing. Even the twins had snickered, but the joke quickly grew thin, partly because Andy was becoming more daring, too serious about it.

'Stop it,' Vanessa said crossly. 'We've all seen.'

'Yes. Pack it in, Andy,' William said. 'It's not funny.'

'Sod off,' Andy shouted. Then, to the girls, 'Look. I'm a flasher. Look. Look.'

'I'll tell your mother,' Vanessa threatened him. She and Amanda drew together, talking in whispers.

William stood in front of him, ordered him to do up the kimono. A fight seemed imminent and the twins joined in, arguing loudly.

Their voices carried to Lois in the barn. She had broken the golden rule and brought matches with her. She had lit the hurricane lamp that Mr Young and Mrs Beatty had left behind and placed it on the circular nursery table. It was okay. She could break the rules. For a special occasion. In front of it she had placed the Chalice: a shallow ice-cream dish on its own pedestal, made of some light, gold-coloured alloy. Now, with a look of fierce concentration on her face, she was carefully filling it from the Thermos flask which she recorked and hid amidst the hay. Finally, she took a long upholstery needle from the hem of her dress and laid it, reverently, beside the Chalice. Satisfied that everything was prepared, she put on her mask and hat and sat cross-legged at the table, waiting.

And that was how they first saw her as, one by one, they climbed the ladder into the loft. Her face was lit from below so that the ghastly green mask seemed to glow and tremble. The lamp threw her shadow back against the wall, up into the dark roof so that it loomed over them as they climbed, dominating.

'What's all this?' William asked, trying not to sound impressed. He bent over the table, inspecting the lamp, the Chalice.

'Gather round and sit,' Lois said in her deepest voice.

They obeyed, impressed by her stillness, the authority of her appearance. William, moving last to the table, felt a tingle in his spine, a creeping feeling of excitement. When they were all seated, Lois unclasped her arms and placed her hands, palms down, on the table.

'Okay,' she said, in her normal voice which, whether she intended it or not, broke the tension.

'Where'd you get the lamp?'

'What's that?'

'What are we going to do?'

'Be still,' she shouted. 'This is a very solemn and important moment.' She glared at them, her eyes appearing disembodied behind the static mask, until silence fell. 'I, Witch Lois, Queen of all the Darkness,' she intoned, 'command you, on this most solemn day, to join with me in a solemn dedication . . .'

'What's she on about?' Jason asked.

'Search me,' his brother replied.

Lois rapped the table sharply with her knuckles.

'Okay, dummies. This is Vanessa's birthday, right? And we're supposed to be a gang, right? Dedicated and loyal to each other.' They exchanged glances, looking for dissent or affirmation. All except Amanda, who stared, wrapt, at Lois. 'Now, when each of our birthdays comes around, we have to solemnly pledge ourselves to the gang, get it?'

'Why don't we all just swear an oath or something?' William said.

'Because this way is more fun. The really important thing is that each one of us will dedicate him or herself to the rest, individually. Just like you all made me walk that ledge,' she reminded them. William's face paled. 'And tonight it's Vanessa's turn.' She looked at Vanessa, smiling.

'What . . . What do I have to do?' Vanessa asked nervously.

'Swear your loyalty and allegiance to all of us. And swear that if you ever betray us or anything we do, you hope to die.'

'All right,' Vanessa said more confidently. 'I promise.'

'Not yet,' Lois snapped. 'First we have to make a blood bond.'

'How?' Andy asked.

'What sort of blood bond?' Vanessa shifted uncomfortably on the floor.

'Into the sacred Chalice,' Lois said, lowering her voice and cupping her hands around the dish, 'which contains the Potion of Loyalty, each of us will squeeze two drops of our mortal life blood and this you will drink down, so that our blood may become part of yours, bonding you to us forever.'

'No,' Vanessa said, shaking her head so that her wired pigtails seemed to dance.

'Terrific. Me first,' Andy said, thrusting out his hand.

'You must,' Lois told her, her voice rising as she pushed Andy's hand aside. 'You must, or forever be banished from our sight.'

There was a silence, tense with excitement, as they all looked at Vanessa.

'A couple of drops won't hurt you,' William said. 'You won't taste it, or anything.'

'Banish her,' Andy said. 'I vote we banish her. She's an outcast.'

'Shut your mouth, Andrew Mercer. It's not for you to say,' Lois yelled. Then, placing her hands under the bowl of the cup, she demanded, 'Banishment or Devotion, Vanessa. Choose.'

'Yes,' said Jason.

'Choose,' said Julian and William together.

Vanessa looked uncertainly at the Chalice. Her palms were damp with sweat. Her stomach felt tight, yet liquid.

'Only two drops each?' she asked.

'No conditions,' Lois said. 'We demand your trust, your loyalty, your secrecy.'

'All right,' Vanessa agreed, in a very small voice.

'You have chosen well, Witch Vanessa. William, you first. Give me your hand.'

Surprised, William held out his hand.

'The left,' Lois said, and picked up the upholstery needle. 'Give me your thumb. Right. Now hold still over the sacred Chalice.'

The boys craned to see, but Amanda closed her eyes. Gripping William's thumb tightly, Lois pressed the point of the needle against the fleshy pad and pushed. Then, removing the needle, she squeezed. A bead of dark red blood stood on his thumb, dropped into the Chalice. A second.

'Good,' Lois said, releasing him.

William stuck his thumb in his mouth, sucking.

'Now you, Amanda.'

'Do I have to? Won't it hurt?'

'Don't be such a baby,' William said, haughtily.

Lois took her hand, held her tiny thumb tight. Amanda closed her eyes and cried out when Lois pricked her.

'Baby,' William said, as he saw her blood flow.

'There you go,' Lois said cheerfully, releasing her. 'Andy.'

Amanda bit her lip to stop the tears. She nursed her thumb in the palm of her right hand, trembling.

'Why the left?' Andy asked, extending his hand.

'Because that is the hand of magic,' Lois replied. 'The hand sinister. Hold still.'

Andy grinned as his blood shone in the lamplight. Julian's hand was ready and waiting when Andy's drops had been gathered. William held his breath, watching, not understanding why he felt so excited and not caring. Jason was next. His hand shook a little, but he did not flinch.

'Now you,' William said to Lois.

'I know,' she told him. With ceremony, she held the needle by its point, offered it to Vanessa. 'You must shed my blood, Vanessa.'

'No. I couldn't.'

'It's an honour,' Lois said. 'You must. Otherwise the bond won't hold.'

'What do I do?'

'Just prick the skin and squeeze, dummy.'

Reluctantly, awkwardly, Vanessa took the needle and Lois's proffered hand. Her own trembled as she advanced the needle close to the skin.

'Don't jab me,' Lois protested. 'Here . . .' She tried to cover Vanessa's hand with her own, to steady it, but her sudden movement only startled the girl. 'Ow!' Lois cried as the needle sunk in further than any of them had experienced. Frightened, Vanessa snatched the needle out. Blood flowed, a steady trickle, running down Lois's hand. She held it over the Chalice, shaking it.

'I'm sorry,' Vanessa whispered.

'It's okay.' Lois folded her thumb into the palm of her hand and gripped it tight. 'Give me the needle. Right. Now, with this blessed needle I stir our blood into the

Potion of Loyalty and Vanessa shall drink.' She stirred slowly, three times, from left to right, and then set the needle on the table.

'What is it?' Andy asked.

'I told you already.'

'What's *in* it?'

'That's a secret never to be revealed.' Lois sucked her thumb clean and then lifted the Chalice reverently, with both hands. She held it out to Vanessa. 'Take it and repeat after me. I'll tell you when to drink.'

Vanessa's throat was tight. She could not speak. She took the Chalice as though it might explode or bite her. The liquid in it was dark and thick-looking, like some vile soup.

'I, Vanessa . . .' Lois began.

'I, Vanessa . . .'

'Drink.'

Slowly, she dipped her head to the cup, barely tilting it. The moment the liquid touched her lips, she withdrew, licking them clean with her tongue.

'Drink,' Lois repeated.

'I did.'

'You did not.'

'No,' William said. 'You only just wet your lips.'

Vanessa took a deep breath, raised the bowl to her lips and took a small sip, swallowing quickly.

'What's it taste like?' Andy asked.

'Shh,' Jason said.

'. . . do solemnly swear by the blood of my friends, Amanda . . . Then drink,' Lois ordered.

'. . . do solemnly swear by the blood of my friends, Amanda . . .'

She raised the cup again, barely sipped. The drink smelled funny, sort of stale and bloody. She felt her throat contract.

'. . . and Andrew . . .'

'. . . and Andrew . . .'

'More this time. You've got to do it properly,' Lois insisted.

Summoning all her courage, Vanessa drank. The potion swilled into her mouth but she could not, dare not swallow it. As her stomach seemed to rise into her throat, she turned her head away and, coughing, spat the contents of her mouth on to the floor. Jason and Julian laughed.

'Come on, Vanessa,' William said impatiently.

Lois stood up, her tall hat seeming to make her tower over them.

'That is an insult,' she said. 'To spit out the blood of friends, to break the solemn oath.'

'I can't,' Vanessa said. 'It's horrible. Please don't make me.'

'That's just what we will do,' Lois said. 'Right, gang?' She waited, her eyes fixed on Vanessa who was trembling and swallowing compulsively.

The twins looked at each other, the same impossible thought in their separate heads.

'Yes,' said William, surprising even himself. He stood up. 'If you won't do it yourself, Vanessa, we shall have to make you.'

'You taste it,' she pleaded. 'You wouldn't drink it.'

'Don't be stupid,' he said. 'Come on, you lot. Help me.'

Vanessa began to cry then, and to struggle. William caught hold of her wrists and pulled them back behind her.

'Give me something to tie her with,' he demanded.

'Here.' Andy pulled off the belt of his kimono and tossed it to William. Jason helped him, binding the soft material tightly around her wrists until they were helpless. William knotted it. 'Sit on her legs,' he told Andy, pulling Vanessa, who had started to scream, roughly along the floor, away from the table. Andy leapt to obey, straddling the kicking girl.

'Don't,' Amanda said. 'Please stop it.'

'Shut up,' Jason said. 'Or we'll do it to you.'

'Okay, come on,' William shouted. He was pinching

Vanessa's nose between his thumb and forefinger so that her mouth was forced open.

'Wait,' said Lois, who had taken no part in this but had watched with an unimagined sense of power and triumph. Whirling in her green dress, she retrieved the Thermos flask from its hiding place and filled up the Chalice. 'Ready,' she said, breathlessly.

'Hold her head steady,' William told Andy.

Vanessa's eyes rolled terrified in their sockets. A gargling noise came from her open mouth. Lois approached, dogged by the curious, fascinated twins. Amanda remained by the table, crying quietly, not understanding why it had all gone wrong. She had liked it when Lois was chanting in the lamplight, the magic Chalice in front of her. But now . . .

'In the name of Andrew,' Lois boomed and tilted the Chalice against Vanessa's lower lip. 'And of William and Amanda, of Jason and Julian . . .' The thick, brownish-red mixture flowed into her mouth and even though she tried not to swallow, it trickled down her throat. '. . . and of Lois, you, Vanessa, do solemnly vow, by their blood, the blood of chicken and of liver . . .' The twins drew together, their eyes wide with fright. Julian shook his head sharply, as though to deny it. '. . . that you will always be loyal and never reveal our secrets on pain of death and torture.'

The Chalice was empty. Lois held it up with a triumphant flourish. The bloody concoction was dribbling from the corners of Vanessa's mouth. She was forced to swallow, again and again, but as she did so the contents of her stomach rose, choking her. The sounds she made frightened William, who let go of her nose. Andy jumped up, his robe falling open. Vanessa's head fell forward. A stream of blood, of half-digested food, of sickly bile gushed in a torrent from her mouth, on to her knees, the floor.

'Ugh!' Jason said and turned away, clutching his stomach.

The vomit spattered against Andy's naked legs.

'Watch out,' he said, dancing away, looking down at himself in disgust.

Again Vanessa's stomach contracted and a second rank geyser spewed out, spattering and plashing. Her nose began to run uncontrollably, streaking her face. She sat, with her head hung forward, making retching noises and spitting, swallowing against the empty rise of her gnarled stomach.

They were all looking at her, shocked and afraid. William's face was chalk-pale. He could not tear his eyes away from her. The twins stood close together, wanting to hold each other. Amanda sobbed, sniffing, not knowing what to do. Andy clutched his penis, squeezing it rhythmically through his underpants. Again Vanessa vomited, but nothing came away but the terrible sounds of coughing, retching, sobbing, all mingled. She swallowed repeatedly and they could hear then that she was crying. That and the slowly pervading stench of what she had sicked up acted upon their senses, freeing them.

Lois snatched off her hat and dropped it to the floor. She tossed her mask away into the shadows.

'Okay,' she said. She was breathing very hard and her voice sounded faint. There were two spots of red on her cheeks and her eyes had the glazed look of someone who has experienced a transport of joy or terror. She stepped towards Vanessa.

Andy bent and began to clean his legs with the skirt of the kimono.

'William, take the others on home. Make sure they don't say anything.' Lois spoke quietly but urgently, looking at Vanessa. William lifted his head. His eyes were enormous and deeply troubled.

'What . . .?'

'I'll take care of Vanessa. Go on home now.' Her voice rose, cracking. 'All of you. And remember. The vow Vanessa made is binding on all of us. We had a good time. Okay? You can say she threw up if you have to. That's all.'

'But what about her?' Julian said.

'Yes.' Jason.

'I'll take care of her.' Lois bent down and began tugging at the knots which held Vanessa's wrists.

'I'm going to be sick,' Amanda wailed.

'Get her out of here.'

'It's the awful pong,' Jason said. 'I feel sick, too.'

'Go. Scat. William,' Lois yelled.

They began to leave then, William shepherding them down the ladder. Only Andy remained, clutching himself and watching. Lois looked up at him and when she saw what he was doing a chilly smile curved her lips.

'Stop that and go home.'

'I want my belt,' Andy said miserably.

Lois tugged it free and tossed it to him. He fastened the kimono and went quickly towards the ladder.

'Okay, Vanessa. Come on. Let's get you up.'

As Andy's head disappeared from sight, Vanessa, supported by Lois, got unsteadily to her feet. She moaned with distress and disgust as vomit slopped from her lap, slid down her already ruined dress.

'Just stand there, okay? You can stand by yourself?'

Swaying, Vanessa tried to nod her head. Lois left her, ran to the hay pile and filled her arms. Then, crouching by Vanessa, she began to wipe off her dress with bunches of hay.

'It *was* blood, you know,' Jason said, breaking the silence that had enveloped them ever since leaving the barn.

'Shut up.' Julian dug him in the ribs.

'Not really?' Amanda said.

'No. I suppose not,' Jason admitted, glancing fearfully at his brother.

'Shut up. Shut up all of you,' William said, his face red with anger.

'Shut up yourself,' Julian retorted.

'I'll belt you, Shillingworth.'

'Oh yeah?'

‘Pack it in,’ Andy screamed. ‘What . . . what are we going to say?’

It was the question that troubled them all, frayed their over-stretched nerves. William unclenched his fists and made himself be calm.

‘You heard what Lois said. Just . . . Vanessa was sick. They won’t think anything of that,’ he said, suddenly realizing the truth of it. ‘If they ask, say she’s okay now. Lois took her home.’

‘But we don’t know if she is,’ Amanda pointed out querulously.

‘She will be. That’s what you’ve got to say. If you don’t, if anyone says anything else, you know what’ll happen to you.’ William’s voice was fierce and crazy.

They did not know, not precisely, but they could imagine. Imagination sealed their lips, haunted their dreams.

‘Okay, now?’ Lois called, climbing carefully down the dark ladder.

Vanessa was huddled in the open doorway of the barn, where Lois had placed her while she cleared up the loft. The cool, fresh air, Lois had told her, would make her feel better as indeed it had.

‘Yes. I think so.’

‘Come on then. We better be making tracks.’ Lois helped her up, peering into her face. ‘Just think about tomorrow. You’ll have all your presents and things to play with. You’ve been through your initiation. Just think of that. It’s all over now, but you did it. Doesn’t that make you feel good? I know I did when I got to think about being shut out on that ledge on Christmas Eve.’

‘I want to go home,’ Vanessa said.

‘Sure you do. And don’t worry. I’ll explain everything to your parents. Everything’ll be okay. Wait. Just let me get the door. Come on. Lean on me.’

Later that night, while Lois was describing the events of the day to her cassette recorder, Ben Hunter called on the Carradines. He came to apologize for Yvonne's hysteria when Lois had brought Vanessa back. It was only shock. She had calmed down now. And Vanessa was fine, of course, sleeping. He wanted to thank Lois, from all three of them, for what she had done to help Vanessa. He hoped Yvonne had not upset her.

Pearl and Neil shared a proud smile and told him they'd be sure to tell Lois and have her stop over in the morning, to visit Vanessa.

Ben Hunter thanked them again, and said that Vanessa would really like that.

11 MARCH

Vanessa had a temperature, was to spend the day in bed. Yvonne, looking as though she had spent a sleepless night, was reluctant to let Lois see her, but Ben intervened. Just for a few minutes, Lois promised. And not to excite her.

The pretty pink and white bedroom was full of March sunshine. It fell on the row of flounced and staring dolls that sat in a row above the bed. Vanessa, tucked under the pink, flower-sprigged duvet, looked no bigger than a doll herself.

'Hi,' Lois said in a stage whisper. 'I can't stay long. I promised. How are you?'

Vanessa's eyes did not look too small that morning. They were large with instinctively remembered fear. She shifted a little to the other side of the bed. Lois, smiling, sat down, as though Vanessa had been making room for her.

'How do you feel?'

'I've got a temperature.'

'But you feel okay?'

Vanessa nodded, turning her pallid face to the window.

'Maybe you won't have to go to school tomorrow,' Lois said cheerfully. 'That'd be neat.'

'Why . . . why did you make me drink that . . . stuff?'

'So's you'd really be a member of the gang. You wanted that, didn't you? You remember, Andy wanted to banish you? You just imagine how that'd be. Wow, I'd do *anything* not to be pushed out. Just think what it would be like. No one talking to you. No one to play with. Anyway, you can't have a gang unless everyone is initiated.'

'But blood,' Vanessa protested, her lower lip trembling. 'You were horrible, cruel . . . How could you make me drink blood?'

'Is that . . .? You didn't . . .? Oh no.'

She began to laugh then, clutching her stomach, making the bed quiver with the paroxysms that shook her.

'It's not funny,' Vanessa protested, her face acquiring a hint of colour.

'I know. I'm sorry. It's just such a wild idea.' Her eyes wet with tears of laughter, Lois fought to subdue the desire to shout and roll around on the bed. 'Where did you get such a crazy idea?'

'You said,' Vanessa accused, pushing herself up in the bed.

'That was just talk. Ritual talk. Listen, what you drank was just some stuff I mixed up.'

'Your blood was in it. Everybody's.'

'Sure, but that was nothing. That was symbolic, Van. You couldn't have minded that.'

'I thought . . . you said . . . chicken's blood . . .' She had grown pale again, could not go on.

'Listen . . .' Lois bounced on the bed. 'It was Coke, some chocolate powder, some red colouring, raspberry sauce . . .'

'Honestly?'

'Cross my heart and hope to die.'

Vanessa slid down under the quilt.

'Where would I get chicken blood? Would I make you drink anything so awful? Yuk. It makes me feel bad just thinking about it.' A look of studied alarm came over Lois's face. 'Oh, I'm sorry. I thought . . . I thought you were sick because the boys were too rough on you. I thought you got scared and . . . But now I see . . .'

'Yes.'

Lois looked at her sadly, chewing her lip.

'Well, it's over now. You're initiated. And just think, the rest of the gang still have theirs to come. Doesn't that make you feel better?'

'I suppose. Yes.' Vanessa managed a half-smile. 'Will they have to drink it, too?'

'I don't know. Maybe we can think of something better. Why don't *you* think about it?'

'All right.' This time Vanessa managed a proper smile.

It was still there, wreathing her face, making her look well again, when Yvonne came in to tell Lois it was time for her to go. Some of the tension eased in Yvonne as she watched the girls say goodbye.

'Thank you again, Lois,' she said, holding the front door open.

'I guess she just got too excited. It was a really great party, though, Mrs Hunter. Still, I guess she'll be okay now.'

'Yes. I expect so. Goodbye, Lois.'

' 'Bye.'

Marge Beatty had spent a sleepless night. Three times Amanda had woken, screaming and calling for her. Incoherent, bad dreams that could only temporarily be soothed away. At dawn, when at last she seemed settled, reassured, perhaps, by the grey light, Marge had returned to her own room to find John awake, watching her.

'What's wrong?'

'She had another nightmare.'

'No. I meant, with you.'

'I'm exhausted. What do you expect?' Marge got heavily into bed.

'Let's talk.'

'What about?'

'You. Us. I can't pretend any longer. I don't think you should, either. Marge, what's making you so . . .?'

'I'm not one of your students, John. I don't have to put up with your concerned counselling, your instant solutions.'

'Please, Marge. All I'm asking is . . .'

She had thrown back the bedclothes, escaped his comforting arm.

'I'm going to make some coffee,' she announced, 'since you won't let me sleep.'

And she was still drinking coffee now, hours later, with

the sun shining in the garden where John was studiously digging the rich, black earth. Amanda was watching him, silent and thoughtful. Marge stiffened as she saw Lois Carradine approach them.

'Hi, Amanda, Mr Beatty.'

Amanda looked, Lois thought, much more sick than Vanessa did. Her features were pinched and there were dark smudges under eyes.

'Lovely morning,' Mr Beatty said. 'No excuse for not making a start on the garden.'

'I've been to see Vanessa,' Lois told them. 'She's stopping in bed today. But she's okay.'

'What a shame she was sick,' John Beatty said, pressing down on the big fork he was using. 'Must have spoiled the party.'

'Not really, eh, Amanda?'

Amanda would not meet Lois's eyes.

'No,' she said. And then, as her father turned a forkload of soil over, 'Oh. Ugh. Daddy, look.'

'What?' Lois said.

'It's all right, Amanda,' John said in what, for him, was a sharp, almost an impatient voice. 'Worms won't hurt you.'

'I hate them. They're horrible.'

'Don't be silly. Lois isn't afraid of them, are you, Lois?'

Lois looked at the long, fat worm, sliding and slipping on the soil. It was pink but parts of its nearly transparent body showed patches of mauve, like bruises.

'No,' she said. 'They're good for the soil, right, Mr Beatty?'

'Kill it, Daddy. Please.' Amanda backed away, her eyes filling with tears.

'I certainly won't.'

'It won't hurt you,' Lois said. 'Look.' She bent down, reaching for the worm.

Amanda screamed.

Marge threw open the window.

'Amanda. Amanda, whatever's the matter?'

'It's just a worm,' Lois called, holding the wriggling creature up for Marge to see. 'Morning, Mrs Beatty.'

'Come inside, Amanda. Come in here, darling.' Marge called, ignoring Lois.

'I'd better see to her,' John said apologetically, and went towards his daughter.

Smiling to herself, Lois dropped the worm and watched it wriggle away, seeking shelter among the crumbled soil.

The cramps began that night, after supper. At first Lois thought it must be something she'd eaten, a green apple maybe, but the pain was lower and somehow deeper inside her. There was an attendant dull ache, like nothing she had ever felt before, in the small of her back. Her whole body felt tight and tender. Nothing, it seemed, could prevent the pain spreading, growing tentacles, reaching up to squeeze her head. She was afraid and cried out for her mother.

Pearl saw at once what it was. After all, she had been expecting it. Holding Lois's hand, smoothing her brow, she reminded her of the talks they had already had. She fetched a sanitary towel and helped her pale, trembling child to fix it. The irony, Pearl thought, was that she was no longer a child. Nor yet a woman. Lying down again, she looked vulnerable and bewildered. Lost, Pearl thought, in that strange and inaccessible place between childhood and womanhood.

'Just try to relax,' she said. 'Don't fight it.'

'Why does it have to hurt so? Just so's we can have babies?'

'It doesn't always. I'm sure it won't next time. The first time, the body has to adjust. Try to think how grown up it makes you. And you'll be glad one day, when you're married and more than anything in the world you want a baby of your very own.'

'Will I?'

'Of course.'

'It'll be like this every month?' Lois asked, turning her head on the pillow.

'No, darling. I'm sure not.'

Pearl hoped not. She'd been lucky, blessedly free of the agonies some women experienced and she hoped she had passed that accident of body chemistry, or whatever it was, on to Lois.

'I'll get you some aspirin,' she said. 'They'll help.'

She thought Neil looked frightened when she told him, alarmed by a mystery he had never tried to fathom.

'She'll be all right? You don't think we ought to call the doctor?'

Pearl laughed easily.

'Of course not. It's perfectly natural, not an illness. But I'll stay with her for a while.'

'Yes. Do that,' he said, relieved to hand the responsibility over, to retreat from these female concerns.

Lois sat up and swallowed the aspirins without fuss or protest.

'We'll keep you home a couple of days,' Pearl said. 'See how things go. Try to rest now.'

'Mommy? Will everyone know? I mean, does it show?'

'No, darling, of course not. You know that. I shall have to tell your gym teacher, but no one else need know.'

'They'd laugh at me,' she said.

'Only because they don't understand. You should be proud.'

'I don't see why. It hurts!'

'That's enough now,' Pearl said, straightening the bedclothes over Lois. 'Would you like me to stay with you?'

'Yes, please.'

More like a child than she had seemed for a year. Soft and frightened, yielding. For a moment, Pearl resented that she should be so, now, when she was leaving childhood behind. And she resented the school, their circumstances that placed Lois with girls for whom this watershed was still far off, unimagined. But she was careful not to let any resentment show. She wanted Lois to be proud and confident, to accept the workings of her body and grow into the fine and happy young woman Pearl knew she could be.

'It feels better now, Mommy,' Lois said drowsily.

'Try to sleep then. I'll be right here.'

She released Lois's hand and tucked her arm inside the covers. She sat beside her, watching and wondering, but for Lois that evening would chiefly be remembered as the first time ever Daddy did not come to say goodnight. As though she was infectious, out of reach, no longer his little girl.

APRIL

The Carradines held the barbecue Pearl had dreamed about that Christmas Eve, on a Saturday night in mid-April. As soon, in fact, as the weather permitted. The tiled patio at the back of the house was screened by pre-cast Spanish arches which Pearl had decorated with Chinese lanterns inside which, after sunset, the lights from the Christmas tree would glow. Everybody had come, except Marion Young, but her absence from the fairly frequent social gatherings of the Crescent inhabitants was no longer remarkable. Pearl had scoured London's better stores for the makings of a real American barbecue, substituting lamb chops and spare ribs for the steak she simply could not afford. She had made her own sesame buns for the children's hamburgers, chopped onions and set out an array of relishes. On impulse, she had bought Neil a laminated apron on which was printed the stylized outline of a woman's body, clad in black bra and lacy pants, black suspenders. Neil wore it with good grace, parrying the hearty, would-be jocular remarks of the men. The children had thought it hilariously funny, except Lois. Pearl refused to let that worry her. Lois was going through an awkward time just now. It would pass, and she hoped that the barbecue would serve to make her feel at home. She moved among her guests, a bottle of white and another of red wine in her hands, topping-up glasses.

'Smells good anyway,' Gerry Shillingworth remarked, sniffing.

'I do think you're marvellous, Pearl,' Yvonne complimented her. 'I could never organize anything so complicated.'

'Oh there's nothing to it. It's just a matter of practice.'

'I suppose this is pretty standard sort of fare in the States,' Nigel Mercer said.

'Except that out there they have it by their swimming pools,' Gerry added.

'With the big difference that in California you can still afford steaks,' Pearl said, moving away. She had learned to ignore and avoid the sniping at all things American which, from her limited contact with them, seemed to Pearl to be Gerry's and Nigel's main topic of conversation.

She went over to Marge Beatty who was leaning against one of the arches, looking away down the garden where the children were gathered around a trestle table, borrowed from the Hunters.

'Drink, Marge?'

Laconically, Marge extended her glass. She looked tired, older. She was still stunning, but the make-up, once discreet, had become thicker, more obvious. Pearl was struck by two wedges of orange-tinted rouge on her cheeks. A few months ago, Marge had not needed rouge.

'How are you? I haven't seen you in ages.'

'Fine. Busy.'

Pearl followed her indifferent gaze back into the garden. Luke Mercer was running back and forth across the width of the lawn, totally absorbed in some world of his own.

'He's a funny kid,' Pearl said. 'Don't you think?'

'Not as funny as some.'

'Oh?'

Marge glanced at her but instead of taking up the invitation to explain, drank from her glass.

'Nice party,' she said.

'I just hope the weather holds. I'm afraid it'll get a bit chilly later on. Still, we can go inside.'

'I have a bit of a headache,' Marge said. 'You won't think me rude if I don't stay too late?'

'Oh I'm sorry. Can I get you something?'

'No. Nothing works. Maybe it won't develop.' She sketched a smile that did not reach her eyes and turned away, walked towards the barbecue.

Not for the first time, Pearl wondered why Marge did not like her and, as always, told herself not to be so sensitive. Marge was simply – what a strange word, she thought, in this context – simply unhappy. Unhappiness was never simple.

'Since Mohammet will not come to the mountain . . .' Ben Hunter held out his empty glass.

'Sorry.' Pearl poured red wine for him.

'You look very contemplative for such a jolly occasion.'

'Not really. How are you, Ben?'

'Fine.'

'Yvonne looks well. Seems more relaxed. I'm glad.'

Ben's face softened as he looked away, over Pearl's head, to his wife, smiling, a scarlet shawl clutched around her shoulders.

'Yes. She's improving. And what about our daughters, eh?'

'How do you mean?'

'As thick as thieves. All Vanessa ever talks about is Lois. Lois did this. Lois says . . .'

'I'm glad,' Pearl said. 'Lois is at that age when she needs a girl-friend. Oh, don't get me wrong. I'm delighted she mixes so easily with the boys but . . . well . . .'

'It's good for Vanessa, too. Being an only child . . .' He stopped, aware of the ghost he had summoned up. 'Just look at them,' he said quickly, turning to the garden. 'Thick as thieves.'

Lois and Vanessa were sitting together on the edge of the paper-covered trestle table. Lois swung her long, jeans-clad legs in time to pop music playing from her cassette recorder. With the jeans, she wore a check shirt and a stetson hat, now hanging loosely on her back.

'So,' Lois said, keeping her voice low, 'did you think of anything?'

'I wondered,' Vanessa said, glancing over at the twins who, with William and Andy, were standing apart, 'if we could make them walk the plank.'

'How? I mean, what happens when they get to the end?'

'That's what I couldn't decide,' Vanessa admitted.

'Stop looking at them. They'll know we're talking about them.'

'I don't care. They're always doing that lately. Going into huddles, pretending they've got secrets.'

Lois giggled and Vanessa joined in, dipping her head towards her friend.

'What's funny?' Amanda asked.

'Nothing.' Vanessa's face became secretive, bland.

'Shall we play something?' Amanda said. Vanessa used to be her friend, and she didn't understand why she wasn't anymore.

'No,' Lois said, slipping off the table. 'We're gonna dance. Come on, Van.' She turned up the volume on the cassette recorder.

'No. Everybody'll see,' Vanessa said.

'So what? Come on.' She tugged Vanessa's hand. 'You go to dancing classes, don't you?'

Giggling, blushing, Vanessa let herself be pulled out onto the lawn. Lois, taller, swung her out, drew her back. They faced each other, swaying.

'Look at them,' Jason said, his voice harsh with scorn.

'Show offs,' Julian shouted.

'Ignore them,' Lois said. 'Dumb boys.'

'May I have the pleasure of this dance?' Andy said, mincing. He burst out laughing when Julian pushed him away.

'Don't take any notice of them,' William said. 'They're only trying to attract attention. Anyway, what do you think?'

The twins exchanged a look but came, apparently, to no firm conclusion.

'What sort of gang would it be if we boycotted it?'

'Oh very funny,' Andy jeered. 'Boys' boycott, get it?'

'If I was as thick as you,' William sneered, 'I'd keep my mouth shut.'

'Why don't you then, since you are?'

'I wasn't talking to you anyway. Julian, what do you

say? Jason? Look, there are more of us. Why should it be her gang? What do we get out of it?'

'It's all right,' Jason said.

'I think it's good. I'm not joining any boycott,' Andy said.

'That's because you're not a boy, pouffe,' William said.

Andy's cheeks flamed. 'Hark who's talking,' was all he could think to retort.

'There they go again,' Vanessa said, dancing past. 'Fighting and quarrelling. Boys *are* stupid.'

'Oh yeah? And I suppose you think you're not?' Julian said, imitating her movements.

'Oh Julian,' Lois exclaimed. 'I didn't know you could dance. Why don't you ask Amanda?' Laughing, she whirled away.

Amanda stared at him gravely, hoping.

'Why don't you, Andy,' William said, pushing him. 'You'd like to dance with the girls, wouldn't you?'

'Piss off.'

'Leave him alone, William,' Jason said. 'He's all right.'

'Suit yourself. If you want to go around with a pouffe . . .'

'You say that once more, William, and I'll . . .'

'Knock it off, you two,' Lois said, dancing her way between them. 'They can hear you up there,' she said, rolling her eyes at the patio. 'You want to get sent home or something?'

'Suits me,' said William. 'It's boring here. Barbecue. Stupid idea.'

'Okay. If you feel that way, just go,' Lois said and stalked off, taking Vanessa with her.

'See?' said William. 'Well she can stuff her stupid gang. From now on I'm not having anything to do with it. And if you had any guts, you'd do the same.' He strode angrily away, up the lawn.

'Ah, William. The very person.' Ella Mercer swooped on him. 'The hamburgers are all ready. You can help me carry them down.'

'Yes, Mrs Mercer.'

'Isn't this fun? You children are really very lucky. In my day, we'd nothing like this,' she said, leading him to where Pearl and Neil Carradine were loading two paper-covered trays with hot-dogs and hamburgers.

'He'll soon get fed up,' Andy said, 'when he sees he's all by himself.'

'He's just jealous,' Jason said.

'He's got a point, though,' Julian argued. 'There are more of us than them. We shouldn't always have to do what she wants.'

'Don't, then. Tell her. Go on. I dare you. You go and tell her she can't be boss,' Andy challenged.

'Look. William's coming back already,' Jason said.

'Oh great. Grub. Come on. Bet I can eat more hamburgers than you,' Andy said, darting towards William and helping himself from the loaded tray he carried.

'Not eating?' Holding a plate of barbecued ribs, with French bread on the side, Doug Young stood beside Marge Beatty.

She gave him a cool, sidelong glance.

'No appetite.'

'That doesn't sound like you. Don't tell me you've changed.'

'What if I have? It's obviously of no interest to you.'

'On the contrary. I should be very disappointed.'

'Well, since you're not the first consideration in my life . . .' Marge walked away, deliberately cold-shouldering him. Doug caught up with her as she was helping herself to another glass of wine.

'You look as though you need a real drink,' he said, 'or do I mean man?'

Marge caught her breath sharply, surprised not so much by his cruelty but his ability to hurt her.

'Doug, I've got a headache. I don't . . . Some other time, perhaps, I'll feel up to bitching with you.'

'That's not what I had in mind. Marge?'

'No. Don't think you can just walk back into my life when you choose.'

'I never walked out.'

'Then where the hell have you been all these weeks? What's the matter, Doug? Has your new girl-friend got tired of you? Or is it just the fact of a whole weekend with Marion getting you down?'

'It's you. Just you. You knew we had to cool it. You knew it was too . . .'

'Bullshit,' Marge said. 'You got scared or bored. Or both.'

'Listen to me, all right? Just listen.'

'I don't want to hear. Don't you understand?'

He caught her arm, preventing her from walking away again. Aware of Sylvia Shillingworth's eyes on her, Marge smiled.

'They'll be expecting me to get home to Marion. You've got a headache. We could meet up later. Just to talk. Please, Marge.'

'John . . .'

'You could go for a drive. Nothing like it for clearing the head.'

He released her arm and Marge moved away. Damn him. Damn the need in her, the response his voice, the pressure of his hand on her elbow, could arouse. Him? Who are you fooling? she asked herself. It could be anyone. Boring old Gerry Shillingworth, doting Ben. Anyone except John. As an act of penance, Marge went and stood beside her husband, accepted a mouthful of his food.

'Don't the lights look pretty?' Amanda said. She had not been able to eat all of even one hamburger. Andy asked if he could have what she had left and she let him. 'Are you going to dance again?' she asked Lois.

'I will if William will,' she said, looking at him.

The twins sniggered and nudged each other.

'Is William going to be your boy-friend?' Amanda persisted.

'Yes. Are you, William?'

'Oh Lois, Lois, I love you,' Andy said, clasping his hands passionately to his chest.

'Well, William?' Lois teased, smiling. 'Don't take any notice of them.'

'When I want a girl-friend,' William said, the blood draining from his face, 'I'll get a pretty one.'

'You horrible beast, William Young,' Vanessa burst out. 'You ought to be ashamed of yourself.' She tugged at Lois's sleeve. 'Don't take any notice of him, Lois. You *are* pretty. He's just a pig.'

William felt himself trembling inside, but he remained where he was, watching the play of emotions across Lois's face. Strangely, he did not feel pleased that he had hurt her, but the bitter twist to her mouth, the look that promised he would pay for his insult, robbed him of any triumph. He walked away, heartily sick of them all, towards the Chinese lanterns which glowed in the dark.

'Dad,' he said, locating his father on the patio, 'I want to go home now.'

'Okay. I think I ought to be getting back to your mother. Excuse us, Ella, Yvonne. We'll just go and say goodnight to the Carradines.'

Marge, standing with John and Gerry, watched him steer his handsome, look-alike son towards Neil, heard him raise his voice so that she would know he was leaving. She did not join in the general chorus of 'good nights' but helped herself to another drink. If he thought she was going chasing after him . . .

'What about Amanda?' John said, at her elbow. 'Didn't she ought to go to bed now?'

'Oh leave her. She can sleep in tomorrow. Look, she's having such a good time.'

Like moths, the children had drawn nearer the lights. The cassette machine stood on the grass. Andy, Lois, Amanda and Vanessa were dancing together. Foolish grins on their faces, the Shillingworth twins stood watching them.

'Join in, twins,' Marge called. 'Are you having a nice time, darling?'

'Yes,' Amanda said.

'Oh don't they look sweet?' Yvonne said.

'I know how to get those two young men dancing,' Ella said. 'Come on, boys. I'll teach you the Gay Gordons,' she called, laughing at herself as she tripped out onto the lawn.

'I've got a terrible headache,' Marge whispered. 'You bring her home later.'

'No. We'll all go. I'm sorry.'

'Please. You stay with Amanda. All I want is some fresh air, some quiet.' Marge pecked his cheek. 'Go and dance with her. That would really make her day.' She felt almost warm towards him as she saw the slow dawning of surprise and pleasure on his face. 'Go on.'

She hurried away, making her excuses to Pearl, who saw her to the door.

Fresh air? John thought. Where would the air be fresher than here, in the Carradines' garden? But he shrugged and went to claim his daughter for the dance.

William did not know who he hated most: them or himself. From his unlit bedroom window he could see into the garden of Number Five, could see them, so many prancing ghosts in the lantern-lit dark. Lois's white stetson was much in evidence as she swung down the line in some kind of barn dance. And Mrs Mercer making a fool of herself as usual. He hoped Andy felt shown up by her. With half an ear, he heard the front door close, heard his father start the car. He wanted to throw open the window and shout to them to shut up, to go to bed. How could anyone sleep with all that noise going on?

Instead, he left the window and threw himself down on the bed. Grunting, he pulled the pillow over his head, smothering his ears. If they had any guts they'd have joined him, the twins and Andy. Too late, he realized that he had been banking on it. Rehearsing it in his head, imagining how it would be, William had become too confident of his own powers of persuasion. He had underestimated Lois, the hold she had on them. Why had he said that? Why try to humiliate her like that?

The answers lay in an area too confused and painful for William, yet, to cope with. It had to do with the long, uncertain week after Vanessa's birthday party, when both she and Lois had remained at home, 'under the weather'. Their absence had altered the structure and the loyalties of the gang. Amanda was outnumbered, hardly seemed to belong at all. Jason had talked, in spite of Julian, about blood, blood collected for Lois and given to her in secret. William, still deeply impressed by the ritual and the excitement of that evening, naggingly conscious of the part he had played in subduing Vanessa and how strange and thrilling that had made him feel, had defended Lois, pooh-poohed the twins' suspicions. By so doing, by exercising his natural authority, he had become the leader of this truncated gang, the top man.

Although he had never admitted it to himself, he had expected Lois to be grateful when she was well again, when she returned, but instead she seemed indifferent. Her sudden confiding, giggling, feminine rapport with Vanessa confused him. She no longer seemed to care about the gang, yet to assume that nothing had changed, that it was still hers for the commanding. She had made William feel special, had made him her deputy. It was not just that he expected her to be grateful to him, but that he did not understand what she saw in Vanessa, how she, a stupid girl, could have replaced him.

He did not like to think about Vanessa at all. He could not do so without re-experiencing the helpless flutter of her hands against his thighs as he knelt to bind her, the plea, the helplessness in her eyes as he gripped her nose, forcing her pretty pink mouth open. He blamed Vanessa for the disturbing and very intense feelings he had experienced that night. Those feelings continued to disturb him, had awoken in him a curiosity that had led to shame and misery. In an illogical but seemingly very direct way, William blamed Vanessa for Andy, too.

Soon after that party, William had got permission from his father to keep a pet rabbit. William had never been allowed pets, much as he longed for them. His mother did not like dogs. Caged birds were messy. The thought of mice and terrapins made her flesh crawl. She was allergic to cats. Hamsters bred and William had no interest in goldfish. But because his father was in a good mood, because William could demonstrate his thrift by displaying the carefully hoarded pocket money, his father had agreed to a rabbit, as long as it never came indoors, was never any bother to his mother.

There remained one problem to cloud his elation, a happiness which took the sour edge off his feelings about Lois and the gang. For all he was clever, William lacked virtually all manual skills. Andy Mercer, on the other hand, could make anything. He could make a super rabbit hutch without thinking. William's economies had included the cost of the hutch. He approached Andy, who agreed to do it. The wood was acquired, along with the wire netting. William promised to help. After school, he had joined Andy in the back of the Mercers' garage, marvelling at the younger boy's dexterity and skill with wood and nails. William could do nothing but hand him the hammer, pass the nails. He had felt admiration for Andy, without realizing it, and a gratitude he was too embarrassed to express, even had he known how.

Even then William, being the private child he was, would have been impervious to Andy's advances had it not been for Vanessa, for those tingling, swimmy moments in the barn when she had been so completely and so oddly in his power. If he did not learn to be a carpenter by observing Andy, his knowledge of sex was greatly expanded. Andy, talking, confiding, had created with his words an atmosphere of forbidden, shared delight. On any other occasion, had Andy grabbed him like that, between the legs, William would have pushed him away, or treated the whole incident as a joke. But it wasn't a joke to Andy, and William had been powerless against the violently seductive response of his own body.

The incidents, for there had been two of them, were a scalding source of shame to William. Unable to understand or to control his own body, he blamed Andy. He hated and despised Andy. And the memory of Vanessa, her mysterious collusion with Lois, shamed him, too. Shamed and excited him.

William could not analyze these events and the emotions they set warring within him. He experienced them only as shame and loneliness, a sense of injustice which made him need to dominate the gang. He had taken a leaf out of Lois's book. He had planned to lead the boys in revolt, to form with them a union that would parallel that between Lois and Vanessa. But he had failed. Or rather, they had failed him.

Slowly, William pulled his hot, flushed head out from under the pillow. There was no music now. He sat up, rubbing a certain moisture that could not possibly be tears from his eyes and groped his way in the dark back to the window. The Chinese lanterns were still lit. He could see only a part of the patio, Mrs Shillingworth's blonde head, Mr Carradine, holding a glass. There was no sign of Lois or the other children. The conversation was muted, suited to the hour, the end of a party. Mrs Mercer's ready laughter grated through it for a moment. Glasses tinkled.

With a sigh, William turned away from the window and began to unbutton his shirt. It was very late. He heard his mother moving around downstairs, vaguely wondered where his father could have gone. He undressed and climbed into bed in the dark. He did not want to put his light on, did not want anyone at the Carradines' barbecue to know that he was awake, lonely, miserable. It would have comforted him, though, to put the light on, count for the umpteenth time the money he had saved, re-read the list of all that would be required to make the rabbit comfortable, keep it healthy. He lay down, admitting that it was all memorized and accessible anyway. Another week and he would be able to buy some hay, sawdust, bran. Another two weeks, and he would be able to buy the rabbit.

He wanted a buck. He could not decide what colour. Of the list of possible names he had made, currently he could not decide whether he preferred Oliver to Henry. Perhaps Oliver. Perhaps not. He turned over, pressing his face into the pillow. He knew one thing. It would be the best, the most handsome and cared for rabbit in the world. With it, he would never be lonely. He would have no need of gangs and other childish pastimes. As sleep tugged at him, he imagined himself holding a large soft-furred rabbit in his arms and telling them all, Lois at their head:

'Sorry. I'm too busy. I've got to see to Oliver.'

Or Henry.

'Well? Can you fix it? *Can* you?'

Lois was sitting on the floor of the loft, her legs swinging in space. Below her, Andy was making a minute, considered examination of a chair, a carver which Mr Shillingworth had given them. One spar was broken. The upholstery was torn and wads of greyish-white stuffing protruded from the seat. Andy tilted the chair forward, crouched, peered underneath it, let it fall back, jarringly. He tested a joint between the upright back and one of the half-padded arms.

'Andy? Can you fix it up?'

Lips pursed, a craftsman's frown of concentration on his brow, Andy circled the chair. He rubbed his chin to denote deep thought. Then he plumped down in the chair, wriggling his bottom back and hooked his heels over the undamaged spar.

'Yes,' he said. 'I could make something of it.'

'Terrific. You sure took your time, though.'

'You can't rush a good job,' he said, echoing his uncle who had taught him most of what he knew.

'When can you start?'

'Soon as I get the materials. I shall have to think about it, of course. It needs planning.'

'I'll help,' Lois said eagerly.

'And we'll have to get it over to my place.'

'Oh no!' Lois had brought the chair to the barn herself, balanced awkwardly on a wheelbarrow. The thought of trudging back with it again made her exclaim, 'Can't you fix it here?'

'Use your head,' Andy retorted. *'They'd* see. They'd be bound to cotton on. You want it to be a surprise, don't you?'

'We could hide it, put a tarpaulin over it.' She hadn't thought of that and she should have done.

'And when could I work on it? The only time I can come here is when you lot are here.'

'Right,' agreed Lois. 'We'll just have to get it back, I guess.'

She twisted a little, raised her left foot to the level of the floor, preparing to stand up, get on with it since it had to be done. Her skirt slipped down the slope of her thigh, exposing the curved, inner surface.

'Wait,' Andy said.

Tugging her skirt ineffectually towards her crooked knee, Lois turned her head sharply to Andy.

'The sooner . . .' she began, but he cut her off.

'I said I *can* do it. I haven't said I will.' He leaned forward, elbows on knees, his chin in his hands, which gave him a slightly better view of her exposed leg. His stomach and chest felt tight, pleasurably so.

'You said you could begin right away,' Lois accused him, puzzled.

'*Could*. I never said I would.'

'What are you talking about, Andy?' Lois asked, with a heavy show of thinly-stretched patience, mimicked from her mother.

'Well, why should I? What's in it for me?'

Lois shook her head, looked away, out through the open doors of the barn. She did not know how to handle this because she did not understand what he wanted. A thought occurred to her, a slightly alarming one.

'It's not because of the twins, is it?'

'No.'

'Well then?'

'There ought to be some reason for *me*. Look, if I was a grown-up, you'd have to pay me.'

'But you're not and besides I don't have enough money. You're doing it for the gang.'

'No.' Andy shook his head. 'I'd do it for you . . .' Lois looked down at him, her curiosity caught. 'If . . .' His face was flushed. For the first time Lois realized that he was not looking at her, at her face, but . . . She felt his eyes on her leg and reached automatically for her skirt, pulling it towards her knee. 'If you'll show me . . .' He had no need to be more explicit. Lois rolled on to her side, showing the backs of her thighs as her skirt fell away from them, and scrambled up.

'Why should I?' she said, embarrassed that he had been looking at her.

'Because you want me to fix up the chair,' Andy said reasonably, leaning back and folding his hands in his lap. 'No one else can do it. William couldn't.' His poise quavered as he became defensive.

'We'll see,' Lois said and walked deeper into the loft.

'Then we'll see whether I do the chair or not.'

'Andy . . .' she protested angrily.

'That's my last word,' he said. 'Take it or leave it.' He folded his arms across his chest and turned his head towards the sunlight outside, whistling quietly between his teeth.

Lois did not know what to do and she hated the trapped feeling Andy's ultimatum roused in her. He had no right! Lois liked things to be simple, black and white. To know where she stood. She had laughed, that first time, laughed him into shame when, out of the blue, he had asked to see her pants. But she could not laugh now. Why couldn't she? She sat down on the circular nursery table, nervously tucking her skirt under her legs, keeping it low and taut across her knees. Because things had changed. Because she was a woman now. A young woman. Her Mom had said. She had to be careful now, modest, leave behind the natural and careless immodesty of childhood. Because it would be a violation to let him and somehow dangerous. Unbidden, jumbled images of Mrs Beatty and Mr Young rose spectre-like in her mind. She shuddered. Maybe Andy meant . . . No. He could not. He was only a kid. The whistling had stopped. She did not want to do it. If she agreed then she would be giving way to him, she would be giving away a piece of her control, her territory. But one day – Lois had never consciously thought of this before – some guy would have to look at her, touch her. She wished she had not thought of it now. Presumably then, when it happened, she would want him to. She could not imagine that at all. She pressed her knees defensively together. But since it had to happen, maybe it would be okay to practise with a kid, with Andy? Maybe she could get used to it, understand why he should want to?

'I'm off now,' Andy called. 'See you.'

'Wait. Andy.' She jumped up and moved to the edge of the loft floor. He was standing nonchalantly between the chair and the doors, his hands in his pockets. 'You promise to do the chair?' He nodded. 'Just like I said?'

'Yes.'

'Promise. Say it.'

'I promise to fix the chair.'

'Okay.' She backed off, away from the edge, not knowing how it could be accomplished, how begun.

Andy came to the foot of the ladder, began to climb, slowly. His face was set, pink, his eyes very bright, searching.

When he was only halfway up the ladder, Lois said, 'Stop. Stop there.'

She came forward again. The expression on his face was a preparation for anger, frustration. She stopped at the top of the ladder and stared straight ahead. For the first time she became aware of the vertiginous danger of the loft. She felt dizzy, as she had that night on the Hunters' window ledge. There was nothing but space in front of her. She concentrated on it as she lifted her skirt, pulled it up, up until it was bunched in her sweating hands around her waist.

Andy gasped with pleasure and astonishment. He leaned his weight against the left upright of the ladder, his head tilted back, breathing through his mouth. He let his eyes crawl upwards from her knees. The pale smooth thighs, slightly parted. To the leg of her knickers gripping and indenting the flesh. There was a narrow little band of pale green trimming edging the legs, the waist. They were white, spotted with little green and pink flower sprigs, like apple blossom. Above them, her bare stomach, the hollow of her navel. And between her legs where the knickers were drawn tight, a slight, a voluptuous hump. He gazed. His eyes devoured her. He was panting and hot. He pushed his left hand hard into his groin, making the stretched back of his knees tremble.

Lois saw the space go up into the shadowed rafters of the pointed roof, stretch away to the far end wall, slip down to the distant floor.

I wondered if we could make them walk the plank.

Yes, of course. That was it. At the time the idea had seemed impractical, no fun. But now, she saw it all. She glanced down at her own feet, the edge of the loft floor. She saw Andy's red face, his wet, shining eyes, with shock. For a moment she had forgotten. She saw that he was trembling, quivering, as though mortally afraid. Something like an enormous smile began in her stomach, rose up fluttering her chest, blossomed on her face. She let the bunched skirt fall and squatted down, grasping the edge of the floor.

Andy let his head fall forwards, his forehead pressed against a rung of the ladder.

'Andy, could you fix something up here? I don't know what it would be exactly. Something that turns but would hold. Straps maybe, or things like those little cage things – what do you call them? – that you put your feet in on racing cycles. Andy?'

She realized that he had not heard or taken in a word she had said. Like someone in a trance, she watched him gather himself, come out of himself.

'I did it, Andy, didn't I?'

He swallowed, nodding his head. His smile was small and shaky.

Lois did not know what prompted her to ask, 'Did you like it?'

'Yes. Great.'

He began to descend the ladder as though the intimacy he had just shared with her was something he could not discuss.

'Wait. Andy, I want you to come up here and take a look at the floor here.'

'What for?'

'There's something else. I can't figure out how it could be made to work, but you can.'

He hauled himself up the ladder again until his head was on a level with the edge of the floor. Excitedly, everything else forgotten, Lois explained what she wanted, what she had in mind. Andy listened, nodded, narrowed his eyes and felt the bevelled piece of wood which sealed off the ends of the floorboards. It was strong enough. Suddenly, he had a vision of what she wanted and how it could be put to his own most secret use.

'Yes,' he said, enthusiastic. 'It'd be great. I'll work on it. I'll think of something. Don't worry.'

'You're terrific, Andy.'

'But . . .'

'What?'

'You'd have to let me again. Just now . . . that was only for the chair. This is extra.'

Lois stood up, holding her skirt flat against her legs to make sure that he could not see up it.

'No, Andy,' she said. 'You've got to figure it out and fix it. Then, if it's real good, I might let you.'

Their eyes locked. Lois was smiling. Andy tried to think of an argument to counter her ultimatum but he could not. He could only think of the possibilities, the barely imaginable delights his invention could provide. He realized that he couldn't lose.

'All right,' he said, suddenly business-like. 'Now let's get that chair over to our garage.' He went down the ladder. 'We can manage it between us.'

Lois smiled. It didn't seem so bad now, what she had done, might have to do again. She had experienced the power of her body, the power it, through no will or thought of her own, exercised over Andy. She felt sort of proud of herself as she scrambled down the ladder, not even caring if Andy peeked up her skirt as she did so. She had discovered another weapon in her armoury, one she would nurture and treasure. She wondered, as she jumped down to the ground, how many other people might be susceptible to it. In a way, she felt grateful to Andy.

30 MAY

Jason woke first. It was still very early. He could tell this from the angle at which sunlight entered the room. It sketched the shadow of the window on the blue wall at the foot of his bunk. There was a knot of excitement deep in the pit of his stomach and beyond that, a sense of dread, dark and amorphous, which he tried to push away, did not like to think about. Above him, in the upper bunk, Julian stirred. It was always like that. The twins woke and slept within minutes of each other. They would have been alarmed had it not been so. That it was, that Julian awoke and sighed, turned over, made Jason feel better. The dark dread receded a little.

'What's up?' Julian asked. He had turned over on to his back, stared at the white ceiling. Had anyone asked him, he would have been unable to say how he knew that his brother was awake, was anxious about something. Jason did not need to ask.

'Just thinking.'

'What about?'

'Do you remember that time you were in hospital?'

'That was yonks ago,' Julian said, not seeing how ancient history could be the source of present worry.

'It was awful. It was all right for you. You didn't know anything about it.'

'All right for me? I was ill. I might have died.'

'I know. But for me . . . being left all on my own like that . . . it was really frightening.'

'Well?'

'Well, I was just thinking: what is the worst thing that could ever happen to us?'

'To be dead, I suppose.'

'Not if we both were.'

'No.'

'I think it would be to be split up, separated.'

Julian frowned at the ceiling, considering it. Unlike Jason, he had no memory of it, no experience. Trying to imagine it, he felt peculiar, disabled, as though something was badly wrong with him. He twisted over and looked down at his brother's serious face.

'What brought all this on?' he asked. 'It's our birthday.'

'I know. That did.'

Julian looked comical upside down, with his hair hanging away from his head, but Jason did not laugh. They looked at each other, silent, and then Julian's head disappeared and Jason knew that he understood. Some of the dread, his dread, had entered his brother and worked there, as it did with him, putting everything else – anticipation, excitement – into bleak perspective.

Julian sighed heavily.

'Well, they won't try to make us drink blood.'

'No.'

Unspoken, the question hung between them: What then? It was like a third, ominous presence in the room.

'We could just stay clear?' Jason suggested tentatively. He sensed Julian shaking his head.

'We said we'd go down to the barn.'

'Perhaps we won't be back in time. We could fix it.'

'There'd be tomorrow. Or the next day,' Julian said, fatalistically.

They were going out for the day. The twins were surprised by their mother's unusual willingness not to do the right thing, not to insist on a party with twin birthday cakes. But it suited them, had seemed a good idea at the time.

'Put off the evil hour,' Julian said.

'Scotch'd the snake but not killed it,' Jason replied.

Julian giggled.

'What's that mean?'

'More or less the same. I don't know. I heard it on some quiz programme.'

'Snakes?' Julian suggested, leaping ahead, confident that Jason would follow.

'No. Where'd they get snakes?'

'Don't mind them anyway, do you?'

'Don't know. Don't think so.'

What then? They lapsed into silence, thinking.

'Perhaps it won't be so bad.'

'Perhaps they've forgotten all about it.'

No.

'It's just . . . so long as we're not, you know . . . split up.'

'You're not really scared, are you?'

'Aren't you?'

'A bit.'

'Right.'

'The thing is . . .' Julian said, sitting up.

'. . . to remember that it's just a game . . .'

'. . . no matter what happens.'

'No matter how awful it seems.'

'Not to be frightened by it.'

'Right.'

But what?

'I bet it's something pretty crummy, really,' Jason said, trying to boost his own and Julian's confidence.

'Or they couldn't think of anything at all.'

'Right.'

'You going back to sleep?'

'Don't think so.'

'Shall we get up then?'

'If you like.'

They did not move.

'Happy birthday,' Julian said.

'Yes. Happy birthday.'

Having cleaned the hutch thoroughly and put down fresh bedding, a dish of water, another of bran, William lifted the rabbit out of the cardboard box which served as a temporary home during cleaning operations, and hugged him gently to his chest. The rabbit was not yet full grown, mostly white with a few black spots and patches. He was, after all, called Oliver and his ears were very pink, having only a faint dusting of white hair on them. William stroked his ears gently, smiled at the wriggling, perpetually-curious little nose. The sun was already warm on his back and he looked critically at the hutch to check that it would indeed be in full-shade by noon. With a certain reluctance, talking softly, William put Oliver back into the hutch and fastened the door. He cleared away the tools he had used to clean the cage, emptied the soiled sawdust and stale bedding into the dustbin and then lingered for a while beside the wire netting of the hutch, watching the rabbit wash his face.

All the time he was listening. Listening for the familiar slam of the Shillingworths' 'Medieval-look' front door, the clear, carrying sound of Mrs Shillingworth's voice. There was no special reason why he wanted to be sure the twins had gone before he went over to the barn. It just seemed important to him, a sort of talisman. Checking his watch, he went to stand in the shadows beside the house. He could see the tail of the Shillingworths' four-door family saloon and perched himself on one of the dustbins to wait.

In a way, he'd rather not go to the barn at all. He would be quite content just being with Oliver, talking to him, stroking him. But he had to go. He had to go because already there was that little uncomfortable-pleasurable tingling feeling at the base of his spine. Something more than curiosity tugged him to the barn and this enforced wait was a sort of delicious penance, like rationing the pages of a really good book to postpone that moment when the reader knows all and the book is done, never to be read in the same spirit of excitement again.

He heard Mrs Shillingworth's voice, saw Mr Shillingworth come out to the car and put a laden bag inside. Then Jane, followed by the twins, shoulder to shoulder, as though glued together. The front door slammed and then rattled as Mrs Shillingworth pushed it, to make sure the latch had caught properly. After fastening the deadlock, she would push it again, William knew, but Mr Shillingworth had already started the car so he would not hear the click of the lock, the second, different rattle of the door. He glimpsed Mrs Shillingworth's blonde head and waited, tapping his fingers against the dustbin, until the car left.

He ran then, ran as though the Devil was at his heels, leaping tussocks of grass in the uneven field, pretending they were hurdles on the Crystal Palace track. He arrived at the open barn, panting and flushed.

'They've gone,' he shouted. 'The twins have gone.'

'Big deal,' Lois answered from the shadowed loft. 'What d'you think, Andy?'

Blinking against the sudden dimness, William walked curiously into the barn to see what they were doing. Hanging from the loft floor was a lumpy-looking sack. Andy was kneeling, inspecting some mechanical contraption fixed to the loft floor. Lois hovered anxiously over him.

'What's this?' William said.

'Hey, make yourself useful,' Andy called down. 'Can you reach the sack?'

William stood underneath it, estimating.

'If I jump for it.'

'Okay. See if you can get hold of it and just swing on it. Put all your weight on it.'

'Careful,' Lois said. 'It's got rocks in it.' To Andy she added, 'You'll have to fix it so you can lower it.'

'Rocks?' William pulled a face.

'They're heavy, aren't they?'

William shrugged and jumped, his arms stretched above his head. He failed to get a grip on the sack but set it swinging with a rattle of metal chains.

'If you fixed it nearer the ladder . . .' he said.

'It would have been no good at all, stupid,' Andy shouted.

'You've got to make it lower,' Lois repeated.

'I will. Don't keep on. This is just a test.'

William jumped again, caught one side of the sack and swung with it, monkey-like.

'See?' Andy said triumphantly to Lois. 'It'll hold.'

'He only had one hand on it. I want all his weight on it. I want it tested properly.'

'It's still got all his weight, stupid.'

'Don't call me stupid.'

'How's that?' William called as he dropped to the ground.

'Fine,' Andy said.

'*If* you make it go lower,' Lois reminded him.

William climbed the ladder.

'It will go lower. It's *meant* to go lower,' Andy said, exasperated.

'How's it work?' William asked from the ladder.

'Hang on. Let me drop the sack off first. 'Ware below,' Andy shouted.

The sack crashed onto the barn floor, splitting in a cloud of dust. Stones and rocks spilled out. Lois clapped her hands and shouted at the noise.

'Okay. See here, William,' Andy said, 'the chains pass through here and are fixed with this pin . . .'

William peered at the complicated gadget, which looked like two adapted hoists, but he could not make sense of the principle or the technical terms Andy used to describe it. He had seen for himself that it would work, that it was strong enough, and that was all that mattered. He pretended to listen, though, nodding and saying 'yes' every now and again; but his mind was occupied with the tingling sensation which had begun to spread up his back now, like a slow-motion shiver.

'One of you guys help me with this mattress, please,' Lois said, puffing with the weight of the old mattress which she was dragging clumsily across the floor.

'I'll do it,' William told Andy and went to help her.

They carried it to the edge and dropped it over. It landed with a soft, dull sound and sent up an even bigger cloud of dust than the sack.

'Okay. Now we've got to get it into position,' she said, starting down the ladder.

'You don't *need* it,' Andy grumbled.

'Just fix the chains, okay?'

Muttering, Andy began to fiddle with his machine, rattling the chains on the floor. William climbed down and helped Lois clear the rocks and stones out of the way with an old shovel and two rusty buckets.

'If he'd fixed the thing properly first,' Lois complained, 'there wouldn't have been all this mess.'

The dust made them cough and sneeze and they were soon sweating from their exertions.

'What are you giving the twins for their birthday?' Lois asked William.

'Some new bits they wanted for their Meccano.'

'I wanted to give them something really wild,' Lois said, 'but my Mom said I had to give them book tokens because that way Mrs Shillingworth would approve.'

'That's not fair,' Andy said. 'Didn't you tell her?'

'There's no point. You can't talk to her lately. And will you just please get that thing working right?'

The rocks cleared, Lois picked up one end of the mattress and together she and William half-dragged, half-carried it around the ladder and placed it below the point where, with a clicking of ratchets, Andy was paying out the heavy chains.

'Jump down,' Lois told him, watching the swinging chains, 'and see if we've got it right.'

'And break my leg if you haven't? No thanks!'

'Well, does it look right?'

'Yes. But you won't need it.'

Lois rolled her eyes towards heaven and adjusted the mattress a little. The chains were now low enough for her to touch easily. They descended another few feet.

'That's it,' Andy said.

'I guess that'll have to do,' Lois said, trying to estimate the distance between the ends of the chains and the mattress.

'Oh, thanks a lot,' Andy said, ironically.

'You did terrific, okay? Now take 'em up again.'

William, his back to her, was staring at something square and solid, draped in an old, stained tarpaulin.

'That's the chair,' Lois said. 'Want to see?'

'Yes.'

'Leave it,' Andy shouted. 'Let me. You'll only mess it up.'

'I will not so.'

'You have to lift the tarpaulin, not drag it.' Andy sounded near to tears of frustration. He scrambled down the ladder as fast as he could and pushed Lois aside. Gently, he lifted one end of the tarpaulin, nodding to William to take the other end. Carefully, they lifted it back. William stared at the chair.

'Isn't it neat?'

Andy went to the chair, again engrossed in his work, and examined a festoon of leather straps, some of which had small metal discs or plates fixed to their inner surface.

'It looks just like the real thing,' Lois said, almost fondly. 'I saw a real one once, in a Museum of Horrors. And look, William, back here's the little generator . . .'

'Leave that. Don't touch it. You'll only mess it up,' Andy shouted.

'Oh excuse me for breathing,' Lois said and flounced away. She sat down on the mattress, ignoring them.

Andy showed William the little box-like contraption he had made, with its sinister-looking coils and terminals.

'Help me put the tarpaulin back,' he said. 'And no one's to touch it, understand? No one but me.'

'No,' said William, helping with the tarpaulin, shrouding the chair and its attachments.

He would not dare to touch it. The chair made him feel sick and yet it thrilled him, too. He continued to stare at it, feeling the shivers build and gather in his body, even when the tarpaulin was in place.

Andy went back up into the loft and began to raise the dangling chains.

'What're you going to do now?' Lois asked William. 'Everything's just about ready, I guess, and it'll be hours before they get back.'

William shrugged. He didn't know. He wandered out into the sunlight. Doubts floated and exploded in his mind, like flashes of electricity, but he knew that they were powerless to make him change his mind or argue. He was too interested, too excited.

'You can come and see Oliver if you like,' he told Lois over his shoulder.

'No, thanks.'

'Stay here then, I suppose.'

'Maybe we should have a rehearsal,' Lois said, grinning.

The twins walked slowly right around the horseshoe curve of the Crescent from their house to William's. The day had passed in a flash and they had enjoyed it. Already, though, it seemed to be fading, slipping away from them: everything that had gone before was an overture to this moment, the main, unknown action of the day.

By silent agreement Jason waited on the pavement while Julian went to call for William. His father opened the door and against a background of the baby's wailing, told him that William was out, over at the barn, he thought. He forgot to wish the twins a happy birthday.

They went together to the Carradines' front door, like condemned men, and received Neil's good wishes with muted thanks.

'She's already over at the barn, waiting for you,' he said, winking as he pronounced the death sentence. 'Planning a big surprise, I bet you. So get on over there and have a really good time, you hear?'

'Thank you,' said Jason.

'We will,' said Julian.

They retraced their steps to the pathway between Numbers Three and Four. Jason looked at Julian, who forced a smile.

'Better get it over with.'

'Yes. It'll be all right. You'll see.'

'Come on, then.'

They turned into the path between the houses and then went out into the sunlit, open field.

'Here they come,' Lois said. 'Everybody ready?'

They were all gathered outside the barn, clutching their gifts and watching the slow approach of the twins. Some nodded, some said 'yes' in voices tight with excitement.

'Okay, here we go. Ah-one, two, three.'

Happy birthday to you
Happy birthday to you
Happy birthday dear Jason 'n' Julian
Happy birthday to you.

The twins were surprised by the ragged singing which drifted towards them. They exchanged a glance of pleasure and relief and began to walk more quickly towards their waiting friends.

'Again, and louder,' Lois commanded. 'Ah-one, two, three.'

They repeated the traditional song, Andy and Amanda this time substituting:

Squashed tomatoes and stew

for the second line, and then breaking up into giggles.

The twins stood, with foolish grins on their faces, as the song died away and their friends crowded around them, shouting greetings and questions, thrusting packages and envelopes into their hands. William and Andy thumped them on their backs. Amanda demanded that they open their presents.

'Let's go inside first,' Julian said.

'No, there's more light out here. Come on. Open up,' William said quickly.

So they sat down on the grass outside the barn and opened their presents. Lois loudly disclaimed all responsibility for the book tokens, but the twins immediately knew what they were going to buy with them. The Meccano pieces were exclaimed over, as were the matching slimline pocket torches from Amanda. Andy provided pen and pencil sets, one blue, one red, and Vanessa waited expectantly as they unwrapped her soft, flat packages. She had stitched them herself, large square bags of black cotton, each with a drawstring and embroidered, in shaky chainstitch, with their names in gold.

'They're shoe bags,' she explained, 'for when you have to take gym shoes and things to school.'

'But you can use them for lots of things,' Andy said, and snickered.

'She made them all herself,' Lois added.

'They're very nice,' Jason said.

'Lovely, thank you,' Julian agreed.

They examined their presents again, switching on the torches, discussing what they would be able to make with the new Meccano pieces. Andy got up casually and slipped unnoticed into the barn. William looked at Lois, but her eyes were fixed on the twins, on their bent, identical heads.

Together they formed something, a union she did not know and never would know, something that shut her out. Being a twin, she thought, was not like having a brother or sister. She'd often thought of that possibility, imagined how it would be and didn't like it. The thought alone made her jealous, scared her even, but to be a twin . . . It would be like having yourself there always, the self you saw in the mirror but who couldn't talk back, could only mimic you. She realized that the twins did not know what it was like to be lonely. They did not know how it felt to be alone in a room, looking out, seeing everyone else having a good time, going places, belonging. They could turn their backs on all that because they had each other. Lois did not know how it could be, how it must feel . . .

William stood up suddenly, breaking her concentration. The twins' companionable murmuring ceased. They looked up startled, aware of the silence, of Andy's absence, the taut expression on William's face.

'Yes, well, thanks a lot,' Julian said.

'Yes. Thanks, all of you.'

They began to gather their presents together, instinctively making separate but identical piles. William leaned down and snatched Jason's black bag.

'Let's have a look,' he said, pushing his hand inside it, opening it up.

'You haven't forgotten, have you?' Lois said, frowning. 'You have to make your vow of loyalty on your birthday.'

'That's right,' Vanessa said eagerly. 'Like I did, remember?'

'No. I mean, yes.'

'We hadn't forgotten,' Julian said.

'Good. We've got it all planned out for you. A proper, solemn ceremony.'

The twins looked at Lois mutely.

'First, you've got to be blindfolded,' William said.

'What for?'

'These bags'll do nicely.'

He held the bag bearing Jason's name open, the drawstring loose.

'Right,' Lois said, plucking Julian's bag from his pile of presents. 'Amanda, you take care of this stuff,' she said, indicating the remaining presents as she shook open the bag. 'No, hold still,' she told Julian. 'This is just a blindfold, okay?'

Julian held himself rigid, allowed her to slip the bag over his head. She drew the drawstring tight and knotted it.

Jason ducked his head as William advanced on him with his bag.

'Good job you worked their names on, Van. Otherwise we wouldn't have known which was which.'

'It's all right,' Julian said to his brother, his voice muffled by something other than the bag.

Jason nodded, closed his eyes. William pulled the bag roughly down over his head and fastened the drawstring.

'Now we're going to help you up. We'll guide you so you

don't fall or stumble or anything. Right, give me your hand.'

Lois took Julian's hand and helped him up, steadying him. William did the same with Jason. Once on their feet, the twins reached for each other, their hands groping sightlessly until, guided by some instinct, their fingers touched and laced. Lois watched their hands, caught William's sneer, then she stepped smartly between them, breaking their clasp, and took Julian by the shoulders, guiding him towards the barn door, which Vanessa held open.

Jason opened his eyes when he felt the cord tighten around his neck. His immediate reaction was panic. It seemed to him that he could not breathe either. When he sucked in air through his mouth, the cloth cloyed against his lips, threatening to stifle him. He raised his hand and tugged at the drawstring but it was quite loose. His fingers slipped easily under it. William snatched his hand away, but that didn't matter because his other hand touched Julian's searching fingers and gripped them. The panic subsided a little then, and he tried to breathe normally so that the cloth did not stick to his face or billow out hotly from it. But it returned when somebody pushed between them and he felt his brother's hand torn from his. Immediately, he lost all sense of space. He imagined Julian drawn away from him very quickly, saw him becoming smaller and smaller, sucked into some science-fiction vortex until he was just a pinpoint of light, then gone.

William gripped his upper arm, told him to walk. He seemed disconnected from his feet, which felt clumsy and uncertain. He heard laughter as he passed into the barn. He thought it was Vanessa. Certainly a girl, giggling at the sight of him, faceless because of the hood, identifiable only by the stitched letters of his name. He knew he had entered the barn because he could no longer feel the sun on his back and, more disturbingly, because the darkness created by the hood became absolute. He wished then that he had been more aware of the little light which had penetrated it before. A little was better than nothing.

'Stop. Give me your hands.'

William did not wait for him to obey but seized his wrists and guided them until they felt smooth wood.

'That's the ladder, see?'

He could not go up the ladder blindfold. He could not. He saw himself falling, losing his footing, slipping, dying.

'I'll come up right behind you so you won't fall. Just feel for each rung carefully. All right? Ready?'

The first rung felt sharp and unsafe under his foot. William steadied him, moved behind him. He began to sweat. He could feel it on his back, under his arms, in his groin. His hands were slippery. He tried and failed to remember how long the ladder was. He had climbed it so many times, so carelessly. He could only think of the yawning space on either side. How far had he climbed? How much further? He leaned against the ladder, trembling.

'Go on,' William said. 'Keep going.'

He wanted to say that he could not, dare not. He said, 'Julian?'

There was no answer.

William dug him in the ribs, swore at him. He reached up into nothing, knocked his hand against the next rung, lost it.

'Just slide your hands along the uprights,' William said, impatient.

Somehow he could not. Finding each rung was blind chance. When he did, he gripped it with a grimness, a determination that made his arms shake with the effort.

'Go on,' William said, prodding him.

Jason's hand waved in front of him, feeling nothing. He had a terrible vision of the ladder ending suddenly, leading nowhere. When you got to the top you fell off. He felt queasy and knew that he was going to fall. He had to. It would almost be a relief.

Two hands gripped his arm, held it tightly.

'Come on. I've got you. You're here now.'

He did not recognize Andy's voice but gripped the shoulder to which his lost hand was guided for dear life. Hands took his other arm. He let all his weight rest on this saviour. Hands guided his feet, turn by turn. One rung. Two rungs. There was no connection between his hands and his feet. None. He crumpled up, fell. Whoever had tried to save him was not strong enough.

His knees struck the floor of the loft with a loud thud, surprising him. The impact jarred his spine. He heard someone, alarmed, say, 'What's that?'

Julian?

'Julian?' he shouted, his voice singing in his ears.

There was no reply.

Hands hauled and pulled him to his feet. Voices told him to sit. Groping with his hands, terrified of falling, he felt the painted surface of the nursery table and lowered himself gingerly. It seemed to take forever. All co-ordination was lost to him. His bottom and the table collided.

'What?' he said. 'Let me . . .'

Someone was fiddling with his feet. He snatched them away, frightened.

'Hold still,' William said crossly. 'I've got to take your shoes and socks off. Can you do it?'

He didn't know. Why?

'And roll his trousers up,' Andy said.

Why?

He had to bend down, to find his own feet. The hands tugging off his shoe frightened and angered him.

'Ugh. Your feet smell,' William said.

He felt around, trying to reach his feet. Leaning forward into nothing, into darkness, made him feel sick and dizzy. His hand brushed against flesh, warm and smooth.

'Get off. I'll do it.'

His left foot felt suddenly chill as his sock was removed. The floor was rough and ugly under his sole. 'Lift your leg up.'

William punched him, just below the knee. He obeyed, distracted by the touch of fingers against his ankle, his calf, as someone else rolled his trousers up.

Why?

'All right,' William said.

Jason felt him moving away. There was no one near him. He was all alone.

'Come back,' he said. 'Don't leave me.'

'Jason?'

His name, spoken in fear, was muffled, a cry across space.

'Julian?'

'Shut up,' somebody snarled. 'Shut up or else.'

Hands gripped his arms. Both arms. Hands on either side of him. People.

'Where? Who?'

He knew they were not going to answer him, that he was condemned to silence. They raised him and they made him walk. His feet, cringing against the dirty, rough boards moved in spite of him, obeying the reflex of habit. By sharp pressure on his arms, his captors indicated he should stop. His teeth were chattering. He heard a metallic rattle as something was fastened around his left ankle, and he heard it again as the process was repeated with his right. He lifted one foot experimentally and found it heavy. He recognized the sound then. It was the rattle of chains. He shrank back instinctively, but the unseen, unknown hands gripped again, forcing him to remain where he was.

'Jason?'

It was Lois's voice but it sounded very small and far away. He turned his head, trying to catch the direction. The hands gripped him again and he sensed panic in their touch.

'Careful,' she warned. 'You must be very careful now, Jason. You're in great danger. If you don't do exactly as I say, when I say, you could fall and you could have a really nasty accident. You'd be sure to break your legs. You might even die. I don't know for sure. So, you do just as I say and then nothing will happen to you.' She waited a beat. 'Jason?'

He had to speak, to say that he understood. He wanted to ask her to let him go, to beg her, but he could only make a sound, inarticulate and terrified.

'I want you to sit down now, Jason. Just lean on Andy and William and sit down.'

He didn't think his legs would hold him anyway, and just hearing their names, knowing who they were, made it easier for him. He bent his legs, squatted and sat down. Automatically he straightened out his bent legs and, with a cry of terror, he realized there was nothing there. The chains rattled, the most awful sound he had ever heard, and weights snapped, then dragged at his ankles, pulling him forward, down into nothingness.

He found his voice then.

'Oh please, please . . .' he sobbed, turning his hidden face towards William or Andy, whoever held him back from the dragging weight at his feet.

'I told you, Jason,' Lois said. 'I told you to be very careful. You nearly fell then, didn't you? You nearly fell, Jason.'

'Please let me go . . .' he said and heard his voice as though it belonged to someone else. It was the trembling voice of a frightened child.

'Let you go? Let you fall? Is that what you want, Jason?'

'No, no, don't let me . . .' He flung out his arms, trying to grab William or Andy. Whoever it was danced away from him.

'You must be still,' Lois told him. 'Then everything will be okay. Now, here's what I want you to do. I'm only going to tell you once, Jason, so you'd better listen good . . .'

'I can't,' he sobbed. 'I want Julian . . .'

'Julian can't help you now, Jason. That's what this is all about. Only we can help you, Jason. The gang. Say it, Jason.'

'Wh . . . what?'

'Tell me you know that only the gang can help you.'

He tried, but the words got all muddled up with his babyish tears. And his nose was running so that he had to sniff and that made it difficult to catch his breath.

'That's not good enough, Jason, so I'm going to have to teach you to trust us. Now listen and do exactly as I say. You've got to let go, Jason. You've got to fall. So that we can catch you. And you mustn't struggle or anything or we might drop you. I hope you understand that, Jason, because it's going to happen . . . Now.'

He struggled then, without sense of objective. He kicked his legs against the dragging weights. He twisted to fight off the hands that were pushing him towards the edge, towards nothing. It was no good. He heard his scream, an unearthly shriek of terror and anguish and knew that he was going to die. It was the sound of death itself.

He dropped suddenly, leaving his stomach behind. He pitched forward, seemed to turn over and over. Everything happened very slowly. Something caught him, held him. Something broke his fall. He heard voices shouting, the panting roar of breath overlaying the scream. He turned completely over and there was pain in his ankles. His knees seemed to snap and pop apart. The scream grew louder and louder as all around him he felt nothing. Like a swimmer, he stretched his arms and encountered only space and air. That was all there was. That and the straining grip on his ankles. His head began to pound. The darkness became red and, as it began to fade, he realized that the scream was issuing from his own mouth. He clamped it shut. Instead of silence there was a roaring sea in his head, pounding and deafening. The red increased. The red before his eyes was the pain in his legs and there was nothing else in the world at all. He was lost.

They stood in a loose circle, William and Lois, Andy and Vanessa, Amanda, and watched as Jason swung, upside down, from the chains.

At first, Julian wasn't really scared at all. There *was* nothing scary about walking into the barn with Lois, registering the change in such light as penetrated his hood.

He knew they'd be bringing Jason along behind him, at that time assumed that whatever was going to happen would happen to them both, equally and together. Then there was just too much happening to leave him time to be scared. She positioned him and pushed him down into the chair. It was quite comfortable and it never occurred to him to resist when they – for there were two of them then – fastened his wrists to the arms of the chair, his ankles to the legs. It was only when he heard William explaining about the ladder that he became seriously alarmed. He struggled against his bonds but they remained tight. He knew, by some instinct of brotherly preservation that he must not, as all his instincts cried out for him to do, shout Jason's name. If he startled him, did anything to alarm him, he would fall. They were crazy, he thought, crazy and vicious to make anyone climb that ladder blindfold. The time it took was incalculable, forever. He heard some of William's instructions, Andy's voice and then, when he heard the thud, his heart seemed to stop and he could not prevent the words escaping.

'What's that?'

'Julian?'

So he was all right. A hand clamped over his mouth, pressing the cloth of the hood unpleasantly against his nose and mouth. It was not an effective or, indeed, particularly serious attempt to gag him, but he remained silent, not answering when he should have done.

They would pick on Jason, he thought. It would have been easier on him and they knew that. Not that Jason was a coward or anything, but just because he . . .

They said something about taking his shoes and socks off. Why? He kept very still, almost holding his breath, trying to milk every noise, each word or partial sentence caught, so that he would *know* what was happening. Realizing that the blindfold acted as a distraction from concentration, he squeezed his eyes shut, straining his ears. The sounds made no sense, or rather, in the enforced blackness and total immobility, they took on sinister and monstrous overtones, like the disconnected soundtrack of a nightmare. Voices mingled with the bumps and scuffles but he could hear only the tone, not the sense, until five words cut straight through his mounting sense of dread.

'Come back. Don't leave me.'

'Jason?'

He had meant it to be much louder than it sounded, to give comfort and confidence.

'Julian?'

The answer, his brother's faint and quavering voice stabbed him. He really tugged against his bonds then, knowing that something dreadful was about to happen.

'Shut up. Shut up or else.'

That was Lois, no mistaking her, and simultaneously, hands loosened the hood, pulled it up, admitting light. He was too afraid to look, closed his eyes again. The material was caught tight, pulled back so that it cut into his upper lip, seemed to squash his nose. They were not going to take it off, then. What now? He heard a ripping noise, recognized it and yet could not place it.

Sticking plaster sealed his lips.

He identified it more by the smell and the feel. The hood was pulled down again, but not fastened. It was like a challenge to him. He had to discover what, how much noise he could make, see if he could dislodge the plaster. It was difficult breathing just through his nose. If he took deep breaths, the cotton bag was sucked unpleasantly against his nostrils. The only sounds were muffled grunts, trapped in his throat, only partly articulated. They increased his panic. He had to concentrate, had to make himself breathe regularly and slowly.

The chains clattered and rattled.

He identified that sound at once and he cried out as best he could, struggling. Metal and what he thought was leather bit into his flesh. His cry was a stifled moan, weak and useless. He saw damp stone walls and flickering torches, the evil machinery of torture. Jason's sobs, his wet, childish sniffing only lent a bloody relish to the picture. He tried to blot it out, to hang on to the sparks of reason that told him he was in the barn, that there was nothing very terrible they could do.

How long since he had heard Jason weep like that? He could not remember. The sounds were galling, seemed to tease and twist his nerves. He associated them with pain and strangeness, with an engulfing oblivion that separated him from his brother.

Do you remember that time you were in hospital?

The memory, insubstantial as a dream, swept over him. He began to tremble with a cold sweat and tried to escape the cloying remembrances by listening to the worse reality of Jason's sobbing, the shaking, terrible fear and the rattling chains.

'Jason?'

Lois's voice steadied him. He focused all his anger on her. She was standing close to him. He knew that she must be able to hear his not entirely silenced curses and cries. He did not listen to what she said but tried, by moving his lips as much and as violently as possible, to get the sticking plaster off. He made himself think of Jason, hold on to the certainty that if they hurt him, he, Julian, would kill them. He would kill Lois especially.

The scream razored through his head. It appalled him as he knew that madness was immobility, helplessness, silence and blindness. Without realizing he was doing it, he shook his head from side to side, denying the scream, absorbing it into himself. He became the scream for a moment, his whole body shaking with its tearing force.

He was aware of movement around him. His skin crawled with fear as their voices, breathless and out of control, broke through the scream.

'Get him.'

'Hold him.'

'Careful. Don't drop him.'

'His legs.'

'I told you it wouldn't work . . . I told you . . .'

'Oh shit.'

'You idiot!'

'Shut up. Just shut up. Gently now. Gently.'

Their heavy, laboured breathing pressed against his ears. He could smell his own fear.

Where had the scream gone?

Into the grave. Into silence.

He threw his weight back against the chair, rocking it, trying to throw it over, smash it. They had killed Jason. He knew it. He knew it by the scream's silence.

They were all around him then. Somebody leaned against the chair, steadying it, clamping it to the ground.

'Be still,' Lois shouted at him, and he struggled all the more fiercely. 'Don't you want to know what just happened to Jason?' she said, and he froze, his body became ice. 'Sit still and I'll tell you.'

He did not believe her, knew it was madness to do so, but he had no strength left. He heard them moving around, heard a tiny motor start up, he thought it came from behind him. The sort of motor he and Jason used – had used – to power the cranes and armoured tanks they constructed out of Meccano, working together, always together, like one person with four hands.

It happened then. Something stinging and growing shouting through him. His arms felt numb.

'Julian, listen to me. Did you feel that? Did you?'

Her voice sounded crazy, thick with emotion, as though she was about to scream herself.

It happened again. Stronger this time. In his legs. A shock wave that made him flinch and shudder.

'You're in the electric chair, Julian. Did you know that? That's how we execute criminals back home. We fry 'em, Julian. How's it feel?'

It came again. He gritted his teeth together, determined to ride it out. When it passed, leaving him weak and trembling, he refused to listen to her. He made himself think and understand. With a motor that small, they could not generate much electricity. No more than he had received. Not enough to harm him.

The next shock was already less powerful, a tantalizing tingle of unpleasantness, running up his left arm, making him cringe.

'Because you're not loyal to us, Julian. You're always off with Jason. You and he are against us, Julian, and we can't have that.'

'Like a couple of fairies, holding hands and whispering.'

It was William who spoke, his voice vicious, bending over him.

'You must put us before him, before everyone. You've got to dedicate yourself to us. You have to sacrifice Jason.'

The shock came again, in both legs, making him catch his breath and nip the side of his tongue. It seemed that it would never cease, that he had been wrong. Imagination made it build until he waited for the explosion, the flash that would obliterate him.

His head fell forward. His mouth was full of saliva and he could not swallow it quickly enough. Somebody pushed his head back and, incredibly, he was able to see again. The hood was lifted free of his face and he was able to see his brother suspended from the loft floor, unmoving, upside down. Dead.

Something soft and furry climbed down his back. Why was his back naked? How could it be? He wasn't dead. Where was he? The roaring in his ears had steadied to a rhythm. The pain in his legs had settled to an ache. It seemed that it had always been there. The furry thing meandered across his shoulder blades, making his flesh creep. He flapped with his hand, trying to knock it away. His whole body swung sickeningly and the pain in his ankles increased sharply. Somebody laughed. He tried to call out but found his mouth clogged with spittle and mucous. He bent his neck awkwardly, swallowed.

Now it was something wet and slimy, inching, oozing down his back. It made him feel sick. He began to cough, wriggling hysterically.

'That's enough,' someone said.

The slime became a trickle running down towards his neck.

He wasn't dead. Julian felt that *he* would die with relief when he saw his brother's flesh quiver, his arm lash out at the soft brush with which Vanessa was gently stroking his back. His shirt had come loose from his trousers, hung down over his shoulders, partly obscuring the black hood. Amanda giggled, shivering, as though it were her flesh that was being tantalized and tortured. Vanessa pressed a wet rag against the small of Jason's back, moved it slowly, slowly along his shuddering skin. He began to fight and wriggle. Julian could see the leather manacles biting into his ankles, could imagine the pain empathetically in his own. His eyes rolled wildly in his head, trying to communicate his terror, the imminent danger. His eyes met William's. They were blank, fascinated, but slowly a new light came into them. Julian implored him.

'That's enough,' he said, and moved towards Vanessa.

She squeezed the rag, leaving rivulets of water trickling down his brother's back.

'Okay, Julian. I'm going to take the plaster off now. When I do, I want you to make the vow. You have to do it for you and Jason. And when you do – only when you do – we'll let him down. Okay?'

Her fingers hovered, teasing him, brushing his cheek. He closed his eyes, unable to bear the wait. She fiddled with the corner of the plaster, unable to get a grip on it. He felt her scratch at it with her nail, ease it up until there was sufficient for her to grasp. It felt as though his skin came away with it. With one swift movement, she tore the plaster from his mouth. The stinging pain exploded across his lower face seconds later.

'Let him down, you bastards. Let him down, please.'

'Language,' Amanda said, gazing at him with a slack smile on her face.

'You take that back, Julian, or we'll never let him down. We'll leave you both here . . .'

'Julian?'

Jason sounded breathless, more muffled than the black hood could possibly justify.

'It's all right, Jason. They're going to let you down.'

'When you've made the vow,' Lois said, placing herself squarely before him.

'All right. Yes.' He swallowed, moistened his dried, flayed-feeling lips. 'I promise to be loyal and devoted . . .'

'No. Not like that. You've got to repeat it after me.'

'All right. Only quickly, please . . .'

'The sooner you do it right, the sooner we'll let him down.'

Julian nodded.

'I, Julian, make this solemn, binding vow . . .'

He repeated the words, trying not to gabble them.

'. . . for myself and my brother, Jason . . .'

'. . . for myself and my brother, Jason . . .'

'. . . that we will always be true and loyal . . .'

'. . . that we will always be true and loyal . . .'

'. . . to Amanda and William . . .'

Their names seemed endless, a chain of syllables enmeshing to prolong his brother's agony. His mouth felt dry and he had to force saliva into it.

'. . . and never to reveal anything that takes place . . .'

'. . . and never to reveal anything that takes place . . .'

'. . . between us in Solemn, Secret Session.'

'. . . between us in Solemn, Secret Session.'

'On pain of torture and death.'

'On pain of torture and death.'

'Good. Okay. You can let him down now.'

Julian could not watch. He was terrified that they would hurt him, drop him. He closed his eyes, even wished for the blindfold again. He was shaking and he knew he was going to cry as Amanda began to free his wrists.

Lois crouched beside Jason, holding his shoulders steady.

'You heard that, Jason? We're going to set you free now. But you've got to swear too. On pain of death.'

She put her ear close to his covered head and just about made out the exhausted, whispered words:

'I swear. Please . . .'

She supported his shoulders, pulling them towards her. Above, the chains rattled. Andy and William took the strain, paying out the chains through the special ratchets Andy had so carefully made. At last, the strain of his own weight was taken off his raging legs. He felt the softness and recognized the sour smell of the old mattress under his shoulders and back. He had to lie there for what seemed ages, his legs in the air, while they undid the straps around his ankles. But then they were free and began to throb.

It was Julian who pulled the bag off his head, Julian he saw first, crying and unable to speak.

She watched them. She thought they'd done pretty good until then. She felt let down. Around her, the others were clearing up, dismantling the equipment they had so carefully got together. So much effort for so little, she thought, angry. She was disappointed. She'd really had to wheedle those goddamn chains out of Farmer Applegreen, spent all her allowance on other stuff . . . For what? Oh it had been good. It had worked. But watching them – and she couldn't help watching them – huddled together on the mattress like that, she knew they would heal and she hated them for that. There was no way she could take that away from them, but at least they knew now, had some idea how it felt, who really mattered around here.

'You paid your dues,' she said, standing over them.

Julian looked up at her, his face streaked and flushed with baby tears. For a moment she saw the start of fear in his eyes, something else she would not let herself acknowledge.

'You did really well,' she said, raising her voice so they could all hear. 'That was a really tough initiation and you did it. Didn't they, gang?'

They all agreed. They all gathered around the twins then. Jason struggled to sit up and Julian saw that he was smiling, basking in their congratulations. William offered his hand to be shaken. He took it, embarrassed, not understanding how any of this could be. Not understanding how Jason could be smiling, even while rubbing the sore weals on his legs. Vanessa brought his shoes and socks. He put them on, blew his nose. They were all talking at once, excited and full of themselves, as though the party was only just beginning. Julian was worried about Jason. He didn't think he ought to be sitting up yet, standing. He *was* standing, swaying a little, touching his head. Julian's heart skipped with fear.

'No. I'm all right. It's just that . . .'

He never finished what he was saying. A funny, blanched look came over his face.

'What?' Julian struggled up, hampered by the resilient softness of the mattress. He thought Jason was going to faint or collapse or something.

The others fell back silent, as frightened as Julian. Then they saw it, the damp stain spreading down Jason's left thigh. In the awful silence, they actually heard it, the trickle that became a splash, and saw it, the pool of urine spreading unstoppable around Jason's feet.

Julian felt the blood rush to his face, scorching him, as Lois threw back her head and began to laugh.

JUNE

The sky became sullen and what Neil Carradine called 'an inconveniencing rain' fell day after day: a persistent drizzle which did not prevent you doing what you had or wanted to do, but which made it unpleasant. This unseasonal weather seemed to prolong the let-down feeling, the sense of anticlimax which followed the twins' birthday. If it was experienced most keenly by Lois, the other children were by no means unaffected by it. Her behaviour and attitude left them uncued and uncertain.

Unable to cope with this pervading sense of dissatisfaction, of no achievement, Lois withdrew into herself, developed a sudden interest in and concern for her schoolwork. On the journeys to and from school she shunned the others, with her nose in a book, and parried their hesitant invitations to 'do something', to 'come out to play', by pleading that she had to catch up on her work or by invoking the dreary weather. Unconsciously, Vanessa voiced all their feelings when she said:

'Nothing seems fun any more.'

They had just left the school bus and were walking together, wrapped and buttoned against the weather, into the Crescent, the evening stretching without focus before them. Instinctively, Vanessa bit her lip and looked shyly at Lois who felt William's eyes on her, too.

'Oh I don't know . . .' Andy began, but the sentence was stillborn for lack of conviction.

'It never was anyway,' Lois said brusquely, and hurried away towards her house, leaving them in a surprised and unintentional huddle.

'We could do something,' Andy said, the first to break the silence.

'What?' Vanessa snapped, feeling that Lois's desertion was her fault.

'Well . . .' He scraped the side of his shoe around the contours of a pitted puddle. 'We could go to the barn.'

The twins drifted away at once. Their house was the nearest and their younger sister had already reached the front door. They muttered a desultory 'goodbye' and moved as one person up the short garden path.

'Come on, Amanda,' Vanessa said, walking off as though Andy had never made a suggestion.

'You can come to my house,' Amanda said, trotting behind her. 'We could . . .'

'No, thanks.'

'I don't see why not,' Andy said stubbornly to William.

'I've got to feed Oliver,' he said. 'See you.'

Andy watched him go, looked at Luke's impassive moon-face.

'I don't care,' he said. 'Sod 'em.'

Lois's third period was late. For a brief time she allowed herself to hope that it was all over, a false alarm, but when Pearl explained that irregularity was common at this stage in her development, she became morose and difficult.

'Yeah, and it'll hurt a whole lot worse than the others.'

'No, darling,' Pearl said, trying to comfort her. 'Look, if it doesn't start in a day or so, I'll take you to the doctor.'

'I don't want to go to the doctor. You said it wasn't an illness. You said it would get better. You just lie to me. Both of you.'

'That's not true. It's just that sometimes, when menstruation's difficult . . .'

'I don't want to hear. I hate it.'

Pearl drew a deep breath and looked at the angry, round-shouldered hump of her daughter's back.

'I didn't know,' she said, deliberately trying to lower the tension, 'that you'd talked to Daddy about this. What did he say?'

'Not about this,' Lois mumbled, pushing the heel of her right moccasin off with the toes of her left foot and bending the soft sole under the ball of her foot.

'Then what did you mean? How did he lie to you?'

'It was nothing.'

'Lois . . . You said your father had lied to you. Now that's a serious thing to say and I . . .'

'He said everything was going to be okay. He said I'd make friends and everything would be as it was back home.' She spoke rapidly, viciously, her eyes screwed up so that her face looked mean.

'I'm sure he never said that,' Pearl said and almost instantly acknowledged the possibility that he had with a sense of angry defeat. 'Besides, you have made friends . . .'

'Well, maybe he didn't use those exact words, but that's what he meant.'

Pearl nodded, recognizing the truth of that statement by the lessening of anger in Lois's voice.

'And you have made friends, yes?' she persisted.

'I guess. Only . . . I don't know, Mom, it's just not right somehow.' Her eyes were wide now, confused.

Pearl went to her, placed her hands lightly on the hunched, resisting shoulders.

'I know it's difficult . . .'

'They laugh at me.'

'Why, sweetheart?'

'This bra . . . Do I have to wear it? I hate it. It hurts.'

'If that's so, we'll get you another one. Now, who laughs at you?'

'The girls. At school.' Her voice dropped to a defensive mumble.

'When you're changing, you mean?'

Lois nodded, and let her head rest against her mother's stomach. Pearl slipped her arms around her.

'I'll speak to Miss Jordan again. But you mustn't mind. It's only because they're embarrassed, even envious. They don't understand and you must try to remember that, even though I know it seems cruel.'

With perfect seriousness, Lois said, 'If we were back home I could burn it. All American women burn their bras. I read about it.'

Pearl could not stop the laughter that rose in her. She hugged Lois closer and was quite unprepared for the violence of her reaction. Lois pulled back against her arms while thrusting out with her own. Pearl staggered, her laughter cut off.

'Lois . . .' she protested, steadying herself.

'It's true. And you know it. Everything would be all right if we just went back home only you're just mean and won't let us. I bet Daddy'd take me, if only you'd let him.'

She flung herself round, hiding her face in the pillows.

'We are home,' Pearl said, her voice sounding cold and harsh to her own ears. Shaken, she walked out of the room, closing the door behind her.

'What does Neil say?'

Yvonne Hunter was surprised by Pearl's visit, at being taken into her confidence. She felt that her question was lame, might even seem to be an expression of indifference. She wanted to help but did not know how.

'I didn't tell him,' Pearl answered and looked up from her hands which were tightly clasped on the kitchen table. 'I can't. You see, I thought we'd got over that. I think *we* have. It's just Lois. But I'm scared of starting it all up again. He found it difficult at first, too. Especially his job. Oh God, I'm being cowardly. I'm scared that if I tell him about it he might agree with Lois.'

'No, you're not. But you definitely want to stay here?'

'Yes. Very much. I can't explain it. But maybe I'm just being selfish. Maybe I ought to . . .'

'I think you have to talk about it,' Yvonne said gently.

'I know. You're right. And I shouldn't burden you with it. I'm sorry. I honestly didn't mean to.'

'I'm glad you did. It's just that I don't know what to say. I don't think I'm very good at giving advice.'

'What I actually came for was information. I wondered if Vanessa had said anything to you about Lois.'

'No.'

'Some of the girls have been teasing her about wearing a bra. That's what brought all this on, really. She's begun to menstruate.'

'Oh.'

'She's not having a very good time of it, I'm afraid.'

'Poor thing. I remember how awful it was. I'll certainly speak to Vanessa . . .'

'Oh, I didn't mean to imply that she was involved. Lois never said that. It's just that they seemed to be such good friends only a few weeks ago and now . . . I wondered if they'd quarrelled or anything.'

'I'm sure not. Vanessa would have said. Don't you think that it's probably just that Lois feels awkward, embarrassed? I know I did.'

Pearl nodded.

'I'm sure you're right. I've let it all get out of proportion.'

'I just wanted to lock myself away. I remember praying for my periods to stop. But it passes.'

'Thanks. That's just what I needed to hear. I'm sorry I bothered you.'

'It's no bother. I'm glad. And I will talk to Vanessa. Just to make sure she understands. After all, it'll be her turn soon.'

Vanessa did not like hearing about it. It made her feel squirmy inside and, no matter what her mother said, she associated it with bad things. For the first time in ages she thought about her initiation and wondered if Lois had told the truth about it *not* being blood. This doubt tempered her feelings of sympathy for Lois and made her Saturday morning call at Lois's house more of a duty than a pleasure.

The rain had drizzled out during the night, leaving the Crescent looking damp and new-washed under fast-moving, fluffy white clouds. That, and the fact that Yvonne had seen Pearl and Neil drive away from the house without Lois, had prompted her to suggest to Vanessa that now would be a good time to call on her. As she emerged from the shadow of the big tree in the centre of the Crescent, Vanessa saw William emptying sawdust and rabbit droppings into the dustbin beside his house.

'Hello,' she said. 'What are you doing?'

'Cleaning Oliver's hutch out.'

'Can I see him?'

William's face brightened visibly.

'Okay. You'll have to wait, though, till I've got the hutch ready. He's in a cardboard box while I do it and you can't really see him there.'

'That's all right. I've got to call on Lois. I'll come round afterwards.'

William smiled, noting the imperative in Vanessa's statement.

'Fine. You can bring Lois as well if you want.'

'Okay.'

William walked away and Vanessa, feeling better, went up to the Carradines' front door and rang the bell. While she waited, she pushed her toe against the tiled doorstep, wishing she was at her dancing class, practising her pirouettes. Lois opened the door a few inches and stared at her, frowning.

'Hello. Are you coming out?'

'Why aren't you at dance class?'

'It's cancelled.'

'Oh. Why?'

'Miss Settle had to go somewhere. She's judging a regional competition.'

'Why aren't you in it?'

Vanessa shrugged.

'Aren't you good enough?'

'It's for older girls. Anyway, you said you were going to come to the class and you never did.'

'I did not. Is Amanda in it?'

'No. I told you. It's for senior grades.'

Lois looked disgruntled and not fully convinced.

'I said I *might* come. I said I'd *think* about it. I never said I *would*.'

'Who cares? Are you coming out?'

'What for? Out where?'

Vanessa shrugged again, pushed her hands into the pockets of her pink dungarees.

'William said we can go and see his rabbit if we want.'

'Oh, big deal.' Clowning, Lois opened the door wider, leaned against the jamb, pretending to faint. 'Spare me the excitement. I don't think I can stand it.'

In spite of herself, Vanessa giggled and saw an answering grin on Lois's face.

'It's something to do,' she said and could not prevent her eyes moving downwards to the firm thrust of Lois's breasts under her T-shirt. Involuntarily, she blushed and all her mother had said came flooding back into her mind.

'What's wrong? Why are you staring?' Lois straightened up, reached for the door as though to close it in Vanessa's face. Her arm veiled her breasts.

'I'm not,' Vanessa said. 'Are you coming?'

'No, I'm not. And you were.'

'I said I'd go.' She moved tentatively away.

'Go then,' Lois shouted. 'Just because you haven't got anything to do since your stupid class is cancelled doesn't mean I've got time to go looking at dumb rabbits.' Unaware of how loudly and angrily she was speaking, Lois associated the look of shock on Vanessa's face with her staring, with her own new awareness of her body. 'I hope you didn't think I've been moping around here every Saturday morning, waiting for *you* to get back from class. Because if you did, you are absolutely wrong.'

She slammed the door, unable to bear Vanessa's eyes on her any longer. She stood behind the door, trembling and vowing to herself that she would never, ever speak to Vanessa Hunter again.

*

Gently, William lifted Oliver out of the cardboard box and held him against his chest.

'Oh, he's beautiful,' Vanessa said. 'Can I hold him? Please, William.'

'No. Better not. He doesn't know you – do you, Oliver? – and he might try to get away. You can stroke him though.'

Vanessa reached out and felt the soft fur, barely brushing it with her fingers. Oliver stiffened and his claws dug into William's arms. He spoke soothingly to the rabbit.

'Stroke his ears. He likes that.'

'They're all silky,' Vanessa said as she moved one finger along the flattened ears.

Slowly, William felt him relax. After a few moments, he raised his head, looked around, nose quivering. Vanessa smiled with pleasure.

'It'll be all right to stroke him now,' William said and watched her small hand move over the rabbit's humped back. 'Lois didn't want to come, then?' he asked casually.

'No. And I'm glad. And I bet Oliver is, too, aren't you, Oliver?'

'Why? I thought you two were best friends.'

'Well, we're not any more. She shouted at me as though I'd done something awful when all I'd done was ask if she wanted to come out. I think she's mad.'

'I said that the first time I saw her,' William said, recalling that dark night and the extraordinary mixture of feelings his first sight of Lois had conjured up in him.

'Well, you were right,' Vanessa said. 'We all should have known. Jumping out at us like that. Honestly, I was so scared.' She shivered at the memory of it, of Lois's crooked and pointing fingers demanding *trick or treat, trick or treat.*

'I'd better put him in the hutch now,' William said, his voice gratefully dispelling the awful clarity of Vanessa's memory. 'I expect he's hungry.'

'He's lovely,' Vanessa said as she watched Oliver hop from the platform of William's arms into his hutch.

William latched the door and squatted down by the wire

netting front, watching Oliver's nose-quivering investigation of his clean home.

'So you're really not friends with her any more?' he asked, keeping his eyes on the rabbit.

'No. I wouldn't have gone over there this morning only Mum made me. You know what she's been like lately. I've not really been friends with her for ages.'

'Why did your Mum make you call for her?' William questioned, looking at her out of the corner of his eyes.

'Oh . . . no reason. Just something Mrs Carradine said.'

'What?' William stood up.

'Nothing.'

'It must be something. Oh, come on, Vanessa. I let you stroke Oliver. Next time you can hold him.'

Vanessa looked longingly at the hutch.

'I can't,' she said.

'Why not? I won't tell.'

And suddenly she wanted to tell him.

'Promise?'

Her need to get back at Lois was suddenly stronger than her embarrassment or her mother's warning not to talk about it.

'Yes. Come on. Tell us.'

'I don't know . . . It's . . . rude.'

She blushed then, turning away from him. William caught her shoulder.

'Come on, Van. You can tell me. We're friends, aren't we?'

She looked at him, her cheeks flushed, biting her lower lip.

'All right. But you've got to swear that you won't ever, ever tell.'

'I swear.'

'On Oliver's life?'

Nervously, William agreed. And as she began to tell him, blushing, hesitating, in whispers, William rather wished that he had not asked. He had only the most sketchy idea of what she was talking about anyway and he did not like to think about it. As he listened, nodding, pretending to understand more than he did, it reminded him of that time in the Mercers' garage, with Andy, and before that, with Vanessa herself, when he had subdued her and Lois had forced her to drink . . .

'. . . blood,' Vanessa was saying. She stopped, surprised and curiously touched by William's awkward, solemn expression. 'And, you know, she's got . . . you know . . . bosoms . . . All the girls at school tease her. And I don't blame them,' she added, remembering her anger against Lois.

William nodded. He had not really been listening. He had already noticed Lois's breasts for himself. They made him feel the same light-headed, misty way he had that other time.

'You won't tell?' she asked nervously, not understanding the funny look on his face.

He shook his head sharply.

'Vanessa? Come to the barn with me this afternoon?' he blurted out.

'Yes, William,' she said, dimpling. 'I'd like to.'

They were so dumb they didn't even realize that she could see straight into Mr William Stuck-Up Young's garden from her bedroom window. She watched them fooling with the stupid rabbit and almost turned away in disgust when William squatted down by the cage. Only Vanessa didn't go, as she had thought she would. And then something she said obviously interested William and she drew back a little, just to make sure that if they should happen to glance up – which they wouldn't do anyway because they were too dumb and stupid – they wouldn't get to think that *she* was watching *them*.

But she moved back closer to the window, her resolve forgotten as they walked together down the garden, William's head inclined towards Vanessa who was talking, confiding . . . Her hands gripped the white sill. She burned to hear what they were saying. She strained her ears, willed them to hear through glass, across distance. She felt herself tremble when she saw William's expression. It was as though she had stumbled upon some secret. And she could tell he wasn't listening, was thinking something private and personal. She longed to know what it was, wanted to be inside William's head. William was *her* friend. She had made him her deputy. Of all of them, William . . . Then Vanessa stopped talking, looked uncertain, guilty even, and Lois screwed her eyes up, tight shut.

They were talking about her.

She knew it. Like steel, the certainty of it entered her, hurting and tearing at her so that she brought up her hands, not knowing they were white-knuckled fists, and almost beat against the window glass in her rage and pain. And then she saw them move off together, Vanessa smiling up at William in a funny, special way that made her feel . . .

They disappeared, went around to the front of the house and she pressed her fists against the glass, lowered her forehead to its biting coldness.

. . . that made her feel like she had when she was watching the twins that time.

She got it then. She knew what it was. A private smile of complicity, of closeness and togetherness and sharing.

William and Vanessa.

She scented danger and it made her straighten herself, push away from the window, stand tall. But beyond that, she did not know what to do about it.

She had no idea how long she stood there, letting the knowledge and the hurt and the fear all join together and root themselves in her. Then she heard her father's voice calling. She responded automatically, like a zombie, walking out of the room and down the stairs, seeing him lugging a big box of groceries into the kitchen. And then her mother, carrying bags that bulged with mysterious, almost threatening shapes.

'Hey, we just saw Vanessa and William,' her father was

saying, looking up at her. 'Why didn't you go out with them, honey? You look like you could use some fresh air.'

Then he was gone, outside again, and the stairs seemed to grow longer and her mother was talking now, saying, 'Vanessa said she'd called for you. Why didn't you go?'

Her mother's head floated up towards her and then, dizzyingly, receded as the stairs got longer and longer.

'I don't feel good,' she wailed. 'Oh Mommy, I think it's starting again.'

The barn felt damp and chill. They opened the doors wide because William said that would help to air it. Vanessa wished she had not come. The sudden, unexpected intimacy of that morning had gone and there was a constant little nag of nervous fear in her chest because she had told William about Lois. She walked around, aimlessly tracing patterns in the dust on the floor.

William had regretted his invitation sooner, knowing that what he needed was time to think, to sort out what was happening to them all and to plan some strategy for it. More importantly, the actual impulse that had prompted him to ask Vanessa to come to the barn now scared him. At the last moment, he had run over to ask the twins to come as well, but they were going to a cricket match with their father. He did not want Andy there. That would only have made it worse. Ignoring Vanessa, from whom boredom seemed to emanate like an odour, William climbed the ladder and stood on it, looking at the upper floor. The chains from which Jason had hung still lay there, scattered like slumberous snakes on the floor. It all seemed so long ago, so much longer than it really was.

'William?'

'What?'

'What are you doing?'

'Nothing. Just looking.'

'What *at*?'

'Nothing. Just . . . up here.'

Vanessa kicked her toe rhythmically against one of the supporting pillars. William climbed up and walked around, looking at the few items they had brought there.

'Remember,' he said loudly, his voice surprising him by echoing a little, 'how we were going to do this place up, make it really good?'

Vanessa walked out beyond the ladder until she could see William's head floating palely in the shadows before answering.

'Yes. Why?'

'I was just thinking – we never did much, did we?'

'That was Lois's fault. She never wanted to do anything really interesting. She just wanted to be horrible.'

'You are changeable,' William said, coming forward and standing looking down at her, a sort of smirk on his face.

'I'm *not*. It's *her*. She didn't have any cause to go shouting at me and carrying on . . .'

'Don't you think you'll ever be friends again?' he asked. It was important, a part of all that Vanessa's confidence had set moving in his mind.

'Never,' she swore.

'We ought to get the others to come over here. It's stupid not to make use of the place.'

'I hate it,' Vanessa said. 'I don't care if I never come here again.'

'We could still make it nice,' he said, beginning to descend the ladder. Without *her*, he thought, and then knew immediately that that was wrong, not what he wanted at all.

'I suppose,' Vanessa said.

'If I ask them – you'll come?'

'I might.'

'Well, it *is* a good place. We ought to use it.'

'Why did you ask me to come today?'

William had hoped that she had forgotten. He swung his feet free from the ladder, just above the ground, and hung from his arms, trying to think of an answer.

'I thought it might be because of that time, you know, my birthday.'

William dropped down to the floor, forced the air out of his lungs with an exaggerated grunt. He could feel the blood draining from his face, the awful fluttering feeling of fear in his stomach. She couldn't know. She couldn't have guessed. To his relief she spoke again before he absolutely had to say something.

'Shall I tell you something? I really thought it was blood, you know. *That's* why I was sick. I thought about it again this morning.'

'It was,' William said, and immediately wished he had not spoken. But he had no choice. By saying it he could divert her, remove the risk that she might ask him about his part in that first ceremony.

'You *knew*?' Her voice became a sort of squeak.

'No. Not then. Not till later . . .'

'She said it wasn't. She swore to me . . .'

'Well, I'm not absolutely sure,' William said quickly, feeling as though a chasm had opened before him.

'What do you mean? You said it was.'

'I meant . . .' He paused, scuffing his feet, trying to think of a way out. 'I mean *I* thought so, too. I've never been really sure, though.'

'Somebody must know,' she said miserably.

He shrugged and walked towards the open doors.

'Lois,' he said casually.

'Well, I'm not asking *her*.'

'No one else could know . . .'

'You *said*.'

'I wasn't thinking. I suspected . . . no . . . not even that . . . I wondered. That's all. Look what does it matter now?'

'It matters to *me*. If she lied to me, if she really made me . . . drink blood . . . I'd . . . I'd . . .'

'What?'

'I'd do something even worse to her.'

'Revenge,' William said, beginning to feel safe.

'Yes. I would. I mean it.'

William strolled outside, tugged one of the big doors away from the wall and closed it. He leaned against it, looking at Vanessa.

'The gang would all have to get together again. You'd have to be friends with Lois,' he told her.

She looked crestfallen, walked slowly past him, out into the pale afternoon.

'Wouldn't you?' he prompted.

'I know. All right.'

'Don't take it out on me. I haven't done anything.'

Vanessa felt like crying. Whatever she had expected of this afternoon, it had not been this. She blamed the barn, wished she had never come. She turned to William as he let the other door slam shut, noisily.

'Why *did* you ask me to come here? You never answered.'

'I . . . Because we're friends. Aren't we?'

He thrust his hands in his pockets and stared away towards the Crescent. It looked like rain again. The sky above the houses was low and grey.

'Yes,' she said softly.

'And if the others will come . . .'

'All right. Yes. *I'll* come, too.'

'I'll have to think about it,' he said. 'Whose birthday's next?'

She frowned, trying to remember. The question prompted a sinking, excited feeling. After all, it wasn't fair that all the others should get off scot-free when she and the twins . . .

'You haven't had yours yet,' she said.

'I know. But Amanda's next.'

She caught William's eye and suddenly they both broke into spluttering giggles.

'Come on,' he laughed, 'let's go back before it starts to rain.'

'You can come and have tea at my house, if you like,' Vanessa said, hurrying after him.

'Okay. But I've got to get some dandelions for Oliver first.'

'I'll help.'

'Okay.'

'If she's that bad she ought to see the doctor.'

'I'll take her next week,' Pearl said. She felt as though her head was full of spikes which were slowly being driven into her brain.

'No. I mean have him come here, now.'

'She's asleep. It's all right,' Pearl said tiredly. 'Besides, he won't come out on a Saturday night. Not for something like this.'

'Oh great. So much for your wonderful National Health Service.'

'Please, Neil. Don't shout.'

She leaned back and closed her eyes. Neil walked to the window and looked out through the rain-spattered glass.

'I'm worried,' he said.

'Now it's started, she'll be all right.'

'But is this going to happen every month? My God, she could have hurt herself. If she'd been at the top of the stairs instead . . .'

'I know. I'll take her to the doctor and he'll see. He'll give her something if it's always going to be like this. But once she adjusts, once the body . . .'

'Okay, I'm sorry.'

He did not want any more details. The whole business made him feel edgy, impotent. He just wanted for Lois to be all right, not to have to go through this every time.

'What you should worry about,' said Pearl, pressing her fingers to her temples, 'is her psychological attitude. That's half the trouble, in my opinion.'

'How do you mean?'

'It's a well known fact that if a woman resists or resents or is scared of menstruation, it makes for more tension. I think that's Lois's main problem.'

'So what can we do about it?'

'I don't know. I'll tell the doctor. Just go on reassuring her, I suppose. I think it makes it specially difficult for her, not knowing other girls who've started. It sets her apart from the kids round here.'

'Well, that is definitely not my fault,' Neil said.

'No. I know. It's mine.'

'I didn't say that . . .'

'No. And I didn't promise her that everything would be warm and wonderful and just like California.'

'Pearl, are you starting in again?'

'No. I thought you were.'

'Okay. I don't want to pursue this, but I want you to think about just one thing. Before we came here, before we came to this country, you and I could talk about our daughter's welfare without getting at each other's throats. Now you just think about that.'

He walked very quickly to the door and wrenched it open.

'I do think about it,' she said. 'All the time. Where are you going?'

'To fix us an omelette.'

'I'll do it.'

'No. You rest up. I need to cool off, anyway.'

The door closed behind him. Pearl turned her face to the window and saw the rain, the grey dreariness of it all – and still she did not want to go back.

William lobbied, cajoled and bullied where necessary. They all came to the barn. All except Lois. She had not been invited. She was, in any case, off school, had been to the doctor. William and Vanessa exchanged a guilty smile when they heard this news, but would not tell the others why.

The twins and Vanessa came together, the boys carrying and grumbling about a tall, narrow cupboard, painted pink. As Jason and Julian, puffing, set it none too carefully down outside the barn, William asked, 'What's that for?'

'Vanessa said . . .' Jason began.

'Don't blame us. We only carried it here,' Julian said.

'I helped,' Vanessa said, thrusting herself forward. 'It's for the barn. You said we could do it up, make it really nice. You promised, William.'

'Yes. But a cupboard?'

'It'll be very useful.'

'How?'

'Well . . .' she looked at it doubtfully. 'We can keep things in it.'

'All right,' said William. 'Bring it in.'

'You take it in,' said Julian.

'We carried it all the way here,' Jason agreed.

With a sigh of exasperation, William called Andy to help him and together they lifted the cupboard into the barn.

'Where shall we put it?' Andy asked.

'Anywhere. Just dump it down here,' William said, letting go of his end.

Andy raised his, stood the cupboard upright.

'It's got a key,' Vanessa said, fishing in her pocket. 'We can lock precious things away.'

'Terrific,' Andy said without conviction as she fitted the little key into the lock.

Grumbling at their ingratitude, Vanessa followed Andy up the ladder. The others were just standing around, or sitting, waiting for something to happen. William surveyed them, wondering how to proceed.

'Well?' said Vanessa, her hands on her hips.

They all looked at William.

'What?' he said, grumpy.

'What now?' Julian asked.

'What are we supposed to do?' Jason added.

'I don't know.'

'Oh William!' Vanessa was exasperated.

'We could take it in turns to hang from the chains,' Andy suggested, inspecting his handiwork.

'Thanks for nothing,' said Julian.

'Idiot.'

'I don't want to,' Amanda said quietly, picking at the sleeve of her dress.

'It's about time you dismantled that contraption,' William told Andy.

'Oh yes? And who says so?'

'I do.'

'Get stuffed.'

'Anyway, Mr Applegreen wants those chains back. He only lent them,' Vanessa chimed in.

'Let him fetch 'em then,' Andy said indifferently and walked to the back of the loft, stirring the pile of mouldering hay with his foot.

'We could clean up,' Vanessa suggested.

'Great,' sneered Julian. 'We get enough of that at home.'

'Me too,' Andy agreed.

'Why do we have to *do* anything?' William said. 'What did we used to *do*?'

No one wanted to answer that. Jason and Julian exchanged one of their private, secretive looks.

'We could play something,' Amanda suggested.

'What? Hopscotch? Bring your skipping rope, did you?' Andy mocked her, walking up behind her and tweaking her hair.

'Don't,' she said crossly, and moved away from him.

'You suggest something, then,' William said.

'I already have and nobody was interested.'

'It was your idea, William,' Vanessa said. 'It's up to you.'

'Well . . .' he said vaguely. 'I don't know. I can't think of anything.'

There was another silence. William began to count the seconds as they crawled past.

'Oh this is useless,' Andy said.

'Right. We're off,' Jason said, glancing at his brother.

'Yes. It's boring.'

The twins moved together towards the ladder.

'Me, too,' Amanda announced. 'I don't like it here anyway.'

'And the next time you have a brilliant idea, Young,' Andy said belligerently, 'just keep it to yourself.'

Julian began to descend the ladder. The others formed an unconscious line behind Jason, waiting to go down.

'You see?' William said.

They all turned to look at him.

'This is exactly why I wanted you all to come here.'

'What's he talking about?' Andy asked.

'Go on, Julian,' Jason urged.

'So that you'd see what's wrong,' William shouted. He was suddenly very pale. 'If I'd told you, you wouldn't have believed me. Now you've seen for yourself.'

'I still don't understand,' Amanda complained. 'And I don't care. I want to go home.'

'You won't do what I say,' William persisted, taking a step towards them. 'You don't want to do what Amanda suggests, or Andy. Don't you see?'

Vanessa looked at his eager, almost desperate face, then down at the floor.

'Lois,' he said, almost whispered.

Jason swallowed, sought his brother's eyes. Amanda looked longingly towards the blocked ladder.

'It's no good without her,' Andy said. 'He's right.'

'So? That's not our fault,' Jason said.

'She's sick,' Amanda offered.

'Even when she's better,' William said, 'she won't come back. You see, we *are* a gang, without really knowing it, only it doesn't work without her.'

'There's nothing we can do about it,' Julian said.

'Yes, there is. If we all put our heads together . . .' William crossed his fingers. It was now or never.

'He's right,' Andy repeated and broke out of the line, sat on the old nursery table.

After a moment, Vanessa joined him. Julian looked up

at Jason and nodded. Jason moved back and his twin climbed up the ladder again. William released his breath.

'I want to go home,' Amanda said. 'I don't know what you're talking about.'

'Go on, then,' William said. 'Nobody's stopping you.'

They were all surprised by this but none more so than Amanda. She looked at him, suspicious of a trap.

'Go on,' he repeated.

'All right. I will.'

She went to the ladder and began to climb down slowly.

'Now then . . .' William said, rubbing his hands briskly together, 'let's get on with it.'

It felt like she was carrying something warm and precious inside and she had to be very, very careful for fear it should spill over or break and crack apart. There was no name for this feeling, or if there was, Lois didn't know it and didn't want to. Nameless, it was sufficient: *her* perfect feeling. Hers.

She seemed to float up the staircase, into her sun-filled room. Even the weather smiled. She sat down, just as she was, her schoolcase hugged to her chest and thought about it, savoured it. Just three days back into school and they had all approached her. Well, almost all. But she wasn't going to let William Young spoil anything. William Young was just totally irrelevant. All the *others* wanted her, needed her. They'd said so.

She hadn't thought anything much about it at first. It was no big deal that Vanessa Hunter wanted to be friends with her again. As far as *she* was concerned, she had always been friends with Vanessa. And she said so. And that she didn't see what there was to make such a big old fuss about. Then Vanessa started in asking dumb questions about whether it was really for real blood she'd made her drink that time and that brought it all back to her, The Plan and all, and how it had gone wrong somehow and sort of died on her. So she'd made Vanessa feel bad for ever having doubted *her*, and that cheered her up a little.

And then the twins. Oh, the twins had made everything right again. They'd come up to her, in the schoolyard, when she was deliberately being by herself and Not Joining In. It was so wonderful that she could recall every syllable, every breath they had drawn even.

'Lois?'

'Can we talk to you?'

'Sure.'

'It's just that . . .'

'We went to the barn the other day.'

'Not just us. All of us. Andy and William and . . .'

'She knows, Jason.'

'So? You went to the barn.'

Big deal, she'd thought. Frigging big deal.

'And . . . well, the thing is . . .'

'It wasn't any good.'

'No.'

She had raised her eyebrows.

'It was boring.'

'We couldn't think of anything to do.'

'We used to have fun, you know . . .'

'And we thought . . . I mean . . . that is . . .'

'Are you ever going to go there again, Lois?'

'*Will* you?'

There it was. Like some precious jewel just lying there in the dirt waiting to be picked up. Like something wonderful and transforming out of a fairy-story.

She set her bag down and took her raincoat off. Suddenly she needed to move around, be busy, or she would burst wide open with happiness and excitement.

Then Andy. Of course, he had to make out that she owed him something for having fixed those chains for her, but she'd told him straight out that she was too old and mature for such silly, dirty little games and that if he didn't grow up and stop it real quick, she was going to tell Mrs Mercer all about him and the awful, sick way he was with girls. She'd thought he was going to cry but he didn't. He said he was only joking – which was a lie – and how what he really wanted to ask her was about taking down the chains and stuff. Because William had said that he had to, but he wasn't taking orders from William, but Vanessa said the chains had to go back to Farmer Applegreen and he thought he'd better ask her because he didn't want to get her into trouble by not doing it. If she wanted.

'Why don't you do as William says?' she asked and knew that it was probably the best, the cleverest thing she had said to anybody ever.

'It's not up to William,' he'd said, his face red with anger and frustration then, not embarrassment. 'It's up to *you*. You're the boss, not William.'

It was like a song in her head. So put that in your pipe, Mr William Stuck-Up Young, and go smoke it, she thought, hugging herself and spinning to the song in her head.

And every day – only she hadn't realized the *significance* of it – Amanda had been giving her candy. And today, just this very day, as she drew close to where they were all waiting for the school bus, she'd heard William say, 'Give me another toffee, Amanda.'

'No. You had some.'

'You've got lots.'

'No I haven't. Besides, I'm saving them for Lois, so there.'

How she wished she'd had a camera just so that whenever she wanted she could at that moment look at a photograph of William's face. The look on his face! So she'd sat beside Amanda on the bus, well away from the others, and eaten the candy and promised to be Amanda's friend and said, yes, she would like some more candy tomorrow and played real dumb, as if she didn't know what all *that* was about.

She skipped across the room, pirouetted to face herself

in the mirror. She let her arms fall and looked at herself, at her flushed cheeks and her new breasts and . . .

'Lois. Lois.'

She saw herself transformed, her secret, perfect feeling dashed by annoyance at the interruption.

'What is it?' she yelled right back.

'A visitor for you. Do you want to come down or shall I send him on up?'

A visitor! She saw the gleam of surprise and excitement animate her own eyes before she dashed to the door.

'Who is it?'

'William, dear,' her mother said in that special voice she used when the presence of other people meant that she couldn't yell at her.

William?

'I'll come down,' she said. She didn't want him in *her* room.

'Take William through into the lounge, dear. I've got a hundred things to do in the kitchen.'

She glared at William and walked straight past him. He followed, like a little puppy dog, and when she heard the door close, she turned around, facing him.

'What do you want?'

'To ask you something.'

'Well?'

'Can you come to the barn tonight?' He glanced nervously at the window. 'I don't think it's going to rain. It should be a nice night.'

'So why spoil it with you?'

'Oh please, Lois. You've *got* to. I mean . . . it's important.'

'What is?'

'Amanda's birthday.'

'What has the barn got to do with her birthday?'

'Her initiation.'

'Oh that.' She sat down. 'I'm through with all that. It's just kids' stuff.'

'I agree. Definitely. That's what I want to talk to you about. All that swearing loyalty and things is silly . . .'

'So what do you propose?' She turned her head disdainfully towards him.

'A treat. A special birthday treat. Look, I can't tell you here.' He looked at the door. 'I've got it all worked out but . . . only you could make it work.'

Only you could make it work.

The words dazzled her. She smiled at him.

'Okay, William. I'll come to the barn tonight.'

7 JULY

It was just an ordinary day: a schoolday, a workday, a day undistinguished by the rustle of wrapping paper and the ritual out-of-tune singing. The only sign that it was Amanda's birthday – apart from her father's greeting – was the louder than usual plop of letters on the hall floor.

John Beatty stood by the circular kitchen table, sorting the mail with agonizing slowness and feigning surprise at the number of envelopes addressed to his daughter.

'Miss Amanda Beatty, Miss Amanda Beatty . . .'

'Daddy!'

'Oh and look at this. My goodness, we are becoming grown up. *Ms* Amanda Beatty, no less. Ms.'

Pushing past him, dirty crockery in both hands, Marge said, 'For God's sake get a move on, John, or you're going to make us all late.'

John dropped the consolingly solid pile of envelopes in front of his daughter and shot a look of suppressed anger at his wife's back. Amanda began to tear at the envelopes, her eyes large with excitement.

'Don't drop them all over the floor, Amanda,' Marge snapped, retrieving an envelope and then leaning over the child's shoulder to swab crumbs from the table.

'You might at least let her enjoy her cards,' John said, deadly quiet.

Marge glanced at him, 'I'm not stopping her. I just don't want to have to clean up after her.'

'Look, Mummy.'

'Lovely,' Marge said automatically, not glancing at the proffered card.

'Let me see,' John said, taking the card from her.

Marge left the kitchen, mules clattering on parquet, and for several minutes John quietly admired his daughter's birthday cards, trying by the intensity of his attention to make up for her evident disappointment. He had never really been convinced that it was necessary to postpone her birthday, but had allowed himself to be persuaded by Marge and Amanda's apparent acceptance. He knew now that she regretted it, that Saturday must seem such a long way off and probably wouldn't be the same, anyway.

'Oh.'

'What is it, love?'

Amanda had gone pale. She pushed a card, face downwards, towards him or, at any rate, away from her. He took it from her, automatically telling her to get on and open the others. The card showed a reproduction of a late Victorian illustration of '*Little Miss Muffet*'. The child, who bore a passing resemblance to Amanda herself, was shown happily eating her curds and whey, blissfully unaware of the rather gruesome-looking spider dangling beside her.

'John! For heaven's sake . . .'

Marge burst into the room, her dressing gown exchanged for a livid green sundress.

'We'll be ready when you are,' he said, standing up. 'Come on, Amanda, let's put your cards up.'

'Get your satchel. I'm in a hurry,' Marge called.

Amanda followed her father, clutching the cards.

'Not that one,' she said as he reached up to place the offending card on the high mantelpiece.

'It's only a drawing,' he said. 'A rather good one, actually.'

'No.' She pushed the other cards at him, pleading.

'All right,' he sighed, knowing there was no time to argue now with his daughter's irrational fears. He folded the card back so that the printed greeting and the untidily scrawled, 'Have a *terrific* day, love from Lois XX' showed, and began to line up the other cards in a colourful row.

Marge's perfume filled the car. She was fussing with her hair, fluffing it out at the back.

'I don't ever want that to happen again,' John said, as they drew away from the Crescent.

'What?' Marge said absently, checking her eye make-up in a small hand mirror.

'In future,' John said, raising his voice, 'we celebrate Amanda's birthday on July the seventh, with all the trimmings.'

Marge said nothing, looked at her watch.

'Do you understand?'

'She'll enjoy it just as much on Saturday. Stop spoiling her.'

'I don't spoil her. But God knows I'd be justified, considering how little time you spend with her.'

'Look, it's not my fault Gina decided to hold a summer sale and needs me all day. I can't help it if the country's in recession and you can't give decent clothes away.'

'It's not Amanda's, either.'

'But her birthday's more important than Gina's living, my job?'

'To me, yes. You don't need that job anyway.'

'I don't need it? I don't *need* it?' Her voice became shrill, grating on his ears. 'Oh no, of course not. I mean you're such a wonderful provider . . . Do you realize that if it wasn't for that job, I wouldn't have a rag to wear? Oh, but then that would suit you, wouldn't it? That's just what you'd like – me stuck at home all day, never seeing anyone, wearing madeovers from the jumble sale. Or, I suppose if my luck really held, maybe Sylvia Shillingworth would hand me her cast-offs.'

She turned her head away from him, looked at the summer-green fields passing by without seeing them.

'Since you mention it, yes, I do think you ought to spend more time at home. For Amanda's sake.'

'Well, it doesn't suit me. I'm not a *hausfrau* and you're not going to make me one.'

They approached the outskirts of Olton and joined a queue waiting at the traffic lights by the industrial estate.

'Your selfishness,' John said, 'is amazing. Appalling.'

‘And what about yours? It was your idea to have a baby, not mine.’

‘I managed it without your co-operation, I suppose?’

‘You talked me into it. I never wanted it. Never.’

‘But we’ve got her now and we have . . .’

‘It was horrible,’ Marge went on, ignoring him. ‘It bloody hurt and it was messy and demeaning . . . and . . . and that’s why there’s nothing for me to celebrate on July the bloody seventh.’

The line of cars moved forward.

‘It’s supposed to be Amanda’s day, not yours,’ John said quietly, his anger shocked away by her vehemence and bitterness.

‘And she’s going to have it. Everything’s organized. For Saturday. What the hell difference does it make?’

‘If you can’t see that . . . If you were just to look at her sometimes . . .’

‘I didn’t have time. Let me out here.’

‘I’ll drive you to the shop.’

‘In this traffic it’ll be quicker if I walk down Ellis Street.’

He did not try to argue but drew the car over to the kerb. Marge opened the door immediately.

‘I meant it, you know,’ he said. ‘About next year.’

‘Then you organize it,’ she answered, slamming the door.

She walked quickly away, turned into Ellis Street where, almost at once, her tempo slowed. She checked her watch, glanced back at the traffic, saw it moving at a snail’s pace. She made herself walk on, walk to the next intersection before turning around and retracing her steps. By the time she reached the pedestrian crossing, there was no sign of John’s car. She smiled at the man who braked to let her cross, whose eyes pursued her legs until she reached the far pavement. For safety’s sake she left the main road and made her way to the station through the back streets. There, she knew, Douglas Young would be waiting for her. They were catching an earlier train, so that none of the other regular commuters would see them together. A day out in London. He'd promised her that ever since they'd made it up, after the Carradines' party. And now at last it had come. Shopping – she could do a little, pretend that it came from the boutique. Lunch at a good restaurant and afterwards . . . He had a colleague who had a flat, to which Doug had got the key. They'd have to travel back on separate trains, of course, but she wouldn't think about that, wouldn't allow that cloud to sully the prospect of her day. And she'd buy something extra, a special present for Amanda, she thought, as she came in sight of the station. If there was time.

'Well, I think it's *mean*,' Lois said. 'If I'd known I never would have agreed to hold my present till Saturday.'

'We thought,' Vanessa said, 'you'd have your main presents today.'

'I tell you what, I'll give you mine just as soon as we get home from school. Okay?'

'No.' Amanda shook her head. 'I'd rather wait now, honestly.'

'Oh well . . . If you're sure.'

'Cheer up,' said Vanessa. 'It'll soon be Saturday.'

'It's not the same,' Lois said. 'I know. It's just not the same.'

'It's all right now,' Amanda reassured them. 'Honestly. It was just . . .' She looked near to tears again.

Vanessa put her arm round her.

'I know,' Lois exclaimed. 'We'll have a good time anyhow. We'll go over to the barn and play all your favourite games.'

'Amanda?' Vanessa said.

'Yes,' she nodded, forcing a smile. 'That'd be nice.'

'Leave it all to me,' Lois said. 'I'll fix everything so's you have a great birthday. *Two* birthdays, okay?'

They played musical chairs, using the old nursery furniture, a crate and two of the pails, to the accompaniment of Lois's lusty singing. She timed her pauses so that Amanda won and was ceremoniously presented with a bag of sweets. They played hunt the slipper and blind man's bluff, and then William proposed hide and seek and volunteered to be 'he'. Everyone dispersed, looking for somewhere to hide. Lois had decreed that William should go outside and his voice, counting off the numbers, could be heard above the rustlings and jostlings as the others concealed themselves. Amanda looked around, unable to think of anywhere.

'In here,' Lois hissed. 'Come on, it's perfect. He'll never think of looking for you here.' She gripped Amanda's upper arm tightly, hustling her towards the cupboard. 'Quick, get in.' She held the door open. 'And stay real still.'

Before she could protest, Amanda found herself inside the pink cupboard. The door slammed shut and she heard, with a spurt of panic, the key turn with a faint click. It was dark in the cupboard and she spun around to push against the door. As she did so, her foot caught against something which toppled over with a clatter. She put her hands on the door and pushed against it, rocking the cupboard.

'Let me out,' she said, thinking that Lois was still just outside and would hear her.

Silence. Then she felt it. Something moving across her foot. A tickling just above her sock. She pressed back against the wall of the cupboard and snatched her foot up. Something slid from it. She brushed at the tickling on her leg, felt it move upwards, crawling. When she put her foot down there was something under it, something that squirmed and moved. She looked down but could not make out what it was in the gloom. She sensed, more than saw, movement. Two distinct types of movement. A slow wriggling, purposeless and dreadful. And a fast, panicked scutter. Up the walls. Along the floor. She looked up, to her left and saw, or thought she saw, a spider, large, legs arched as though poised to spring, on the back wall.

She covered her face with her hands, screaming, and threw herself sideways, rocking the cupboard. The flesh on her legs crept and crawled. Her foot slipped as something slimed across her instep. She felt something touch her hair and brushed at it, screaming.

They were everywhere and she knew what they were. Spiders. Worms. She imagined herself ankle-deep in worms, grey and red-blotched. She imagined the spiders crawling up her legs, her dress, her arms. She flung out her arms, beating and screaming. Dizzyingly, sickeningly, the cupboard toppled over. She felt herself contained, trapped, falling in darkness, falling in a squirming, crawling horror. The cupboard hit the ground with a splintering crash and she was lying on her side, screaming. Something cold and wet hit her face, fell away. They ran over her, black and scuttling. She kicked and fought at them, at the obscene brush and run and wriggle of them. On her arms. In her hair. And as she struggled to get her legs away from them, trying to kneel up in her fallen, dark prison, she felt them crunch and crush beneath her, felt her hands sink into them, felt something cling and then dash across her screaming face.

Amanda's continuous scream, the terrified thumping of her limbs against the fallen cupboard, drowned out their voices.

'What is it?'

'Where's the key?'

'It must have fallen out when the cupboard . . .'

'Look for it.'

'Turn it over. Let's get to the door.'

'Yes. Come on. Help.'

The twins and William bent to the cupboard, rolling it and its lashing contents over, so that the door, splintered now in two places, faced them.

'What's the matter?'

'Amanda. Amanda.'

'We're trying.'

Lois dashed forward, flattened her hand on the barn floor and released the key.

'Amanda!'

'Break the door.'

'No, you'll hurt her.'

'Here it is,' Lois shouted, holding up the key. 'Quick.'

William took the key, still warm from her tightly clutching palm and stooped, fitting it into the lock.

'Stand back,' he shouted, waving the others aside.

He turned the key and jumped back. The door fell open with a crack onto the floor.

'Oh, no! Oh!' Vanessa screamed and backed away.

A large spider ran down the door to meet a splattered death beneath William's quick foot.

'Bloody hell,' Andy said, disgusted.

There were worms on her dress, spiders bunched in fear, others dashing from her. Vanessa screamed again and ran for the doors. Jason stepped back, trembling.

'Get her out. Get her out of there,' Julian shouted.

William reached into the cupboard, seized Amanda's arm and pulled her part-way out. Her tense and terrified body resisted him.

'Careful . . . you'll hurt her. Here . . .' Lois went to aid him.

Pulling together, they dragged her free of the teeming cupboard.

'Stand up, stand up,' Lois shouted, knocking a spider from Amanda's dress.

With her feet came a slew of garden worms, cold and writhing.

'Help me,' Lois shouted to Andy. 'Get them off her. Make her stand up.'

Her face still covered by her hands, still screaming, Amanda stood, leaning against Lois. Andy brushed at her clothes, picked a worm from her foot.

'Take her outside,' William advised.

They frogmarched her, the others following, through the doors.

William peered into the cupboard, saw at once the old, shallow paint tin in which a few worms still lay, and snatched it out. A spider ran across his hand and he shook it free. Glancing around, he hurled the telltale can away, heard it rattle in the distant corner of the barn. Then he closed the door of the cupboard and systematically began to kill those spiders he could find. There was nothing he could do about the worms.

Amanda's screams had abated to a series of hoarse, shaking sobs. Lois knelt in front of her, holding up her skirt, inspecting every inch of the material for lurking spiders. Andy squatted beside her, touched Amanda's exposed thigh.

'I'll help,' he said, his eyes fixed on her lace-edged panties.

'Get away,' Lois said, and lashed out at him with her arm. The blow caught him on the side of the head. More from shock than the force of it, he lost his balance and fell on to his side. 'You get away from her. Go on. Go away.' She gave the skirt an angry shake, stood up, pulling Amanda with her. 'You, too,' she yelled at the twins, who stared in astonishment. 'All you boys, get lost.' She put her arm around Amanda, dragging her away, around the side of the barn, out of sight. 'Vanessa, you come help me.'

'I'm scared,' Vanessa said, hovering.

'Fat lot of use that is. Hold still, Amanda. Let me look, okay?' she said, softening her tone. 'Just keep those boys away,' she ordered Vanessa, over her shoulder. She made Amanda turn round, unzipped the back of her dress and pushed it off her bony shoulders. She checked the seams of the dress, peered down the front at the thin, heaving chest. 'There's nothing on you. Nothing at all, okay?'

'My hair,' Amanda wailed, clutching at it, her mouth a pink O of lingering terror.

'Shush now,' Lois soothed. 'Let me see.' She began to part the fine silky strands of Amanda's hair, running her fingers through it. 'There's nothing,' she said. 'Now come on. Stop crying, Amanda, and let me clean you up.'

Amanda pulled away from her, roughly, her fists tight-clenched against her chest.

'You did it,' she sobbed. 'You put me in that cupboard.'

'Only as a place to hide,' Lois said. 'Now let me . . .'

'You put them in there. You knew . . .'

The scream rose again, startling Vanessa who, fearing the discovery of some remaining horror, backed off, trembling, towards the corner of the barn. Then she caught her breath in shock as Lois hit Amanda hard across the face.

'And where have you been?'

Marge stopped just inside the living room door. Her eyes registered her husband, but her mind was totally fixed on the distinctive green and gold Harrods bag which, with several others, hung in full view of him from her fingers.

'You're early,' she said, turning away, masking the bags with her body and trying to disentangle them.

'I asked, where have you been?'

She heard him stand up and looked over her shoulder.

'Where the hell do you think I've been?' She dumped the bags on the nearest chair and turned to face him, standing directly in front of the chair.

'Not at the shop,' he said levelly, then raised his voice as Marge opened her mouth to protest. 'The sale starts on Thursday. I know because I called for you. I came to apologize,' he said, moving steadily towards her, 'and to ask you to come home early as a surprise for Amanda.'

'Yes, well . . . there was a change of plan . . .' she began. Please God, she thought, let Gina have made up some story.

'Where have you been?'

'It was a surprise . . . I . . .'

He seized her arms and literally threw her aside. The high heel of Marge's green plastic sandal turned under her, making her stagger back against the table. Ignoring her, John snatched up the bags, began pulling out their contents.

'I went to London,' she shouted. 'I wanted to get a surprise for Amanda.' Her ankle hurt but she managed to straighten up. She could not bear him tossing her beautiful new things about like that.

'Oh yes?' he said. 'This I suppose?' He turned to face her, holding up a wisp of black lace, the suspender belt about which she and Doug had so often joked and which, that day, he had bought for her.

'Don't be ridiculous,' she said, suddenly calm. 'It's there. You'll find it. But don't throw my things all over . . .'

He hurled the suspender belt at her, turned back to the chair and began to empty the bags, flinging the matching brassière and briefs, a black dress across the room.

'Stop it,' Marge screamed. 'Don't do that.'

Heedless of the pain in her ankle, she began to scramble about the room, snatching up the items he had thrown. For the first time in years she wanted to cry, with rage and disappointment. Panting, she picked up a velour sweater and clutched it, bunched up with all the other things, against her chest.

John looked at the dress, the little girl's pink, puff sleeved dress.

'See?' Marge said. 'Satisfied?'

He gripped the dress tightly and, before he knew what he was doing, wrenched his hands apart. The dress tore in two, straight down the middle from neck to waist.

'You bastard,' Marge screamed.

John flung the ruined dress at her feet.

'I won't have my daughter dressed in his presents,' he said. 'In fact, I won't have you dressing like his whore, either.'

He walked towards her, his arms outstretched for the clothes Marge held bundled against her breasts.

After she hit Amanda, it was only a matter of time before she quietened down. Then, just to keep her happy, Lois had held an investigation but nobody knew anything about how the spiders and worms got in there. Even Amanda could see that the twins and Andy and Vanessa were as shocked and upset as she was. The spiders, maybe, you could explain, but the worms – well, that was odd. But William said he'd check it out in one of his nature books. Maybe they sometimes hibernated or something. By then, Amanda didn't care much anyway. The boys, under William's direction, volunteered to break the old cupboard up and burn it. That didn't please Vanessa any, but it couldn't be helped. Then she and Vanessa cleaned Amanda up as best they could and brought her on home.

They went in through the side door and Lois had her explanation all ready because they had seen Mr Beatty's car outside. That was when Vanessa had chickened out but, as things developed, Lois was actually glad she had. They heard voices at once and Amanda led the way to their living room. Well, truly, in all her life, Lois had never seen anything like it. Mrs Beatty was all scrunched up by the fireplace and Mr Beatty was tearing clothes out of her arms and yelling at her. He yelled, 'Whore. Bitch. I'll tear every rag that shit's ever given you.'

And Mrs Beatty was swearing and kicking at him. Instinctively, Lois had put her hand on Amanda's shoulder. Then Mr Beatty had just caught hold of his wife and shook her and threw her aside so that she fell on the settee, dropping all the stuff she'd been holding. And Mr Beatty snatched up something black and lacy and started tearing at it, all the time cursing and hollering, until Amanda screamed louder than any of them.

'Daddy. Mummy. Daddy. Daddy.'

They'd all frozen then, like when the projector breaks

down at the movies. He just stood there, with this piece of lace torn between his hands and his face looking like it was going to melt. Mrs Beatty was the first to move, after Amanda, that is, who had broken free of Lois and was running towards her mother. Mrs Beatty just pushed herself up and away from that settee and, hobbling a little, like she was hurt, picked something up off the floor and tossed it at Amanda.

'There you are, darling,' she said, in that ugly, witch's voice of hers. 'Happy birthday. You can thank your Daddy for the state it's in.'

He'd sort of crumpled up then, moaning Amanda's name.

And that's when Mrs Beatty spotted her.

'Get out of here you, you monster. Get out of my house, you vile, spying little bitch.'

And she'd gone, you bet, as fast as her legs would carry her.

Later, after she'd related the whole thing to her parents, Pearl said, 'What was it?'

'What was what?'

'Amanda's present.'

'Oh. A dress. A real neat pink dress, sort of silky, you know? But it was all torn . . .'

'Yeah, okay, that's enough now,' Neil said, standing up. 'Now listen here, Lois. What you saw and heard was personal and private between Mr and Mrs Beatty. It wasn't your fault you saw it, but even so it's none of our business. Have you got that?'

'Sure, Daddy. Only I . . .'

'Listen, now. Because it's nothing to do with us, I want you to forget that it ever happened. Mrs Beatty didn't mean or probably even know what she was saying to you, so you must just put that out of your mind. What's more important is that I want you to promise me you will forget all about this. Now only we know about it, so if I hear any gossip or talk at all, I'll know who started it, won't I?'

'Yes, Daddy.'

'And if I do hear any, you are going to be in real, big trouble.'

'I won't, Daddy,' Lois promised. 'Only you've got to promise me something, too.'

'No conditions,' Pearl said, moving towards them.

Lois touched the lapel of her father's jacket.

'Just promise me you and Mommy won't ever be like that. Promise?'

Pearl turned away. Her heart felt like there was a cold hand gripping it as Neil promised.

10 JULY

The sun beat down on Lois where she lay in the back yard of Number Five. It had started up again, the tension, but it wasn't as bad, and with her eyes closed behind enormous sunglasses, she could almost pretend she was back in California. The impression was strengthened by a stack of her favourite comic-books which had arrived yesterday morning from her grandmother. She pretended to be immersed in one of these whenever she sensed or caught William looking at her as he fed his pet rabbit. Not that she really minded. She felt somehow better about her body. Otherwise she would never have dared to wear the black and white halter her grandmother had also sent. She wore it with white shorts and a big straw sun hat of her mother's. The ensemble made her look grown-up and sophisticated. The hat and the glasses had the added advantage of making her feel private, cut-off, so that she could observe William sneaking looks at her. She began to feel drowsy and thought that once William had gone away she might nap in the good sun. Maybe her mother was right. If she rested up, eased herself into it, like the doctor said, it wouldn't be so bad this time. She shifted restlessly, embarrassed suddenly to be even thinking about it with William so close.

'Will you stop staring at me, William Young?' She propped herself up on her elbows, her comic-book clasped across her breasts.

William's startled face appeared over the top of Oliver's hutch.

'I wasn't,' he said truthfully.

'There's just no privacy here,' she said, though not angrily. 'I'm going to ask my Daddy to put up a real high fence. Or maybe yours would like to?'

William came close to the low hedge which separated their gardens.

'This is your boundary,' he said.

'Trust you to have a smart answer.' She flopped down again, with a sigh.

'It's a shame about the party, isn't it?' he said, reluctant to leave.

'I don't care.'

'Mr Beatty took Amanda off first thing this morning.'

'Off? Where?' Lois sat up. The concealing comic-book, forgotten, fell to the grass.

'Her grandma's.'

'I thought she was supposed to be ill? That's why they cancelled . . .'

'She looked all right,' William said. 'Mrs Beatty didn't go.'

'Well, *that* doesn't surprise *me* the least little bit. How long are they going for?'

'The weekend.'

'How come you know all this?' Lois cocked her head on one side, pushed the sunglasses down her nose a little.

'Amanda told me. I got up early, see, to get some dandelions for Oliver. They're freshest if they've got the dew on them and . . .' He hurried on, aware of Lois's flagging interest, 'I saw Amanda get into the car, so I went over and talked to her while he, Mr Beatty, he was getting something from inside the house.'

'Did you ask her if she was sick?'

'No. There wasn't time.'

'Well,' Lois said, pushing her glasses up again, 'it would have been a very boring party anyway.'

'It's just tough on Amanda. That's all I meant.'

Lois did not answer. She lay down, turned on to her side, away from William.

'I'd better go now,' he said after a while.

'Sure.'

'See you, Lois.'

'Yeah. 'Bye now.'

Lois couldn't wait to tell her parents. She could discuss it with them if with no one else and, though they pretended a lofty, adult indifference, she knew they were really interested, had heard them talking about the Beattys' marriage. She chuckled to herself suddenly, thinking that they didn't know the half of it.

Inside the Youngs' house, Doug intermittently saw his son, talking to Lois over the hedge, as he paced back and forth between the big window at the front and the smaller one at the back. Upstairs, the baby had at last stopped crying and he felt a slight easing of tension. He did not dare remain at the front window, much as he longed to, for twice that morning Marion had asked him why he kept looking out into the Crescent. He thought it likely that Marge would appear. He'd wanted her to all morning, ever since William had brought the news of John's and Amanda's departure to the breakfast table. He had not seen her since their day together, although she had phoned him at the office. She'd told him to keep his head down, keep out of John's way. It would blow over, she said. After all, he had no proof. She'd be in touch as soon as it was safe. He'd left the car in the drive deliberately, so that she would know he was at home. All she had to do was go out for a walk. He'd told Marion he was going to clean the car, but he didn't dare start it now in case Marge should suddenly decide to go out. It would be just his luck to have the car half-waxed when Marge decided . . .

'Why do you keep staring out the window like that?'

He started guiltily and turned purposefully away from the window. He had not heard Marion come in. She sat down, an absent look on her face. He guessed, fingers-crossed, that there was no need to answer. She picked up the *Radio Times*.

'I thought you were going to clean the car.'

'Yes. But I don't know . . . It's too hot. I'll run it through the automatic in Olton.'

'I thought we had to economize,' she said, folding the *Radio Times* open at the Saturday afternoon programmes.

'Well . . . What's a quid here or there?' he said, walking round her, his eyes moving to the window.

Marion leaned back against the cushions.

'It's a pity about the party,' she said.

Only half-listening, Doug was taken by surprise. How long was it since she had shown the slightest interest in any social occasion? He'd practically had to drag her to the Hunters' Christmas do, and then . . .

'What party?' he asked, pushing the memory of her public weeping away.

'Amanda Beatty's. Her birthday. You remember. William was going.'

'Oh yes. That.' He walked back to the window, just passing it, glancing out. 'Talking about birthdays, we ought to think about William's.'

'Oh that's ages yet,' she said, vague. 'I think I've seen the film on BBC2 this afternoon, only I'm not sure. I think I have.'

'Less than a month,' he said, bored with her endless TV programmes, knowing that, whether she had seen it or not, she would watch the film and probably fall asleep in front of it. 'He ought to have a party,' he said. 'Like the other kids.'

He saw her shoulders tense, anticipated the whining note in her voice which, no matter how justified, he still could not bear or excuse.

'Here? Oh, no, I don't . . . I don't think I feel up to that.'

'You could try.'

'No, Doug, please.' She turned to him, her hand plucking nervously at the back of the couch, her face all eyes, begging. 'I know you think I'm useless, but I can't . . .'

He couldn't cope with tears, recriminations, the self-accusing monologues that were supposed to justify her grey indolence.

'I'll arrange something,' he said, dismissing the subject.

'Will you? Oh thank you. I know I'm . . .'

'It's all right. I understand. I shouldn't have mentioned it.'

He stood at the window, not caring now even if she did suspect something. He willed Marge to come out.

'What though? You're here so little . . .'

'What?'

'William's birthday. What will you do?'

'Oh, I don't know.' He shrugged. 'Take them all to Macdonalds or something. Don't you worry about it.'

'All right.' She settled back again, into the cushions, the *Radio Times* listless on her knees. 'If I feel up to it,' she said, 'I'll try to come with you. I ought to. I do know I ought to, for William's sake. I'll really try. I promise.'

'Good.'

There was a long silence. Fists clenched in his pockets, Doug mentally implored Marge to show herself in one of the windows, at least.

'I think I'll just have a look at the film,' she said, getting up and moving somnambulistically to the television set.

'Yes. Sure.'

He waited a little longer and then it occurred to him that he could call Marge up from a phonebox.

'I think I'll go for a stroll,' he said, sounding tense when he had meant to be casual.

Marion nodded, apparently absorbed in the BBC test-card.

3 AUGUST

'Many happy returns of the day, William.'

William stared and stared. It was as though his brain had lost the ability to translate what he saw into sense and meaning. A kind of numbness which was also dread, a prescience of horror crept through William's cold veins.

'I *said*, Many happy returns of the day, William.'

Already up and dressed, Lois leaned even further out of her bedroom window. Slowly, as though it cost him an immense effort, William lifted his face. Lois had never seen it so pale. His dark eyes were the only spots of colour and they seemed to glow with something . . . something Lois could not name.

'It's Oliver,' he said, his voice barely carrying. 'He's gone.'

'Wait,' she said after a moment. 'I'll be right down.'

William stared at the hutch, the door hanging open, the latch dangling free. On impulse, he thrust his hand into the bedding, knowing before he felt it that it would be cold. He withdrew his hand and leaned against the hutch, his eyes misted and blurred. He did not acknowledge Lois's noisy, panting arrival.

'Oh wow,' she said, taking in the door, the almost tangible sense of emptiness. 'You must've forgotten to latch it properly,' she added, fingering the latch.

'I didn't. Of course I didn't.' He slammed the door, snatching the latch from her fingers.

'Okay, okay. Well, he can't have gone far,' Lois said and began to stomp around the garden, calling, 'Here, Oliver. Here, boy. Come on, Oliver.' There was something almost comic in the way she peered under bushes, between plants. 'Here. Oliver. Here, boy.'

For a while, William watched her as though she were a

figment of his imagination. Then, 'Stop it,' he yelled. 'Stop it.'

He rushed at her. Surprised, Lois turned towards him, alarm spreading over her face as it seemed he would surely hit her. Instinctively, she stepped back.

'You'll frighten him. You'll scare him away. Just stop it,' William shouted.

'Well, okay,' she shouted back. 'I was only trying to *help*.'

Pearl, attracted by their voices, by something in William's especially, came into her garden.

'What is it?' she asked. 'What's all this shouting about?'

Lois walked around William, giving him a wide berth.

'He's lost his rabbit. I was only trying to help him and . . .'

'Oh dear. Can't you find him? Surely he won't have gone far?' She spoke to William's silent back.

'I was only trying to help,' Lois repeated, petulant.

'Later, dear,' Pearl said, still looking at the boy's back. 'You'd better come and have some breakfast now.'

Lois looked at William – Pearl thought an almost longing look – then turned on her heel and marched up the path at the side of the house.

'I'm sorry, William,' Pearl said gently. 'I'm sure he'll turn up. Perhaps you could put some food out for him or something?'

Still he did not speak. He stood there rigid, his whole body tensed as though to prevent himself flying apart. Pearl, with a sad shake of her head, went into the house.

'I was only trying to help,' Lois complained again, throwing herself into a chair. 'He's no cause to go yelling at *me*.'

'He's upset,' Pearl soothed. 'You know how much he cares about that rabbit. Best leave him for a while.'

'Dumb rabbit,' Lois muttered.

'It's very important to *him*. Now you've got lots to do this morning, so just leave William alone. Let's just hope he finds it.'

'I could help . . .' Lois protested.
'Lois,' Pearl said, warningly.
'Yes, Mom.'

It was true. She did have plenty to occupy her that morning. First, she had to carry the big carton of things she had borrowed from the house over to the barn. One thing, she thought, as she did so, the loss of Oliver would ensure that William obeyed her injunction to stay away from the barn until she said. Vanessa was going shopping with her mother, so that was okay, and Lois was pretty sure the twins would be too wrapped up in each other to have any curiosity about her preparations. The Mercers were away on their annual holiday – she wondered if Andy had remembered to send William a card – and Amanda was once again at her grandmother's. Still, just to be sure, she put the box right at the back of the barn and placed the heavy pile of newspapers she had already brought over on top of it. Then she set off across the fields to the farm.

It was Joe she wanted, Joe she'd fixed it all up with. He didn't ask as many questions as Farmer Applegreen and besides, ever since that time with the chickens, Lois felt that the farmer was suspicious of her. He might have said 'no' to something like this. So she was glad to see, as she drew close to the farm, that the battered old truck Mr Applegreen drove was not there.

Joe, taking advantage of the boss's absence, perhaps, was sitting on a bale of straw, furtively smoking one of his thin, squidgy-looking, hand-rolled cigarettes. As always, his pale eyes took a moment or two to light up as he saw Lois swinging across the yard towards him. The light spread slowly from his eyes to his lips, which he moistened as the smile broadened. He reached up one calloused hand and pushed the old, greasy-looking cap he always wore back on his head.

'Hi, Joe. Did you get it for me?'

'Hello,' he said, smiling, his eyes travelling slowly down her body. 'Yes. I got 'im.'

'Terrific.' Lois waited. The man drew on his cigarette, looking at her. 'So? Where is it?'

'No hurry, is there?' he said. 'Sit a while.' He patted a corner of the bale invitingly.

'I can't stay long,' Lois said. 'Just till you finish your cigarette, okay?' She ignored his invitation but climbed up where the bales were stacked in step formation and sat slightly above him. His eyes followed her, rested upon her. She swung her legs, smiling back. 'It's a beautiful day.'

'Yes.'

'I wish we could go away somewhere but Daddy says we can't afford it this year, not with the move and everything. We're going to save up and maybe go back home next year.'

'Go?' Joe said, his eyes dimming with a frown.

'Just for a vacation.'

'You don't want to go off. I'd miss you.'

'Only for a month, two maybe. I'd miss you, too, Joe. I'll tell you what. I'll send you a postcard.'

He nodded slowly, puffed again on his cigarette. Lois looked around the yard. It seemed sleepy, peaceful, in the morning sunlight. Joe's eyes did not leave her.

'I brought a bag,' she said, worried that he might have forgotten the purpose of her visit, pulling a folded plastic bag from her pocket.

'Oh, yes.'

Joe seemed to be thinking. His eyes left her, moved slowly over to some old stables on the shadowed side of the yard.

'Is it there?' she asked, wriggling forward on the bale, twisting to follow the direction of his gaze.

'Yes.'

To her relief, he stood up, pinching the butt of his cigarette between his fingers and placing it, with almost studied care, into a battered tobacco tin taken from his overall pocket. Lois jumped down, landing bouncily beside him.

'You get bigger and bigger,' he told her, staring into her eyes. 'Growing.'

'I guess. Okay? Can we go fetch it now?'

'Yes.'

He moved off towards the stables, Lois at his side. He walked close to her, his arm brushing hers, going ahead only when they reached the buildings. The top half of the stable door to which he went was open. He reached over the bottom section and unbolted it, dragged the door open.

'In here,' he said.

She went ahead of him into corn-smelling gloom. Bins of feed stood against the walls. In a corner, there was an irregular pile of something, covered with an old sack. Joe, brushing against her, went to it and lifted up the sack.

'There you are,' he said. 'You can take your pick.'

'Oh,' she said. 'So many.'

'Yes.' He looked pleased and Lois saw that he wanted her approval.

'You did really well, Joe. Fantastic.' She bent over the pile and selected one, pointing. 'That one.'

He nodded, picked it up and dropped it in the plastic bag she held open for him.

'Thanks, Joe.'

'Yes.' He took a few steps backwards, placing himself between Lois and the door. 'I got it for you.'

'Yes, Joe. And I'm really pleased. Thank you.'

'Now you . . . you do something for me.'

Something, some sixth sense made her feel scared.

'What, Joe?'

'You . . .' He came towards her, his hand held out.

Lois flinched back, unable to help herself. He caught her arm, just above the elbow and held it, his fingers immediately smoothing the tanned flesh. Joe stared at her, rapt, his hand stroking her arm.

'Touch,' he said, smiling.

She looked at his hand.

'Yes, Joe. Only I really do have to . . .'

He moved more quickly than she thought possible for him. One hand was instantly on her left breast, squeezing. The other fastened around her wrist and dragged her free hand urgently towards his groin.

'Touch,' he said, smiling.

'No!'

Lois twisted round, butted him with her shoulder. Surprise and a child-like knowledge of pain exploded across his face. He tugged at her wrist but Lois was already gone, was free of him, was out intó the light of the yard again, running, the plastic bag swinging at her side.

Joe stood in the open doorway, his mouth hanging slack. He raised his hand and waved, but she did not look back.

Lois sniffed and brushed for the hundredth time at the smudge of dirt on her green T-shirt, over her left breast. The mark did not come off, as she knew it wouldn't. She picked a colander out of the carton and began wrapping it in sheets of newspaper which she fastened with sticky tape. She rubbed the back of her hand across her nose. She had not really been crying, and if she had it was only from shock. Joe had scared her, but not nearly so much as the idea of it, as the prospect of having, ever, to go back to the farm. It was the shock, she realized, the sheer unexpectedness of it. Andy now. If Andy had made a grab at her she wouldn't have been at all surprised. But Joe. Joe had always seemed so gentle and slow. Well, she'd fix him. She'd think of something, she vowed furiously, digging into the box again and pulling out an oval, pink plastic sponge. It was the fact that he had wanted her to touch him. She shuddered, told herself not to think about it. She would just stay away from him, never go near the farm again. He hadn't hurt her. Nobody would know. Her breast had felt nothing but the recoil of surprise. Now it seemed to glow because she was so conscious of it. And she hadn't touched him at all. Even if she had, it wouldn't have been her fault, but she hadn't.

'Dirty old pig,' she said aloud, and sniffed again.

The sound of her voice made Lois feel better. She began to wrap a small pocket comb quickly. She wouldn't tell anyone. She would forget about it and concentrate on William's birthday.

'I hope his hand withers and drops off,' she muttered. 'I hope both his hands . . .' But she couldn't think of anything bad enough.

She looked at the parcels she had made and was pleased with them. Her tummy rumbled and she realized that she was hungry, that it was lunch time. She piled the parcels back in the carton and spread some of the remaining newspapers over them. She came out of the barn, brushing dirt from the knees of her jeans, and began to walk quickly back towards the Crescent, thinking that she would have time to finish everything off this afternoon, before she had to get changed for William's birthday outing. It was perhaps the thought of William that made her notice him. He was walking slowly along the hedge at the back of the houses, stopping every now and again to peer into the thick foliage.

'William,' she called, and broke into a run.

He did not answer but stood, white-faced, waiting for her.

'He didn't come back yet, huh?'

'No.' He would not meet her eyes.

'You looking for him down here? Do you think he could come so far?'

'*I* don't know.'

He turned away and the stoop of his shoulders, the completeness of his misery, touched her suddenly.

'You want I should help you?'

'No.' He shook his head, continued walking away from her.

'William, I *am* sorry.'

He just shook his head again as though it didn't matter,

as though there was nothing anyone could say that would soften the loss. Lois's cheeks burned suddenly and she turned away, hurrying. She wished then – and it was a sincere wish – that she had not let Oliver out, had not carried him, tense in her arms, to the bottom of William's dawn-washed garden and let him go, hopping.

But it wasn't really her fault. How did she know the stupid rabbit would go wandering off? She'd thought it would be like a cat or a dog. Even pigeons had homing instincts. She couldn't know that dumb Oliver didn't. Her conscience began to settle, salved. Anyway, she told herself, it was cruel to keep animals penned up in cages. She really believed that. She *did*. Besides, William could always get another. And that made her laugh a little.

Doug Young reached home shortly before four pm. He was hot and sweaty and thought that there would just be time for a very quick bath before he had to round all the kids up and drive into town. He entertained no hope that Marion would come and help him, despite her promise, even though Sylvia Shillingworth had agreed to look after the baby. He was surprised, therefore, when Marion came hurrying into the hall. Surprised by the fact that she was wearing make-up and a blue dress he had not seen since before she was pregnant.

'Oh good . . .' he began, before the worried expression on her face made him frown and prepare himself for excuses, tears.

'Thank goodness you're home. It's William . . . I can't do anything with him . . .' She glanced towards the stairs, took Doug's arm and drew him into the living room.

The baby gurgled from the carrycot, all ready, apparently, to go.

'Oliver's gone,' she said. 'This morning, William found the hutch open.'

'Oh God,' Doug groaned. 'How did that happen? Well, he can't have gone far . . .'

'He can't find him. He's been searching all day. Look, he wouldn't even open his presents.'

Doug saw the stack of parcels, just as they had been when he left that morning, extra early in order to get back for the party.

'And now he won't get changed or anything,' Marion went on. Almost fearfully, she added, 'He says he won't go.'

'Won't go? What the hell . . . Where is he?'

'In his room. He just went up there . .. I couldn't make him see sense.' She followed Doug out into the hall. 'He's ever so upset.'

'He will be when I've finished with him.'

'Oh no, Doug. Don't be cross. Really, he's heartbroken. I'm sorry. I did try . . .' she called, as he went up the stairs.

'William?'

Doug's anger melted the moment he saw William. White as a sheet, his eyes red from weeping, he was lying immobile on the bed, staring at the ceiling.

'Hey . . .' Doug said, sitting beside him. 'Mum told me. I'm sorry. But it's not the end of the world. Most likely he'll come back . . .'

'No,' William said fiercely.

'Well . . . What about your presents? Actually, they'd better wait now. Get changed, wash your face . . .'

'I'm not going.'

'William, it's all arranged. Jason and Julian and every-one . . .'

'Take them. I don't care.' He threw himself over on to his side, hiding his face.

Doug watched him for a moment and then touched his shoulder.

'Listen to me, son. I know it's hard. And it's bloody rotten luck happening today of all days, but you're old enough now to understand . . . What I'm trying to say is that when something bad like this happens, you have to put a good face on it. We all do. You have responsibilities to people. Your friends, Mum and me. Even if you feel . . . oh, I don't know . . . Being grown-up means getting over things, trying for other peoples' sake. So come on, eh? Get changed and . . .'

'I didn't leave the door unlatched,' William said.

'Maybe he shook it free. Maybe he saw a really gorgeous lady rabbit visiting the garden and decided to elope.'

He felt William relax. Slowly, the boy turned towards him.

'Doe,' he said.

'Yes, well . . .'

'Do you think . . .?'

'There's a lot of rabbits about, wild ones, this time of year. Yes. I reckon old Oliver's gone off to get married.'

'Don't be daft. Rabbits don't . . .'

'All right then. For a bit of the other, since you're so grown up.'

In spite of himself, William smiled. 'But he won't come back?'

'Not until his lady love throws him out and by then, well, he might have developed a taste for it.'

William sniffed.

'Look. I'll tell you what. First thing tomorrow morning – I'll take the day off, okay? – and we'll go into Olton and get a really safe catch for that hutch – a bloody padlock, if you want – and a new rabbit. Two if you like. What do you say?'

A little colour washed into William's cheeks.

'A special present. Your *real* present.'

'Do you mean it?'

'Yes. Provided you are up, dressed and downstairs in ten minutes,' Doug said, standing up. 'And smiling,' he added from the door. 'Right?'

'Yes, Dad.'

'Ten minutes, or else. Marion!' he shouted, going into the hall. 'Take the baby over to the Shillingworths' and round up the kids. We'll be ten minutes.'

'He's coming?' she said, her eyes wide.

'Of course he is.'

Doug began to unbutton his shirt.

Everything considered, Lois thought the party went better than she had feared or expected. For one thing, she thought it was a really neat idea to hold it in a proper restaurant. William's father had fixed everything, reserved tables and all, and the special attention they got from the waiters made Lois at least feel really grown-up and excited. Then Mr Shillingworth, who had come with them because they couldn't all fit into one car, made her laugh a lot with his funny voices and his teasing. And when things got a bit flat and quiet, there was Mrs Young to look at and think about. It was really weird seeing her together with Mr Young. Somehow Lois always thought of her as separate, even from William, and inevitably Mr Young went with Mrs Beatty in her mind. Only she didn't like to think about that because it reminded her of Joe, but she knew that it explained the way Mr Young behaved towards her. It was sort of bland and non-committal. He avoided her eyes and hardly ever spoke directly to her and when he did, or caught her looking at him, he composed his features as though he was holding something in, in back of his face.

Then, when the meal was over and it looked like everyone was getting ready to go home, the waiter came back with an enormous birthday cake, with all the candles lit, and placed it ceremoniously in front of William. He looked like he was going to cry and needed two puffs to blow out all the candles which, she thought, meant that his wish wouldn't come true.

'I didn't make one,' William said.

'Why ever not?'

'Because I've already got it,' he said, beaming, and told them about getting two new rabbits in the morning.

'Yes,' said Lois, 'but it won't be the same, will it? I mean, it won't be the same as *Oliver*.'

And then Vanessa kicked her under the table and they were all looking at her, silent.

'No,' William said, breaking the awkward silence. 'It'll be even better.'

He looked at his father who nodded and winked.

'First,' Lois explained, 'you all have to be blindfolded.'

'Oh no,' said Jason.

'Nothing's going to happen,' she told him scornfully.

'Why can't we just keep our eyes shut, then?'

'Because you could cheat, easy.'

Jason looked at Julian, who shrugged.

'The whole idea is,' Lois went on, 'that you only have the sense of touch.'

'I don't understand,' Vanessa said.

'That's because none of you will let me finish.'

'All right. Shut up, you lot. Go on, Lois.'

'Right. Okay. So you have the blindfold on . . .'

'What'll we use?'

'Shut up, Julian.'

'I brought blindfolds, okay? So, when you're blindfolded, I give each of you a parcel and you have to work out what's in it just by feeling it.'

'Oh.'

'What? Even if it's in a cardboard box?'

'No, dummy, because nothing *is* in a cardboard box. Okay?'

'What about you?'

'I can't play because I know what's in the parcels. *I* wrapped them up.'

'Oh come on,' William said. 'Let's get on with it.'

She handed out the strips of thick bandage and checked that they were all properly blindfolded before she started passing out the parcels.

'I don't know,' Vanessa said, almost at once. 'I give up.'

'It's a ball,' Julian announced.

'Wrong. Try again.'

'It's like a ball.'

'A brush,' Jason said. 'A clothes brush.'

'Right. One point to Jason.'

'Does that mean I've won?'

'No. That's the person who guesses the most objects.'

She took the small package from Vanessa, who dropped out, and passed it on to Jason.

'A box?' William said, turning his parcel over in his fingers.

'Close.'

'I know. A cigarette packet.'

'Right for William.'

'Oh I can't do this. If it's not a ball, I don't know what it is.'

'Okay. Pass it on to William. Here, let me.'

'A comb,' Jason announced.

'Right again. Hey, you're really good at this.'

'This is easy,' William said. 'It's a colander.'

'Right again. You see, Vanessa? Right, now the battle of the champions is on.' Lois made a trumpeting noise that was meant to sound like a fanfare.

Vanessa and Julian, their blindfolds removed, looked bored.

'It's better with more people,' Lois told them. 'But this is the really good part anyway.'

'I don't think it's a very good game,' Vanessa said, stubborn.

'That's because you give up too easy. Here,' Lois said, handing new packages to William and Jason.

Separately, they both correctly identified on old gramophone record and an egg whisk.

'Okay. We'll have to bring in a time limit,' Lois decreed.

'Good,' said Vanessa.

Lois ignored her.

'Here you go. What about this . . . and this?'

'A pencil box.'

'No.'

'Er . . .'

'That's not fair. He said what it was. He can't have another go,' William protested.

'I didn't mean that anyway,' Jason argued. 'I was just thinking out loud.'

'That's cheating.'

William gripped his own parcel tightly. It gave under his fingers.

'A sponge,' he said. 'A bathroom sponge.'

'Right. That means you're out of time, Jason.'

'That's not fair. He was arguing so . . .'

'I've won,' William said belligerently.

'Oh who cares?' Jason said, tearing off his blindfold.

'Okay, William. One more. See if you can get this.'

It was heavy. It lay across his thighs, heavy and sort of floppy. There were hard, stiff bits sticking out from it. His hands moved over it delicately, trying to trace the shape. It was both hard and soft, limp, but rigid and . . .

'Ugh,' Vanessa said.

'What?'

'Oh, it's . . .'

'What is it, William? Come on.'

. . . damp or at least moist. Moisture seeping through the layers of paper. He raised his fingers, which felt tacky, and sniffed at them.

'Stop it,' Vanessa said. 'Stop it. It's bleeding.'

'What?' William said.

'Bleeding,' Vanessa repeated, and clapped her hand over her mouth.

They all stared at it and it was true that the central section of the package, where it was soft and malleable under William's exploring fingers, had become dark red and damp. William reached up and snatched his blindfold off, let it dangle like a too-large collar around his neck. His heart thudded and skipped as he looked down at the bloody package on his knees. Part of him wanted to hurl it away, but a stronger instinct told him that he had to know what it was. He began to tear at the paper, holding his breath.

'No,' Lois shouted. 'That's not allowed.' She went to him, tried to snatch the parcel away.

With a force that surprised them all, William lashed out at her, knocking her arm away.

'Ow,' she said, stepping back and rubbing her arm.

William, whiter than ever, scrabbled again at the layers of newsprint. His fingers touched fur and he stopped. He looked at Lois, his face a set, unfathomable mask. She said, 'You're not supposed . . .'

'Who's going to stop me?'

He stood up and placed the package on his chair. The twins moved closer, craning to see. He had torn the paper in the middle and now it was easy to yank it off. With two savage gestures he did so.

It was a rabbit, dead, its eyes staring, its stomach slit but not gutted.

'It's a rabbit,' Jason whispered and looked at Lois, horrified.

'Oh no,' Vanessa moaned.

'It's not Oliver,' Lois said.

William straightened up. He held the rabbit by its stiff back legs. The twins backed off, together, watching. Vanessa turned her head, not wanting to see it.

'I'll never forgive you for this,' William said, in a terrible voice that none of them had ever heard before. 'Never. Never as long as I live.'

Then, with a speed that made it impossible for any of them to see what he intended, he flung the rabbit with all his strength at Lois. She screamed and dodged but the dead creature struck her hard in the chest. The force of impact made blood spatter on to her dress, her face.

'Never,' William repeated, tears starting, scalding from his eyes.

The rabbit fell with a dull, dead sound at Lois's feet. There was a streak of blood across her breasts, staining her dress. More splattered on to her legs, making her draw back.

William groped his way to the ladder and began to descend, tears running down his face.

Lois looked down at herself, felt sickened by the blood. She held her hands out from her body, not knowing what to do. Then she became aware of the silence, of their eyes fixed on her, solemn and accusing.

The barn door creaked then slammed back against the wall, shuddering.

'It was a joke,' Lois told them. 'I thought it would be a joke.'

The twins moved simultaneously towards the ladder.

'I can't help it if he hasn't got a sense of humour,' she shouted.

Vanessa followed the boys.

Lois looked down at the rabbit, stirred it with her foot.

Outside, sounding already very far away, Lois heard the twins calling, 'William. Wait. Hey, William.'

'A joke,' she told the rabbit. Then she drew back her right foot and kicked it as hard as she could, kicked it into the air, out of sight, into the body of the barn. The damn thing had brought her nothing but trouble, right from the first.

24 AUGUST

'If you ask me,' Andy said through a mouthful of sausage sandwich, 'William's a spoil-sport. Well, he always was, really. I mean, long before you came here.'

Lois, stretched out in the sun, pricked up her ears, attracted as much by a new note of maturity in his voice as by what he was saying. She had remarked it before, since his return from holiday.

'And I'll tell you something else,' he went on. 'I bet the twins'll agree once they've had time to think it over. You'll see. When they get back from Majorca they won't have any time for him either.'

'Majorca,' Lois said lazily, correcting his pronunciation. He shrugged and took another sandwich from the box his mother had made up for them, to get them out from under her feet. 'What was William like, anyway, before I came?' she asked.

'Oh, you know. He was always the one that stopped us doing things. Like the barn, for instance. It was always William who said we couldn't play there and said he'd tell if we ever went near it.'

'He might have got that from his father,' Lois said.

'How? What do you mean?'

'Oh nothing,' she said, sitting up and twisting to look down at the barn, which shimmered a little in the heat. They had meant to go further, 'to have a good ramble about the fields', as Mrs Mercer had put it, but it was too hot. By the time they'd climbed the hill down which they had tobogganed earlier in the year Lois had refused to go any further. 'I didn't mean anything special,' she said vaguely.

'Well, you'll see. The twins'll be on our side,' he said confidently.

'I don't care,' Lois said, lying down again and stretching her arms above her so that the dry grass tickled her bare tanned arms.

Since the incident of the rabbit, the number of her friends had shrunk, though only William was actually not speaking to her. Vanessa was nearly always busy. With the twins away their attitude was open to speculation. Still, she had been glad when Andy returned from Scotland, even if it did mean that anything they did together involved Luke tagging along.

'How can you eat so much in this heat?' Lois asked as Andy selected another sandwich.

'Easy. Do you want something?'

'Save me an apple, huh?'

'Do you know something else? William even tried to blame me. He said the latch on the hutch wasn't strong enough . . .'

'Let's talk about something else.' Lois rolled over on to her stomach and flexed her legs in the air. 'I am entirely bored with the subject of William Young.'

'Me, too,' Andy agreed readily. He pulled his shirt over his head and dropped it on the grass beside him.

'Boys are lucky,' she said, watching him.

'Why?'

'Being able to take your shirt off like that.'

'Nobody's stopping you.' He lay back, hands looped behind his head.

'Don't be stupid. Girls can't.'

'Why not?'

'Oh Andy . . . You know.' She looked down at herself, plucked blades of grass and rolled them between her fingers.

'There was a girl in Scotland did.'

'Oh sure, aged six.'

'No. She'd got . . .' He made a gesture, cupping his hands with an imaginary fullness at the level of his own nipples.

Lois blushed.

'You liar, Andy Mercer.'

'No, honest. She did.' He glanced at her. 'We played "Doctors",' he added.

'Oh, sure.'

'You don't believe me?'

She shrugged.

'I just don't want to hear about it. I told you to cut that stuff out. Where's Luke?' She twisted round, looking for the younger boy.

'Over there.' Andy jerked his head, indicating the direction.

'What's he doing?' She stood up quickly, shading her eyes against the sun.

'Playing.'

She saw Luke walking along the hedgerow, swinging his arms in military style.

'My cousin Hamish's got hair.'

Lois burst out laughing.

'Well, so I should hope. Whoever heard of a bald cousin?'

'No. I mean . . . down there.'

'Oh.' She turned away, feeling the blood rush to her cheeks.

'That was it, you see. This girl, Fiona . . .'

'I don't want to hear about it, Andy,' she said crossly and walked away from him.

'Well, you started it.'

'Me?' She looked back at him, her eyes wide with exaggerated surprise.

'You told me not to talk about William. You said you wished you could take your top off.'

'I didn't mean . . .'

'I don't know what you're so scared about, anyway.'

'I am not scared.'

'Fiona had much bigger ones than you, anyway.'

'Stop it. Just stop it.'

Unaccountably, she burst into tears. They surprised her as much as they did Andy who, kneeling on the grass, stared at her with his mouth open. She did not understand why she was crying but she knew that she could not stop.

'Lois?'

She shook her head.

'I'm sorry. I didn't mean . . .'

She was glad that he did not laugh at her or tease, but that only made her sadder somehow.

'It's all . . .' she said through her tears, 'so weird.'

'What is?'

She did not answer, tried to sniff back the tears. Andy handed her a paper napkin.

'Come on, sit down,' he said. 'You'll feel better.'

Blowing her nose, sniffing, she sat down. Andy shuffled on his knees closer to her. He heard her mutter 'weird' again.

'What is?' he repeated.

'You . . . everything . . . this.' She threw her hands apart in a gesture which might have referred to her body or the surroundings. 'Anyway, I'm not scared.'

'All right.'

He sat back on his heels pulling up grass with a sharp, tearing noise.

'You don't believe me,' she said when the tears had abated a little.

'I don't know.'

She dabbed at her eyes, blew her nose and took a deep breath. She leaned back with her hands pressed flat against the grass and stared away at the barn.

'Well, I'm not anyway,' she insisted, sullen.

'Okay. Prove it.'

'How?' She looked at him.

'Take off your top. Show me.'

'What here? You're crazy.' She looked around the field as though it were full of people.

Andy stood up.

'Okay. Let's go to the barn then.'

'No.'

'See? You are scared.'

'I am *not*.'

'Come on, then.'

'What about Luke?'

'He'll be all right.'

Andy set off down the hill, hands in pockets.

She watched him go, undecided, frightened.

'You're not scared just because you don't *want* to do something,' she shouted.

'Says you,' he mocked, over his shoulder.

The air inside the barn was warm and slumberous, heavy, yet Lois could not suppress a shiver as she passed from the sunlight into the gloom. Light entered in pinpoint shafts through cracks and gaps in the weathered old boards, striping Andy's bare torso as he stood watching her.

'I don't know why you make such a big thing about it,' she said, unable to conceal the tremble in her voice. 'It's no big deal.'

She pulled her unbuttoned shirt out of her shorts and slipped it off.

'There,' she said, with as much boldness as she could manage.

Andy said nothing. He looked superior, smug. After a moment, he went towards the door.

'Okay. All right.'

Angrily, she reached behind her for the clasp of her cotton brassiere. She shrugged the straps from her shoulders and let it slip down her arms. She stood with her eyes cast down, her hands clasped in front of her. After what seemed a very long time she raised her eyes and looked at Andy, but the light slanted across his face in such a way that she could not read his expression.

A terrible cold shame swept over her.

'Get out of here,' she said, her voice a cracking whisper.

She turned her back on him, hitching her brassiere back into place. She fumbled awkwardly with the clasp.

'Get out. I hate you. And I'll make you pay for this if it's the last thing I ever do.'

Andy laughed.

She grabbed up her blouse and pulled it on. Her fingers shook so much that she could not button it. She could feel the tears pricking at her eyes again.

'Get out!' she screamed, moving towards him, her fists raised.

Andy bolted for the door and slipped out.

Lois leant against the warm wall, her head resting on her folded arms, and sobbed.

EARLY SEPTEMBER

The spurt of fairly intensive work which Lois had done during the period of her disaffection proved sufficient to convince the school authorities that, with the start of the new academic year, she should be educated with children of her own age. It meant, in fact, that she would be attending the upper school, wearing the black and grey uniform that would physically set her apart from her friends in the Crescent. She would still travel to and from school with them, of course, but there would be no playground or classroom contact. Pearl guessed that Lois would cope with this pretty well, but she warned Neil to stand by for a period of storms and tantrums until she made new friends and learned to reconcile the two groups. To have friends who were her contemporaries would be good for her, Pearl was sure but, she reminded Neil, being an only child they knew how important friendships were to her and how intense she could be about them. Even anticipating the difficulties, Pearl felt that this move was a turning point. The lure of America, she was convinced, would gradually lose its dazzle now – although she did not say *that* to Neil – and, as the leaves began to yellow in a glorious Indian summer, she felt at ease, that the worst was behind them.

Pearl's mood of contentment seemed to be underlined by her neighbours. The Shillingworths returned from their holiday, tanned and expansive. Sylvia was full of plans, not only for her re-election as Parent-Governor, but for organizing a proper lobby of selected Olton shops to expand their range of 'quality' goods. After all, it was in their own interests in these times to encourage free enterprise and competition. Pearl, smiling, agreed to help her.

Amanda returned from her grandmother's having grown, looking well and relaxed. It became known, by the osmosis of gossip, that the Beattys were going to try again. John had accepted a more senior post at the polytechnic where he lectured and Marge was going to look for a more demanding full-time job. They would have help in the house if necessary. Everyone agreed that the important thing was to keep Marge occupied. Pearl, in her heart of hearts, wished them well.

She was even more delighted by the privately confided news that Yvonne Hunter had finally decided to try for another child. She laughed and blushed when she said it and Ben seemed to have a permanent beam on his face. Pearl hugged Yvonne, told her that she could not be more pleased and promised help and support of every kind, when the time came.

In contrast, the Youngs seemed to have drawn in upon themselves but that, most of the ladies of the Crescent agreed, was exactly what the family needed. Whether Marge's decision had influenced Doug's or vice-versa nobody knew. They marvelled, though, to see him so frequently at home, to see Marion with a smile on her face, William playing with the baby in the garden. Early in September they went away for a few days and more than one pair of eyes noticed that, on their return, Marion and Doug were holding hands like young lovers as William carried his brother to see the rabbits. Pearl crossed her fingers for the Youngs for they still, she knew, had a long way to go. Even so, she felt optimistic.

As for the Mercers, they went on as ever. They, like the devoted Shillingworths, seemed impervious to the storms and tensions that buffeted other families. The boys were healthy and happy. Nigel bumbled about as usual while Ella was always busy, always welcoming. Pearl was glad of and for them.

All in all, she thought, sitting in the garden with a pile of new seed and bulb catalogues beside her, a difficult summer seemed to be declining into a peaceful and promising autumn.

17 SEPTEMBER

Predictably, Ella Mercer put on a full, traditional birthday tea for Andy and invited all the children. Only William was absent, Marion having somewhat embarrassedly pleaded a prior engagement some days before. William had not returned from school with the others, but his absence or separateness was now taken for granted by them and in no way detracted from their noisy enjoyment of the party. By six-thirty, only the younger children and the twins remained. In a huddle, Jason and Julian checked their previously synchronized watches.

'Hey, Andy, let's go out,' Julian said.

'Yes. Let's go over to the barn,' Jason agreed.

'What for?' Andy rather wanted to try out the new additions to his car racing game.

'Yes, off you go,' Ella said, interrupting the clearing of cake-smeared plates.

'But I . . .'

'Be off with you. I happen to know that three bonnie wee lassies are preparing a special treat for you,' she said, winking at the twins.

'What?' Andy's head jerked up. It felt like something tight and cold had lodged in his chest. He looked at the twins but their faces were closed, as though they did not know what his mother was talking about.

'There,' she said, bustling up to her son and smoothing the hair out of his face. 'Me and my loose tongue. Still, I haven't really spoiled the surprise, have I, boys?'

'No, Mrs Mercer,' the twins said in ragged unison.

Ella caught Andy's chin in her hand, forced him to look at her.

'Those aren't sulks I see, are they? No. I should think

not. Now off with you. You're that pale a blow in the fresh air will do you good.'

'Mum, I . . .'

'Come on,' Julian said, making for the door.

'And don't stay out too late, now. It's school tomorrow, remember.'

She guided her strangely reluctant eldest boy to the front door and watched him drag behind the twins down the path.

'Stop lagging, Andrew Mercer,' she called, 'or it's straight to bed with you.'

'I don't mind,' he said, immediately turning back towards her.

'Och, away with you.' She dismissed him with a cheerful gesture and closed the door. She couldn't think what possessed the child when everyone was making such a fuss of him.

She put him from her mind and went back to the clearing up, to supervising Luke and Jane at a game of Ludo.

Andy leaned against the solid trunk of the tree in the middle of the Crescent and folded his arms stubbornly.

'I'm not going,' he said.

The twins, facing him but standing so that they effectively blocked any escape route, exchanged an exasperated look.

'I thought you were suppposed to be my mates, anyway,' Andy said nervously. 'Fancy you dropping me in it like this.'

'Dropping you in what?' Julian asked reasonably.

'We haven't,' Jason said impatiently.

'You're in on it. Well, I'm not going. Not unless you tell me what they're up to.'

'We don't know.'

'Pull the other one – it's got bells on.'

'Honestly.'

'Right, then. If you don't know, you won't want to go

either.' He pushed away from the tree and the twins immediately pushed him back. 'You *do* know,' he accused.

'Only as much as you.'

'The girls are preparing a special treat.'

'Should be right up your street,' Julian said, grinning.

'Shut up,' Andy said. 'You know what that means. You ought to know better than anyone.' He spoke directly to Jason.

'We've finished with all that,' Julian said quickly. 'You know that.'

'Oh yes? Look what happened to Amanda.'

'That was an accident.'

'Like hell it was.'

'It *was*,' Jason insisted.

'All right then. What about William?'

'A joke. You said so yourself. It was you who kept on about how he couldn't take a joke and it served him right.'

Andy could not deny this. He looked down at his feet and repeated that he would not go.

'Coward,' Julian said.

'Baby.'

'You see? There *is* something.'

'No, there isn't. Even if there was, trust you to be scared.'

'Weren't you?' Again Andy spoke directly to Jason.

'Not beforehand,' he lied. 'Anyway, we didn't know anything was going to happen.'

'And nothing's going to happen to you,' Julian said. 'Now come on.' He grabbed hold of Andy's arm and pulled him roughly away from the tree.

'No,' he said, and tried to jerk free.

Jason took his other arm and twisted it swiftly up behind his back.

'Ow!' he cried. 'Let go. You're hurting.'

'Coward,' Jason said.

'Walk, or he'll break it,' Julian advised.

'Shut up, Shillingworth. Let go of me.'

Jason eased the pressure on his arm a little but did not release it. Red-faced, Andy straightened up.

'Keep walking.'

'I am.'

'Faster.'

'You're rotten. You're both rotten sods,' Andy said as they manoeuvred him between the houses, towards the field behind.

'And you weren't, I suppose, when you were making your clever electric chair?'

'That was different. Oh come on, twins. Tell us? What's going to happen?'

'Nothing,' Julian said.

'We don't know,' Jason told him and jerked his arm up again.

'Okay. That's just about everything,' Lois said, pleased.

The nursery table was standing on the lower floor of the barn. A white tray-cloth had been spread and on it rested several shiny knitting needles, a pair of tweezers, nail clippers, a bicycle pump, several rolls of bandage, sticking plaster, Julian's clasp knife and an enormous pair of dressmaking shears.

'What's the pump for?' Amanda asked.

'Emergencies, Nurse,' Lois said briskly. 'In case the patient should experience respiratory difficulties. Now, help me on with these,' she said, producing a pair of rubber gloves. 'Oh, and you, Sister, cover the instruments with the other cloth.'

'Do I look all right?' Vanessa asked as she spread the cloth over the array of implements. She was wearing a long brown overall-coat, back to front, while her head looked as though it had been badly bandaged, though Lois *said* it looked like a real nurse's cap. Secretly, she wished she had a proper uniform, like Amanda's.

'We are here to work, Sister, not to consider our personal appearance,' Lois said as Amanda tugged the left glove up over her wrists. 'Now, I am going to hide,' she announced, waving her pink, rubber-clad hands. 'I am going to make a dramatic entrance.'

Amanda giggled. Vanessa tugged at her 'cap'.

'Now, remember. You stand there, Amanda, at the foot of the operating table, and you, Vanessa, by the instrument trolley.'

Primping out her white apron with its brilliant red cross on the bib – part of an old nursing set she hadn't used for ages – Amanda stood obediently at the foot of the mattress. Vanessa moved to her place with less enthusiasm. She didn't really like it. It didn't seem such a good idea after all.

'And be ready with that tape,' Lois called.

'Where are you going?'

'Just back here, in the shadows, where he won't see me. And remember to do it just like I told you.'

'Yes, Lois,' Vanessa said, pulling a face.

'Shh,' Amanda hissed. 'I think I can hear them coming.'

Andy thought his best chance to escape would come when they reached the barn. He could see that the doors were closed and one of them would have to let go of him in order to open them. He knew he could take on one twin. But, as they drew close to the doors, Jason pushed his locked arm up painfully and secured the other, which Julian had released, tight against his side. He struggled but, before he knew what was happening, Julian had seized his ankles and lifted him free of the ground.

'Open up, Nurse,' Julian shouted. 'Patient for you.'

'Stretcher case,' Jason added.

'Hey, what's going on? Let go of me. You're breaking my arm.'

The door was pushed open and he had a fleeting glimpse of Amanda smiling, and dressed in a nurse's white cap and apron. Then the twins lifted him between them and, at a staggering trot, carried him into the barn.

'Put him down there,' Vanessa said. 'There'll have to be a preliminary examination, of course, but it looks bad to me.'

They dropped him on the mattress. Jason immediately sat on his legs and when he tried to sit up Julian pushed him back down.

'He's delirious, Nurse. We might have to restrain him.'

'I'm the sister,' Vanessa said. 'And, Julian, you're supposed to be the doctor now.'

'I know. Okay, let's have a good look at you, old chap.'

'Get off. Let me up.' Andy lashed out at him.

'Lie still and this won't hurt,' Vanessa said.

He twisted his head and saw her looming over him, a long, shining knitting needle in her hand.

'It's no good, Sister,' Julian panted, trying to force Andy's wrists flat on to the mattress. 'We shall have to use what's it.'

Vanessa giggled and dropped the knitting needle with a clatter.

'Physical restraint,' Amanda said primly. 'Pass the tape, Sister.'

'You shut up. You have to take orders from *me*. I'm Sister.'

'Get on with it,' Julian said curtly.

Vanessa picked up a roll of sticking tape and ripped part of it undone.

'Righto, old chap. Just sit up a minute, will you?'

'Get off. Let me bloody go,' Andy shouted.

'Such language,' Amanda tutted.

Jason reached up and grabbed the back of Andy's head, forcing it down towards his knees, on which he still sat. Julian and Vanessa forced his wrists together behind him.

'Please . . .' he said, in a muffled voice.

'Never mind. It's all for your own good,' Amanda said. 'You'll soon be asleep and won't know anything about the major operation you've got to have.'

'Hurry up, Sister,' Jason said. With both hands he held Andy's wrists.

'I'm doing my best,' Vanessa said as she pressed the free end of the tape home and passed it round. Julian snatched it from her and pulled it up. 'Give it back to me now,' she said.

'Don't . . .' Andy pleaded.

They wound the tape again round his wrists, immobilizing them.

'There.' Julian stood up, brushing his hands together.

'You can lie down now, patient,' Vanessa said.

'Get off me, Jason. Untie my hands . . . You rotten bloody lot . . .'

Amanda squatted and grasped his ankles.

'Right. Now for the examination,' Jason said. 'Let's have his shirt off, Sister.'

'Oh,' Vanessa said, biting her lower lip. 'We should have done that before his wrists.'

'Just open it. That'll do.'

'What do you think you're doing? Leave me alone.'

Julian had to hold his shoulders still while Vanessa unbuttoned his shirt. He swore and cursed at them, thrashing. Vanessa yanked his shirt out of his jeans and pulled it open. A button came off and rolled away.

'Now look what you've done. My Mum'll . . .'

'It's no use, Sister. We shall have to have that injection after all,' Julian said.

'No.'

'Certainly, Doctor.' Vanessa picked up another knitting needle and advanced on Andy's chest.

'Just lie still,' Amanda said, cheerfully.

'Piss off. All of you. Let me up.'

'No, Sister. Not there,' Julian said.

'In his bum,' Jason said, and began to unfasten his jeans.

Vanessa and Amanda burst out laughing.

'Get off. Get *off*,' Andy howled.

'Come on. Turn him over.'

'Wait.' Jason had unfastened the waistband of Andy's jeans but the zip was stuck.

'Hurry up.'

The zip gave with a tearing of metal teeth.

'I'll kill you bastards,' Andy shouted, wriggling and writhing.

'Right. Over we go.'

Amanda grabbed one leg, Jason the other. Vanessa and Julian bent towards his torso. He lashed out with his legs, felt his jeans slip down and instantly went limp.

'Okay. All right. I give up. I won't struggle any more. Just let me go.'

'Ooh,' said Amanda. 'Look at his pretty pants.'

'Just like a girl's knickers,' Jason said, spluttering with laughter.

'You sods,' Andy moaned, close to tears. Then he began to struggle again as he felt something passed around his ankles. 'No.'

Jason stood up, laughing, and yanked the prepared noose tight about his ankles. The knot bit into his flesh.

'Right, Sister. Prepare the patient, please.'

'No,' said Vanessa. 'I don't want to. You do it.'

'Oh, all right. Have the needle prepared.'

'Yes, Doctor.'

Amanda leaned forward over Andy.

'I'll do it,' she offered.

Andy felt the brush of her hands at the waistband of his underpants. Giggling, her laughter melting into that of the twins, she pulled his underpants down. He shouted at them, tried to stop the flow of tears.

'Right. Off you go, Sister,' Julian spluttered.

Vanessa jabbed the sharp end of the knitting needle into his left buttock and wiggled it about.

'We shall need more than that. He's not asleep yet.'

Julian took another needle from the table and poked at Andy's bare bottom. It didn't really hurt but he twisted about until he thought that perhaps, if he pretended to go along with them, to feign unconsciousness . . . Anyway, they'd have to let him up now. They had to. He forced himself to lie still.

'Right. Now for the examination.'

'Roll him over,' Amanda said.

'No. You can't . . .'

There was no holding the tears then. Tears of shame and terror. They lifted him up and dumped him down on his back.

'Oh look, he's crying. I expect it hurts,' Amanda said.

There was no laughter, no gasp of horror. He dared to look down at himself and saw that his pants still covered him in front, covered the swollen, hard source of his shame.

Julian prodded his chest with the bicycle pump, pretended to listen through it. He lay still, not daring to move, terrified that his pants might slip, that one of them would notice. Julian poked his belly with the bicycle pump.

'Oh dear.'

'What is it, Doctor?' Amanda asked.

'I'm afraid . . .'

'Oh no . . .' Jason said.

'What?'

'He needs an operation,' Julian said, giggling.

'Shh,' Amanda said, but they all began to laugh.

'Please . . .' Andy said, screwing his eyes tight shut.

'That means . . .'

'Yes. Send for Doctor Carradine, the world-famous surgeon,' Julian said, still giggling.

Lois! Andy had forgotten all about her. Now he felt the same chilling cold fear that he had fought down earlier. He twisted his head round, looking for her. Amanda ran off, out of his range of vision, calling, 'Doctor Carradine. Doctor Carradine. It's an emergency. Come at once.'

'Surgeons are called Mister, dummy, or in my case, Ms.'

Vanessa stepped to one side and he could see her then, advancing ponderously from the shadows. The lower half of her face was covered with a bandage mask. She held her hands, sheathed in pink rubber, out from her chest. She looked down at him, her eyes sliding contemptuously over his rudely exposed body.

'Please . . .' he whispered. 'Let me go. I'll do anything . . .'

'Notice, Nurse . . . Where are you, Nurse?'

'Here,' Amanda said, trotting up, smiling.

'Notice how the patient babbles in his unconscious state.' Lois spoke in a deep, deliberately gruff voice. 'No one is to take any notice of anything he says, for he can feel no pain.'

'Oh please . . .' Andy moaned.

She moved out of range, floated back into his vision. He saw that she was wearing a white overall, back to front. She bent over him, peering.

'Take down his shorts,' she said.

'No.' He jerked his knees up, twisting on to his side. 'Please don't . . .'

Lois pushed hard on his hip bone, pressed down with all her weight.

'Come on,' she said.

'I can't,' Amanda giggled.

'Jason,' she yelled.

He was laughing, too, and blushing, but he reached out and snatched down Andy's pants, exposing his sex.

There was a moment of explosive silence before the laughter broke over him, scalding, making him small and terrified.

'Ah-hah . . .' Lois yelled, snatching her breath between guffaws of laughter. 'Ah . . . I see . . . what the trouble . . . is. It will . . . it will have to . . . to . . . come . . . off.'

She could not stop laughing either. Jason was clutching his sides and staggering about. Amanda held her hand over her mouth. Vanessa, very red in the face, stared and giggled nervously.

'Right, to work,' Lois said. 'If we act quickly, we may save this boy from a life of sin and wickedness. Forceps.'

She held out her hand to Vanessa who gaped at her.

'Forceps, Sister.'

Vanessa shook her head.

'I'll do it, Doctor Carradine. I know how.'

Amanda pushed Vanessa aside and picked up the tweezers which she handed, with a flourish, to Lois.

'Now let me see . . .' she said, advancing the tweezers.

He was rigid now with fear. It felt as though his backbone would break. He held his breath, tried to make himself blind and deaf. The twins' laughter beat against his ears. They clutched each other, helpless, as Lois tweaked the end of his penis between the arms of the tweezers and lifted it.

'What is all this stuff down here?' she spluttered.

He felt the cold nip of steel on his sex. His whole body blushed. He felt himself growing hard again. It hurt. It was horrible.

'Knife, Nurse. Quickly.'

Amanda lifted the clasp knife and held it out to Lois who transferred the still-gripping tweezers to her left hand. 'Open it, dummy,' Lois said, reverting to her ordinary voice.

He could only stare as Amanda struggled with the knife.

'I can't . . .' she said.

'Help her, one of you,' Lois said to the twins.

'It's all right.'

He saw the blade, sharp and twinkling. Lois took it.

'Now, let me see . . .'

He screamed then. The knife grazed his lower belly, cold.

'Hold still,' Lois hissed. 'Yes . . .'

He was too afraid not to. The cold blade kissed his skin, was drawn in a tantalizing line down his belly, lower, lower. It pressed for a moment against his thigh, hovering, then pricked sickeningly at his scrotum.

'Yes . . . yes . . .' Lois murmured. 'This is it. We have to have this off.'

He realized that they weren't laughing any more. He realized that she meant it.

'Please, Lois, no, no . . . Please . . .'

'But this is no good. I shall need the shears, Nurse. One quick snip is best. He won't feel a thing.'

He screamed again, rolling his head from side to side. He saw the scissors pass from Amanda's hand to Lois's, saw her open them.

'Careful,' one of the twins said in a small, tight voice.

She let go of him with the pinching tweezers and he felt it flop back on to cold metal. He had never fainted in his life, but he thought he was going to then. He sensed movement and opened his eyes. Lois's face was close to his, her lips moving obscenely under the mask.

'I really ought to do it, Andy,' she whispered. 'For your own sake. To stop you being dirty and chasing after the girls, frightening them. I ought to do it to stop you going mad and blind. To stop you getting hairs on the palms of your hand. To stop you weakening your backbone. 'Cos that's what's going to happen to you. You know that, don't you?' She paused, waiting for his answer but he could only moan. 'You know I want to do it, don't you? I could, easy. But we'll ask Amanda and Vanessa. I know what I'd do if it was just my decision. I'd close these shears on you with one . . . snap!' He jumped, feeling his shrivelled sex move against the waiting steel. 'But you've been bad and dirty to them, too, so they have to have a vote. What do you say, girls?'

Andy rolled his head to the side, trying to see them, to beg them. Amanda was staring down at him, at the threatening entrancement of the scissors.

'No,' Vanessa said from somewhere he could not see. 'He's learned his lesson now. No.'

'No,' Amanda said. 'Let him off. *This* time.'

Lois withdrew the scissors.

'Say thank you to your merciful saviours,' she ordered him.

He could not. He could not say anything. One long sob escaped him. He turned on to his side, drawing his knees up to his stomach. He pushed his burning face down into the smelly old mattress, trying to hide, to smother himself.

*

Lois dropped the shears into a cane shopping basket and folded the cloths on top of the instruments. Julian pocketed his clasp knife and picked up his bicycle pump.

'Oh shut up, Andy,' he snapped. 'There's nothing to cry about.'

Jason raised the sobbing boy's limp arms and began to peel off the tape.

'They were right, you know,' Julian said. 'We all know what you're like. It was time you were taught a lesson. It was for your own good.'

'Shut up, Julian,' Lois said.

'Tell him to shut up. Tell him to stop crying.'

'Go away if it bothers you,' she said calmly.

He looked helplessly down at Andy. Jason ripped the last of the tape off and Andy immediately brought his hands up to his face. Jason folded the tape into a ball and lobbed it into the shadows.

'Andy?' Julian squatted beside him, shook his shoulder roughly.

'Leave him,' Lois said.

'Yes. You'd better,' Jason said quietly. 'Come on. Let's go.'

Julian looked at his brother, a mixture of surprise and anxiety on his face.

'We can't leave him like this. Just listen to him.'

'We can't do anything.'

'I'll stay,' Lois said, and turned away from them.

'Come on,' Jason said.

Reluctantly, Julian stood up.

''Bye, Andy,' he said, but Andy just went on sobbing.

Lois pushed the rubber gloves into the pocket of her white coat and rolled it up, then placed it on top of everything else in the basket. She looked around, mentally checking that everything was tidied away. At last, she looked down at Andy.

'At least pull your pants up,' she said. 'You don't want your mother to see you like that. Or do you?'

The mention of his mother acted like an electric prod.

He twisted round, reached down and began to pull up his clothes.

'Mo . . . mother?'

'I told Vanessa and Amanda to go fetch her. There was nothing else to be done.'

She walked casually to the door, pushed it open. She saw Ella Mercer hurrying across the field and went to meet her.

'It's all right, son. Come along now. Calm yourself.'

His mother knelt on the edge of the mattress, pulling him into her arms. He sobbed against her breast, feeling the warmth of her all about him as she rocked him.

'They told me all about it,' she said, keeping her voice steady by an effort of will. 'Well, Lois did mostly. They were wrong to take the law into their own hands and, mind, I've told them that, but your offence was worse. Oh, son,' she said, breaking a little but hugging him tighter. 'Whatever possessed you? You were always such a good little boy. I wouldn't be surprised if that devil Hamish didn't have something to do with this. Am I right? Was he putting filthy ideas into your head? Oh well, never mind now. Stop crying. Come on. It's over with. They're sorry they let things get out of control, but they're nicely brought up, respectable kids. As you're supposed to be. Oh God, if your poor father gets to hear about this . . .' She pushed him away from her suddenly, holding him by the upper arms. 'You realize this could have been a police matter, eh?' She shook him. His head lolled back and forth on his neck and she could not doubt that he had been punished enough. She clutched him tightly against her. 'Wisht, wisht. It won't come to that. They'll not tell on you. But you and me have got to have a serious talk about this. Aye, and don't think I don't mean it. How you could do such a thing I'll never know. I really don't. I blame that Hamish. It must be him. Och, come on now. Come on. I'll stop blethering at you. Calm yourself now and let me get you home and into bed before your father gets wind of anything. Come on now.'

She stood up, her knees cracking, and pulled Andy up after her.

'Where's your hankie?'

He pulled it out of his pocket.

'Aye, that's right. Blow your nose and come away home. Come on.'

She led him out into the dusk. She felt drained, exhausted, did not know how she should punish him, if at all. But to think that he would do a thing like that! She'd see to it that he kept well away from the girls in future. God bless them. Though they were wrong to hit him and tell him off so he became nigh hysterical. But then, they'd had the sense to speak out, to tell her what they'd done. What he'd done. Her cheeks burned with the memory of it. And she was a grown, married woman. What it must have been like for that poor Lois she couldn't bear to think.

Sadly, but gratefully, she led her sobbing son home.

EARLY OCTOBER

'There's Jenny, she's real cute and makes everybody laugh all the time. And Grace. Grace, I guess, is a really fine person. And Cassandra . . .' She sighed. 'Cassandra. I think that is the most beautiful name in the whole world. Cassandra. It really suits her, too. Cassandra's folks are very rich and live in a big old house on the other side of Olton, with stables and horses and a real lake in their garden. I'm going there for tea, soon. And Cassandra has a brother who goes to Sandhurst military college which is sort of like West Point only better. Cassandra's name is Hamilton-Weir, hyphenated, and when she grows up she is probably going to be a Lady.'

Lois let the tape run on, hissing softly. She tried to think of more details to confide about her new friends but other thoughts, the seed of a fear which threatened to bloom and spread, intruded. She reached out her hand and switched the recorder off. She sighed and picked up her pen and carefully, in her very neatest writing, inscribed the name 'Cassandra Hamilton-Weir' in her rough book. Such considerable magic as the name possessed for her didn't work now. It looked lumpen, dead upon the page. She closed the book and pushed it to the back of the desk, away from her. She folded her arms and put her head down on them, sighing again.

What do you want for your birthday, Lois?

There. It was out, admitted, faced. Her father always said that a fear faced was a fear conquered. It wasn't completely and entirely true, but she felt better. She did. The recalled words lacked any innocence, carried with them no spark of excitement. They were not an expression of friendship and care. They were *not*.

She sat up, pushing her chair back from the desk.

They were going to ruin everything, everything, and there was nothing she could do to stop them.

Vanessa's question, posed that morning on the school bus, had brought her thudding back to reality. Of course she hadn't forgotten about her birthday. She had been planning it carefully, with strategy and cunning, waiting for the right moment to spring it on her parents. She had dreamed of a small, sophisticated party, something elegant and refined, with no party games and all the girls in long dresses. There would be soft, low-key lighting, music in the background and a fruit-cup, made with real wine. There would be Grace and Jenny and Cassandra, of course, and possibly Marcia Timson and maybe Sandra Bull. And Barry Carter, if she could figure out a way of asking him without embarrassing herself.

She sighed again, not now with disappointment but at the beauty and rightness of it all. The perfumed, candle-lit air. The sophisticated menu that would be crowned with an ice-cream birthday cake. She saw her mother in a black dress, with white cap and apron, serving them politely from the left and her father, handsome, smiling on them from a corner. She, perhaps, would wear a corsage and gracefully dip her nose into its fragrance from time to time, sharing a secret look with Barry Carter. That was because sometimes, in her imagination, Barry arrived at the door with the corsage held lightly in his hand and Cassandra helped to pin it on, admiring her.

But it was no good. She snapped back into the present and her room looked ugly. The glare from the anglepoise lamp hurt her eyes, showed up the scratches and other marks of wear on her cassette recorder. She switched off the light and went to the window, looking out at darkness, at nothing.

Light spilled into the Youngs' garden and she glimpsed William moving back and forth between the rabbit hutches and the house, heard distant pop music playing from a radio. She felt almost warm towards William. At least *he* wouldn't expect to be invited to some stupid, childish, boring birthday party. But the others, with whom she still shared a pretence of friendship, would obviously have it in mind. The thought of her new friends, of Cassandra especially, mixing with Amanda and Andy, those awful twins, made her skin shrivel with embarrassment. Never. It was impossible. But she knew, without even having to ask, what her parents would say. So there could be no party, no party at all. Her birthday was doomed to be grey and empty, uncelebrated. And it was all *their* fault.

But if there was no party, nothing, she thought, then there could be no . . . Not that they would, not that they could. It wouldn't be fair. She'd already done it. With a shiver and a sinking feeling of panic far worse that anything she had felt at the time, she remembered standing on that window ledge, shut out, in peril. So even if they were crazy enough to think . . . Well, anyway, there would be no chance because no party. Goodbye, dreams, she thought with melodramatic sadness, and turned away from the window.

She started, caught her breath. Her own mirror image startled her. In the room's darkness, the white of her face floated, disembodied, in the waiting mirror. She stood still, faced herself, featureless, pale enough to cause reflection and admitted:

I'm scared.

'Look, if she doesn't want a party she doesn't have to have one.'

'It's not as simple as that,' Pearl argued, stacking dishes. 'She has obligations. *We* do. All the other kids have invited her. We owe them. It's expected.'

'Are you seriously trying to tell me,' Neil said, placing himself deliberately against the draining board, 'that some crazy notion of social obligation counts more with you than what Lois wants?'

'It's not only that,' she said, embarrassed. 'But it's

important. You want us to fit in, be a part of the community . . . It's the way things are done here.'

' "It's not only that," ' Neil mimicked, moving back to the table, 'but it sure as hell sounds like it and I think it's . . .' At a loss for the word, he blew a raspberry.

'You've got a hell of a short memory, haven't you?' Pearl flared, turning from the sink to challenge him. 'Have you really forgotten last year, how miserable she was, what *you* promised her for this year?'

'No. I remember. The point is, kids don't live in the past. They have a different concept of time. To herself, she's an entirely different person now. She won't even remember how she felt then. She's only interested in what she wants now, and that happens not to include a party, whether it pleases or offends your snobbish neighbours.'

'And you think you know her,' Pearl said in disgust, turning back to the sink and beginning to wash the dishes.

'What's that supposed to mean?'

'I should have thought it was simple enough, even for you.'

'I don't know my own daughter, huh?'

'Don't shout.'

'I don't know her just because I *want* to do what she wants. What kind of logic is that?'

'She may want it now,' Pearl said, stretching her patience to the limit, 'but on the day . . . She's trying to be grown-up and sophisticated but she's still a kid at heart and on the day she'll want all the trimmings. That's what knowing her means.'

Neil considered several possible arguments and rejected all of them. He went to the door.

'Just concentrate on the goddamn dress she wants, okay?'

He did not wait for an answer. Pearl shook suds from her hands and pulled out the plug to let the water drain away. Yes, she thought, she'd find the dress and she'd think of a way to make things right for Lois because she could not bear a repetition of last year. She could not and she would not.

'Anyway, Cassandra understands,' Lois told her cassette recorder. Doubt crept into her voice. 'At least, I think she does. She said she sympathized. She remembered how *awful* it had been when she'd had to have all her little cousins and things to her birthday party. Cassandra prefers a small gathering of close friends, but this year her brother was home from Sandhurst military college and he had friends staying so it was much more a grown-up sort of affair and all the young men asked Cassandra to dance in turn. Gee, I wish I'd known her then.' Lois stared into the middle distance, her chin cupped in her hands. 'Anyway, Cassandra said "Que sera, sera" and how they always have a big dance at Christmas, with a proper band and everything, and most probably I'll be able to go to that.'

There was a tap at the door and Neil's head appeared around it.

'Hi, Daddy.' She switched off the machine.

'Am I interrupting anything?'

'No.'

He came into the room, closing the door behind him.

'Homework done?'

'Yeah.'

'I just wanted to check with you that it's really okay about your birthday.'

'Going out with you and Mom, you mean, to a restaurant?'

'Right.'

'Yes, sure. Terrific.'

'Honey . . .' He hesitated.

'No, Daddy. I'd really like that, really. As long as I can have my riding lesson first.'

'Of course you can, sweetheart. We agreed all that.'

'Only that's really important to me and the best birthday present I ever had.'

'Oh . . . I guess we can improve on that.'

'No, Daddy, really. If I can just get to ride, then Cassandra says I can go over to her place any time and ride with her.'

'This Cassandra,' he said carefully, 'she's pretty important to you, huh?'

'She's my best friend,' Lois replied simply. 'Oh, and Daddy, she is just the most sophisticated and elegant person . . .'

'Okay, okay. I'm sold already. I love her. Just as long as you're *sure* . . .'

'I've told you. I really want to go out with you.'

'And me with you, sweetheart. Hey, I've heard about this great new restaurant, too, where you can get . . .'

'Oh yes, I've been meaning to ask you about that. Cassandra says The Mill at Dovington is out of this world. Real medieval timbers and a mill race and the most scrummy *duck à l'orange* in the county.'

Neil looked at her. 'Scrummy' – what kind of word was that? Riding lessons and medieval timbered restaurants? She was becoming another person.

'Okay, Miss Sophisticate,' he said, forcing a grin. 'But you tell Cassandra that her recommendation had better be good.'

'Oh, it will. She said you'd probably enjoy the Chablis, too. It's supposed to be light and distinctive.'

'I'll remember that,' he promised, not knowing whether to laugh or shake her. 'You coming down? *Star Trek* in ten minutes.'

'No. I think I'll stay up here. Cassandra lent me a book about eventing.'

He looked blank. Besides, she never missed *Star Trek*.

'Oh, Daddy, you know – like Princess Anne does.'

'Oh, right. Sure. But do me a favour – learn to ride first, okay?'

She laughed and did not see how he shook his head as he left the room.

Jesus Christ, he thought, I'm getting a fledgling British aristocrat for a daughter, and me a Democrat.

So it was all fixed. It was all going to be all right. Maybe now she could uncross her fingers. Maybe now the dreams would stop. Weird, terrible dreams in which all her former friends had gaunt, death's-head faces, were themselves aged and riven, dying, and looked at her out of the shadows of some vast, empty room. They said things to her that she couldn't understand but that didn't matter or make it any less frightening. She knew that they intended her harm, pain, hurt. She didn't know how it would start or how end, only that it would, that it was unavoidable and would be more awful than anything she could ever imagine. In the last dream, as she perambulated through the endless, shadowy room, fearing at any moment that they would jump her, she had seen salvation, had seen hope. Turning, turning in the distance, spotlit, dancing in a beautiful satin gown, she had seen Cassandra. She had cried her name and run towards her, closer, closer, until she could almost touch her. Cassandra's back had been to her and then, as she slowly turned in the figure of her dance, her face hadn't been Cassandra's at all, but William's, chalk-white. He had opened his mouth in a ghastly smile and blood had run from it, run down his chin and on to the curious dress he wore. His hands had stretched for her throat.

Well, all that was over. She knew about dreams and stuff and now that her mind was at rest, they'd just stop, go away. She'd been lucky, really. She acknowledged it. Her parents hadn't even tried to make her have a party and they'd been super about the riding lessons. Even the kids hadn't been too bad. The twins had moaned a bit and said it wasn't fair, but they hadn't gone on and on about it. She supposed they didn't really care any more. The thought struck her sharply, for the first time. Well, that was good, that was okay. A whole chapter of her life was closing – she could almost feel it – and another was opening. She couldn't wait to be good enough to go riding with Cassandra. Oh, and it would be just great comparing notes with her about The Mill at Dovington and the deliciousness of the *duck à l'orange*, which she fully intended to order. None of the other girls had been to the Mill at Dovington. Marcia Timson didn't even know what *duck à l'orange* was. But she and Cassandra knew and this time next year they'd be riding together, side by side, and would eat *duck à l'orange* every single day of the week.

31 OCTOBER

Pearl came downstairs in a terrific new fitted cotton suit, smelling of her best perfume.

'I've laid out her dress. I think that's everything . . .'

'Relax. You look good enough to eat. Did I tell you that?'

Pleased, she looked up at him, flushing a little.

'Really? You don't think it's too jazzy?'

'No. I think it's gorgeous. I particularly like the way it clings to your ass,' he said, grabbing at her.

'Neil! Oh . . . the corsage. Did you remember the . . .?'

'In the fridge. Go take a look.'

'No. If you say . . .'

'Please. I insist. Put your own mind at rest.'

He sketched a bow and ushered her into the kitchen. There was a frosted pitcher of martinis on the table, two glasses.

'Oh, Neil . . .' she said.

'Go check the corsage, then you can thank me.'

He watched her, eyes shining, as she walked across the tiled floor and opened the fridge. The automatic light caught her under the chin, highlighting her face, making the change from puzzlement to delight dramatic.

'But there are two . . . Oh Neil, darling . . . Oh you didn't . . .'

He reached around the door and lifted out one of the two clear plastic boxes.

'I couldn't have Lois outshining you. Here, let me pin it on.'

'They're beautiful. Gardenias.'

'Hold still.'

He leaned close to her, pinning the three waxy-white

flowers on their bed of shiny green to her lapel. She kissed his cheek.

'This is ridiculous – and wonderful,' she said.

'You know something? I think you're more excited than she will be.'

'And you're not?'

'Maybe. Now, if madam will kindly step this way, we just have time for a martini or two before she gets home.'

'You think of everything.'

'A martini and an apology.'

She took the glass from his fingers and looked at him, momentarily anxious.

'Apology?'

'Yep. You were right and I was wrong. So here's to a great evening.'

'And to Lois. If it wasn't for her . . .'

'I know. But that's the toast for the second drink.'

'Neil, I'll be tipsy before we even start.'

'No, you won't. Listen, we have ten minutes to ourselves. Let's enjoy her birthday our way.' He raised his glass, saluting her. 'I love you.'

'I love you, too.'

They touched glasses and drank to it.

Nobody, nobody in the entire world could fall off a horse that was just walking round a stable yard. It was a physical impossibility. And it hurt.

Standing at the bus stop, her pride battered rather more than her right hip, on which she had landed, Lois wondered what Cassandra *saw* in riding. They were difficult to get on and they put their heads down when you were least expecting it. She would never understand where all those straps and things went and even Miss Jenks, the instructress, admitted they'd all be stiff tomorrow. Maybe, like periods, it got better with time, she thought ruefully. Because she wouldn't give it up, not even if she fell off every week for the next year, no matter how much they laughed at her. She wondered if she should tell Cassandra about the 'tumble' as Miss Jenks called it, or whether she could sort of gloss that over? Maybe tomorrow she could just concentrate on talking about The Mill at Dovington and not mention the riding lesson. She cheered up a little at the thought of the evening ahead. She would be able to wear her new dress and open her presents, though right now she rather wished she hadn't asked for all those riding books.

She saw the bus round the corner, its lights looking smoky in the hazy dusk, and bent down, wincing at the soreness in her hip, to collect up her schoolbag and the plastic bag which contained her school skirt and shoes, her blazer. Loaded, aware of the growing stiffness in her hip, she climbed aboard the bus, flashed her pass at the driver and slumped miserably in a seat.

It didn't *feel* like her birthday at all. All day, chattering every moment she could with Cassandra, it had been anticipation: the riding lesson and dinner at The Mill in Dovington. But the damn stupid riding lesson had gone wrong. It was as though all anticipation, even the possibility of pleasure, had been knocked out of her with the force of impact when she fell and they all laughed. Even Miss Jenks laughed. Why, she wondered, did nothing ever turn out right? Her eyes misted as she stared at the darkling landscape through the transparency of her own reflection in the bus window. She saw familiar landmarks, knew that she would soon be home. None of the kids had given her a card or anything. Even Amanda had not wished her a happy birthday. And, of course, she couldn't say anything. But it hurt, just a little, and it certainly wasn't fair. After all she'd done for them. Just a few crummy cards wasn't asking too much.

The bus slowed and stopped outside the gate to Applegreen's farm. A woman climbed aboard, complaining about the weather to the driver. Lois stared at her dully, her lower lip stuck out.

'Cheer up, my duck,' the woman said as she struggled down the aisle. 'It might never happen.'

Fat lot *she* knew. It already had. And far worse than that was the tight little knot of tension in her stomach. Not the sort you get when you're excited, looking forward to something, but the kind that is a dread, a presentiment of something ghastly to come. Her hands, as she leaned down to pick up her belongings, were surprisingly slick with sweat. Maybe, she thought, she was coming down with a bug or something. That would just about be her luck.

The driver stopped by the verge at the end of the Crescent and wished her goodnight. She answered him and climbed down the steps, her hip paining her, and stood there, meaning to re-arrange her bags but not doing it. Stood there, aware of the bus drawing away, cars passing, and of the unlit entrance to the Crescent waiting for her. Suddenly she did not want to walk up there alone. She was scared. She told herself not to be stupid, redistributed her bags and set off, her steps faltering with more than the nagging ache in her hip.

She passed through the narrow part of the entrance and got on to the pavement where she could see the Shillingworths' porch light on, the glowing upstairs windows of the Mercers' opposite. It was quiet. Quiet enough to hear the wind, which she could scarcely feel down on the ground, rattling the twigs of the big tree which partially masked her own house.

The knot in her stomach grew tighter, larger. There were shadows, people, them, moving under the tree, in the blackest part, where no light penetrated.

She walked on, her heart thumping, not daring to cross the road, not caring how stupid it looked if anyone should see her. She would follow the footpath right the way round, keep near what light there was. She saw Marge Beatty flit across the uncurtained window of her kitchen, and that was no comfort. She could scream and holler until she was blue in the face before Mrs Beatty would do anything to help her.

No lights at all in the Hunters' house. What was that? She spun round, towards the tree, where it was dark and ominous. Nothing rushed out at her but the sense that it might, that it could, would, grew stronger, more certain. It was from that very shadow that she had rushed just a year ago, her Daddy's old raincoat around her shoulders like a witch's cape.

Trick or treat. Trick or treat.

Their blank white faces, cold and staring. Mrs Beatty's imperious manner, her clacking high heels. Oh, how she wished now that she had not. If only she had waited, waited for Cassandra Hamilton-Weir, then none of this would have happened, would be happening.

Her head turned always to the tree, she walked on, past the dark Hunters', round the curve of the Crescent.

There was an explosion, a rattling rush of noise that ended in a crack. She jumped nearly out of her skin and a little cry escaped her.

'Hello, Lois.'

She thought she was going to wet her pants, die.

'Did I startle you? Sorry. Just putting the car away.'

She smiled, somehow, with relief, with a feeling of weakness. It was just Mr Young, standing in front of his garage door.

'And a very happy birthday,' he said. 'Enjoy yourself tonight and remember – don't do anything I wouldn't.'

'Right. Thanks.'

Her voice sounded strange, weak and breathless, but he didn't seem to notice. She began walking then, quickly, past their own car, still out on the road, waiting to take them to The Mill at Dovington and up the path, into the light.

'Here she is. Happy birthday, darling.'

Her father swept her into the hall. The house was warm and good-smelling, safe. She put down her bags, caught the martinis on his breath.

'We've already been celebrating,' her mother said. 'Happy birthday.'

As she accepted her mother's embrace, her father said, 'Now shoot upstairs and get into that tub. You've got a busy night ahead.'

'I've laid out your dress, darling . . . Hurry up now.'

'Okay.'

She moved in a dream of relief, feeling sick and dizzy, to the foot of the stairs.

'Hey, how was the riding lesson?'

It was too much for her.

'I fell off,' she wailed.

Just in time, Neil managed to re-arrange his features, stifle the impulse to laugh. He caught Pearl's warning glance.

'Never mind. Everybody does. It's all part of it,' Pearl said quickly.

'Did you hurt yourself?'

'Yes. My hip. It's all sore and stiff.'

'A good soak'll put that right. Shall I look at it for you?'

'No.'

'Go on then, and make yourself beautiful.'

She nodded and went slowly up the stairs. Neil winked at Pearl, and led her, like a conspirator, into the kitchen.

'One more martini before the balloon goes up?'

'Why not?'

She laughed and checked her watch.

The dress was moss green, speckled with tiny pink rosebuds. It had a scoop neck and big puff sleeves. It was held in at the waist with a velvet sash to which Pearl fastened the corsage.

'You look beautiful, Lois.'

She meant it. There stood before her a young woman, prettily dressed, hair gleaming, skin soft and flawless.

'Go down and let Daddy see you.'

Maybe it was the martinis but there was a lump in Neil's throat as he watched her descend the stairs.

'Happy birthday, Princess.' He folded her in his arms, hugging her tight.

'That's enough, you two,' Pearl said. 'It's time we were going.'

'Right,' Neil agreed, releasing his daughter. 'I'll just go and open up the car. You get the lights and everything, okay?'

He left the front door open and went down the path whistling 'Happy Birthday'. Pearl went to the doorway, peered out as though looking for something.

'It's a bit chilly,' she said. 'I think I'll take my white stole after all. Would you fetch it for me, Lois? I put it in the lounge, just in case.'

'Sure.'

Lois walked across the hall and opened the lounge door. She reached for the light switch automatically but the room was already lit by a fluttering golden glow. She caught her breath. A series of crude, skeletal faces stared at her.

'Surprise! Surprise!'

'Happy birthday.'

'Many happy returns of the day.'

'Surprise!'

She heard her mother's laughter pealing out behind her and turned towards the sound, in flight from them as they surged forward, towards her. She stopped at once, her head reeling. William stood in the open doorway his hands cupped beneath a large pumpkin lantern, inside which a candle flickered. He smiled at her shyly.

'Happy birthday, Lois.'

He walked towards her. She saw her father on the step, smiling.

'Daddy?'

'This isn't your present, of course,' William said gravely. 'I've got that in my pocket. Can I put this down somewhere?'

'Surprised, sweetheart?' Neil asked, grinning and hugging Pearl against his side.

'But I'm going with you,' she cried, stepping around William and running to him.

'No, sweetheart. That was just a cover. The old folks are going out for the night so you can have a proper grown-up party of your own.'

'No!'

'Enjoy it, darling,' Pearl said and blew her a kiss.

'I've got to . . .'

''Bye, darling.'

'Have a good time.'

They closed the door in her face. Not going to The Mill at Dovington? She stared at the door, at the polished grain of the wood as though she had never seen it before, as though it would melt. She heard them whispering and giggling, rustling behind her. The sound, like a cold wind stirring dead leaves, propelled her forward. She fumbled with the door, her sweating hands slipping from the latch.

'Wait,' she shouted.

She got the door open and stumbled out in time to see the twin red tail-lights of the car turning out of the Crescent on to the main road. The knot in her stomach broke then. A sound escaped her, part muffled scream, part sob of desolation.

'Come on, Lois. We want to start the party.'

Very slowly, she turned around. William stepped back, holding the door for her, welcoming. She felt cold suddenly in her thin dress and crossed her arms over her chest. Like an automaton, she walked back into the house. The door closed behind her. They were all in the hall, standing, watching her. Their faces were blank, neutral. All except the eyes. Their eyes glittered, contained an eagerness which made her tremble.

'You go first,' William said. 'Go and see how great it is.'

They formed a sort of guard of honour, two rows fanning out from the lounge door. Still hugging herself, she walked between them into the room and it was like stepping into one of her dreams.

The furniture had been pushed back, re-arranged, giving

an appearance of space, of emptiness. It was lit entirely by candles, most of them in pumpkin and gourd lanterns of all sizes, carved with the hideous features of monsters, some in individual holders. There was a long table against the wall, laden with food, towards which she drifted. The sandwiches were labelled, plates of cold meat, potato salad. Light danced on the cut-glass punch bowl. She stared at these things intently, aimlessly.

'Isn't it beautiful?'

'You are lucky, Lois.'

'Here, let me serve you. You're the guest of honour.'

'Surprised?'

'I nearly died not letting on.'

'You would.'

They gathered around William who stood, proprietorially, at the punch bowl. He filled a small glass and held it out to her.

'It's got Sangria in it. Real hard stuff.'

'Lois?'

She unfolded her arms and took the glass.

'That's a beautiful dress, Lois. Where did you get it?'

'Here you are, Vanessa. Catch hold.'

'I'm hungry.'

'In a minute.'

She moved across the room which seemed to stretch in twisted perspective away from her and sat down on the couch. Her knees were trembling.

'A toast,' William shouted.

She looked up at him, at all of them gathered round him, looking at her, smiling, their glasses held ceremoniously.

'To Lois on her birthday, many happy returns.'

They repeated it after him, a ragged chorus, and drank greedily, exclaiming.

'Can we eat now?'

'In a minute.'

Amanda ran towards her, offered a package wrapped in silver paper.

'Happy birthday.'

'Thanks.' Her throat was dry, her voice cracking. She drank from her glass, not tasting. Somebody took it from her. More presents were thrust into her hands, on to her lap. She did not know whether she smiled, thanked them. The gifts surrounded her, slipped from her lap.

'And here's something from me.'

William stood in front of her, holding out a slim box fastened with a pink ribbon twisted into a rosette.

'Aren't you going to open it?'

'And mine.'

'Yes, come on, Lois. Then we can eat.'

'Oh go and eat.'

'Only leave some for us.'

'Surprised . . .' she said weakly.

'Have another drink.' William held out her glass, refilled.

'Thanks.'

She drank and set the glass aside, slid the ribbon from the box William had given her. The ends of her fingers felt numb, her palms damp. She lifted out a crush of tissue paper.

'It'll bring you luck,' William told her.

'Yes.'

'What is it?'

'Let's see.'

She lifted it out, not touching the stump of fur, but looping the thong about her fingers.

'Oh. What is it?'

'A rabbit's foot pendant,' William said and smiled, pleased with himself.

'Nice.'

'Open the others, Lois. Come on.'

She dropped the rabbit's foot back into its box and put it aside. It was hateful, ugly. She fell upon the other parcels, anxious to get it over with, glad of the distraction. William stood aside, watching her all the time. There was a silk scarf, decorated with twirling ballerinas, a book called *Pam's Pony*, an Elton John album which William took from her and put on the record player. She stared at her gifts, handled them but felt nothing. She did not feel real, was waiting to wake up, for the room to melt away.

William said, 'I wanted to be friends again.' He was sitting beside her, turned to face her. The others were gathered around the table, talking, eating. 'I didn't want there to be any hard feelings, you know?'

She looked at him, her face drawn and pale. He frowned a little, as though he did not understand.

'I'm sorry,' she said and felt tears threatening. 'I . . .'

'Come on,' he interrupted her. 'Better get something to eat before Andy wolfs the lot.'

He caught her wrist, pulled her up, drew her across the room to the table. She stared down at the food, her stomach contracting, knowing that she could not eat.

'Hey, what about your cake? Isn't it pretty?'

She had not noticed the cake or wondered about it. Now she looked at it. White, circular, trimmed in pink, her name in icing across the top, thirteen pink candles in rosebud holders.

'Are you going to cut it now?'

'She hasn't had anything to eat yet.'

'You're still eating.'

'I . . . I'm not hungry. I'd like . . .' She reached for a jug of apple juice and, unsteadily, poured herself a glass. She drank it down in three noisy gulps. As she lowered the glass she saw that they were all staring at her. Their faces were very white. Andy's mouth munched and munched. Julian tried to smile but it wouldn't take. She put the glass down blindly, held by their eyes. It clattered against something, slipped, crashed on the floor, breaking. 'What . . . why are you staring?'

Vanessa looked away, embarrassed. The record player clicked off with a sharp, metallic sound.

'I'll do it,' William said, breaking the silence.

'Have you had one of these? They're great.'

'Hey, that's the last sausage roll . . .'

'Pass the cold chicken.'

'You'll be sick.'

'Don't be daft. I could eat all this and more.'

'Pig.'

It was like they could not see her, as though she had become invisible. As though she was the dream and they . . .

'All right, okay,' she said, the loudness of her voice cutting through their chatter, silencing them. They looked at her expectantly. The beat of the music throbbed in her head so that she couldn't remember what it was she wanted to say. 'Stop staring,' she said. 'Please. Just stop looking at me.' She covered her face with her hands. They did not speak and not being able to see them, only to feel their silence, inquisitive and threatening, was worse. Then she found it, seemed to stumble across it in her mind: the lesson she had learned, on which she must act. She dropped her hands. 'Okay,' she said. 'Let's have it. Let's get it over with.' They stared at her, stupid incomprehension on their stupid faces. She leaned forward, bracing her arms against the table. 'Oh come on . . . You know . . . you know. So let's have it. Let's get it over with. I'm not scared. Come on.'

'What's she talking about?' Julian asked his brother. Jason shook his head.

'Quit fooling,' she yelled and struck the table with her fist, making the crockery rattle. 'What have you been planning and working up?'

'She's crazy,' Andy said. Vanessa dug him in the ribs with her elbow.

'Nothing,' William said, taking charge. 'She thinks we're going to play some trick on her,' he told the others.

'Oh. No.'

'We gave that up. *You* said.'

'I don't believe you,' she said.

'Well it's true.' William took her arm. She shook him off. 'Come and light your candles. We all want a piece of cake even if you don't.'

Lois shrank back against the wall.

'You mean it? You're really not . . . ?'

'Look at her,' Andy said. 'She's really scared.'

'Nothing,' William repeated. He held her eyes for a moment. She shook her head. 'I'll light the candles for you, then.' He kicked shards of glass under the table.

William struck a match and held it to the candles, one by one, until they caught and burned prettily.

'Oh, doesn't it look lovely?' Amanda said.

'Come on, Lois. Blow them out and make a wish.'

Her eyes fixed on the glowing cake, Lois pushed away from the wall, walked towards them.

'Just a minute. I forgot something,' William added.

'Really? Nothing?' she said.

William went over to the record player and switched it off. He took a cassette from his pocket and slipped it into the slot, adjusted the controls.

'Okay, now,' he said.

Their voices, amplified, burst out of the speakers.

Happy birthday to you
Happy birthday to you
Happy birthday, dear Lo-is
Happy birthday to you

She bent over the cake. Her hair swung forward, brushed the flames. She heard it fizz and jerked back. Somebody seized the hand she raised to hold it back, twisted it behind her. William's hand clamped on the back of her neck, pressing and holding her over the cake. Her hair swung again, frizzled. She could smell it.

'My hair . . .'

The heat from the candles tickled her skin. She twisted her head, began to struggle. Only then did she become aware of the many hands holding her. She tried to kick but her foot slipped and one of the little flames licked her cheek, hurting. A hand pushed down on the top of her head. Three flames pricked her cheek. She pushed back against the hands, heard the horrid sizzle of her hair. The flames burned, maddening her cheek, sharper than the savage grip on the back of her neck.

'Make a wish, Lois,' William said. 'Make a wish, go on.'

They pushed then, releasing her. Her face struck the cake, breaking the icing. Cream spurted. Candles toppled. One dug painfully into her right eye. Sponge and cream squidged into her nose, her open mouth. A hand on the back of her head pushed down hard, ground her face into the ruined cake. She coughed and spluttered, swallowed something that lodged in her throat. She heard laughter cutting through the still-singing voices, issuing from the speakers. The old custard pie routine, she thought. Good. A good one, William.

Happy birthday, dear Lo-is
Happy birthday . . .

No one was holding her now. Coughing, she lifted her head. Blind, her cheek smarting, she turned and began to wipe the mess from her face, shaking it from her fingers on to the floor, the table. Absurdly, she thought, Mom'll kill me for this. Kill me. She winced as she touched the burned spot on her cheek.

'Hey . . .' she said, trying harder than she had ever tried to make a joke of it.

She wiped her eyes again, spat. The front of her dress was covered in cake and cream, jam. Looking down, she saw that the corsage was ruined, must have been pressed against the edge of the table. She touched it sadly with shaking fingers, saw a crushed petal fall.

The tape went on and on, endlessly repeating:

Happy birthday to you
Happy birthday, dear Lo-is

'You guys . . .' she said, trying to make her breathlessness sound like laughter. 'You guys sure . . .' She blinked, lifted her head, looked at them.

They encircled her, white-faced, not smiling. They each held a candle. A long red one in Vanessa's hand, in the others' thick, white, stumpy ones. The light of their various flames dazzled her, held her mesmerized.

'Pretty . . .' she said, leaning towards them.

'It *was* blood,' Vanessa said. 'You made me drink blood. Jason and Julian told me.'

The twins murmured, nodded their heads in unison. They stared boldly at Lois, not afraid of her any more.

'Just a little . . .' she whispered. 'Not enough to . . .'

'And then you lied to me, pretended to be my friend. That's the worst of all,' Vanessa went on. 'You lied to me because you wanted me to be your friend. That's horrible. That's the worst thing of all.'

'And you knew what was in that cupboard,' Amanda accused, stepping forward. 'You pretended to make such a fuss and look after me and everything, when all the time you did, you knew . . .'

'Oh no,' Lois said, shaking her head. 'That was *his* idea.' She looked at William. 'You want to ask him about that before you go accusing people . . .'

Amanda turned slightly towards William.

'You killed Oliver,' he said levelly, his eyes fixed on Lois's face.

'No, I never . . . How could you . . . I only let him go. I never killed him. I swear to you . . . I wouldn't do a thing like that. I couldn't.'

'Says you,' sneered Vanessa.

'You could have killed Jason,' Julian said. 'You didn't worry about that, so why should we believe you?'

'How can you prove you didn't kill Oliver?' William asked in the same, unemotional voice.

'I give you my word . . .' she began but they only jeered at her. 'Okay. I can't prove it. But *I* know I didn't. So there.'

'And I suppose that's what you'd've said if Jason had fallen and broken his neck.'

'He didn't fall. It was all safe.'

'Did you try it? Did you test those chains yourself?'

She looked away from Julian's flushed, angry face.

'The point we're trying to make,' William said, taking on the roles of Judge and Interpreter, 'is that you took risks with our lives that *could* have ended in death or injury and you had no right to do that. Worse, you didn't care.'

'And what about you?' Lois shouted. 'I didn't risk my neck when you shut me out on that ledge, I suppose? It's okay for you to go risking people's lives . . .'

'No. It isn't. We've talked about that . . .' William glanced at the others who nodded their agreement. 'I know I was wrong to shut that window. I've apologized and I've never stopped feeling bad about it. But two wrongs don't make a right.'

'Oh, that's easy to say. You just chicken out, William, whenever the going gets rough.'

'You didn't care what happened to us,' Vanessa said.

'You could have injured Andy. You never stopped to think that your hand might slip . . .'

'He asked for it. You all agreed,' Lois protested.

'Why?' William demanded. 'Why did we agree?'

'Because you wanted to, because you were having fun and now you've all got chicken about it . . .'

'We were scared of you,' Julian said. 'We were all scared of you.'

'So? That's my fault? Just because you're a lot of chicken kids . . .'

'That's right. That's what you thought about us, wasn't it? Just a lot of kids who didn't matter.'

'And if anything had ever happened to one of us, you'd have made sure that we took the blame.'

'Sure, because you went along with it. You did it, just as much as me.'

'Just like you did what I wanted, when it suited you,' Andy said.

Lois stared at him in amazement. She couldn't believe this. Blood crept agonizingly up her neck to burn in her cheeks.

'All the time you were saying how dirty he was,' Vanessa said viciously, 'you were letting him look at you and do whatever he wanted. Then you punish him for it, using us to help you.'

'Hypocrite,' William said.

'He blackmailed me . . .'

'How? What did you have to hide?' William challenged her.

Lois shook her head, her cheeks still flaming. There was a long silence during which William looked hard at each of the others in turn. They nodded, as though agreeing to some unspoken proposal or question.

'What's this?' Lois asked, her voice suddenly small and uncertain.

'We've all talked about this,' William answered, 'and we don't care any more that you hurt us and put some of us in danger but we accuse you, all of us, of betraying our friendship. You made us swear loyalty to your gang, but you were never loyal to us . . .'

'Okay. So I screwed up. I'm sorry.'

'You used us,' Vanessa said with hatred.

'You were jealous of us,' Jason said.

'Jealous? Of you? A bunch of dumb kids . . . You think I'd be . . .' She stopped, bit the tip of her tongue. Their stony faces were out of a nightmare, accusing her.

'And you set us against each other,' William said.

'And now,' Amanda piped up, 'you want to forget about us because you've got Cassandra . . .'

'Oh, I get it. You're the jealous ones because I've found a friend of my own age with whom I have something in common at last.'

'You were never our friend,' William repeated.

'No.'

'Never.'

'We weren't good enough . . .'

'Oh yeah? And what about you? Since you're all so riled up about friendship, what did you ever do for me? When I moved in here, did any of you try and make friends? You were all too stuck up and British for that. What did you do, that night, when I came trick or treating? You laughed at me. You said I was a crazy person. All of you were having a good time. You'd all been to your Hallowe'en party and I had nothing. And it was my birthday. But you didn't care. You didn't care that I was miserable and lonely and . . . and . . . had nothing . . . and no one . . .' Tears were suddenly streaming down her face. She stamped her foot in anger. 'You should have tricked or treated,' she wailed. 'You should have.'

'Why? What makes you so special?'

'Cry-baby. Look at her.'

'She's pathetic.'

'Just a big bully.'

'Okay,' she screamed at them, wiping her tears away. 'You're right. Damn good and right. I hated you and I swore I was going to make you as miserable as I was. But *you* started it. A bunch of dumb kids . . . Well, it's over, finished. You can all go back to your stupid homes and your stuck-up parents and take your goddamn presents with you.'

'Not yet,' William said in a voice that made her blood run cold. 'You still owe us. We've planned a little treat for you. Right, gang?' He smiled then, a ghastly, pallid smile.

'What?' she said, her heart thudding.

Nobody answered. Nobody moved.

'If you think I'm scared . . . Go ahead. Do your worst.'

She took a step towards them. Vanessa instantly raised her candle, flicked it under Lois's nose.

'Hey,' she said, backing off, 'go careful. You shouldn't go messing with fire.'

'Or chains.'

'Or spiders and worms.'

'Blood.'

'Oliver.'

'Scissors,' Andy shouted and thrust his candle hard into her face.

Hot wax spattered on to her throat and chest. She jerked back, lurched against the table, sprawled on it. Dishes cracked and broke beneath her. Cutlery and glass fell and rattled, shattered – the percussion of a nightmare.

Happy birthday, dear Lo-is

She tried to raise herself but Jason pinned her down, forcing her shoulders back. Vanessa held the red candle to her hair. It sizzled and flared for a moment. Another flame burned her chin. Hot wax dripped on to her face, solidified there. She saw Amanda's face, lips drawn back from her sharp, almost pointed teeth, before wax hit her already-smarting eye and sealed it.

'Oh God,' she moaned. 'Oh please God.'

They were shouting at her, screaming at her but she could not make out the words for:

Happy birthday to you
Happy birthday to you

chanting on and on.

Hands pulled her up. Crisp black smuts rained from her hair on to her shoulders, the table. Hands pulled so roughly at her arms that she heard the sleeve of her dress tear. They pushed her forward, twisted her unresisting arms behind her. They pushed her so hard that she stumbled, caught her foot in the hem of her dress and fell on to her knees. She heard the material rip just before her knees crashed against the floor, jarring pain through her which flowered in her bruised hip. They pulled her forward, hands in her hair, tugging. She could hear the hiss of their breath beneath the chanting tape. The back of her neck again, the gripping fingers seeming to fit naturally into the bruises already made.

The big pumpkin lantern, the one William had brought, was on the floor before her. It blazed with a host of candles packed into its hollow centre, so many that the skin and the flesh of the pumpkin were beginning to char and smell. The lantern seemed to rise up to meet her. The heat from it melted the wax on her face so that it dripped and ran like rainbow tears, splashing and sizzling into the furnace which fitted about her face. The heat seared her, went on growing until she felt her very flesh on fire. She was burning, taking flame. She saw herself red, gold, blackened. The smell blooming in her nose was the smell of her own roasting skin.

Her body became limp, surprising the hands that held her. She fainted, her conscious mind leaping through a hoop of fire into dark, consuming flames of pain.

Happy birthday, dear Lo-is
Happy birthday to you.

They stood amid the wreckage of the room, panting, drained by their efforts, shocked by her stillness. She didn't look real. She looked like a doll, a rag doll, torn and stained, tossed away unloved, fallen face down in a spew of shattered pumpkin shell and cooling candle grease. She looked, to all of them, smaller, as though she had shrunk.

The tape clicked off, startling them. Vanessa burst into tears.

'Wait outside,' William said. 'Wait in the hall.'

'Is she . . .?'

'Come on,' Jason told his brother. 'Best do as William says.'

They trooped out, in file, without looking back. Jason closed the door.

William looked around him at the broken crockery, the spattered cake, the strewn meats. The air smelled dry with the smoke of guttered candles.

Her foot moved, twitched, and then the whole leg straightened.

He squatted beside her, reached for her shoulder and pulled her over. Her arm fell out from her body, her knuckles rapped the wooden floor. William could hear her breathing, choked, difficult. He was surprised, not alarmed, that she did not cry out or moan. He stood up and walked slowly, with great deliberation, across the room to where a slim purple candle still burned. He lifted it carefully and carried it, with the same deliberation, back to her. By its flickering light he could see her face.

It looked as though her hair had been a wig all the time and that wig had slipped. Her forehead, red and streaked with black stains, had grown. Her right eye was puffed and swollen, milky. It seemed that the lid could not close and she had no lashes. For the rest, he recognized her beneath swellings, the red, crusty patches, the swollen, vicious blisters. As though her face had melted and re-formed. It was lumpy, misshapen, swollen on the right side. Icicles of coloured wax streaked her chin, dribbled frozen stains down her throat, across her chest towards her breasts. Red wax had solidified in the chain of her locket which winked and shone at him in the light.

She excited him, this sight of her. Her mauled, misshapen face latched and chimed with feelings in him that were nameless but which made him light and heady. Burning between his thighs. Hot and hard, jutting. He held the candle higher, to see her better. Her breasts rose and fell. A bubbling sound came from her throat. He put his left hand between his legs and squeezed. His face became dark with blood, tingling. His thighs trembled. The small of his back felt weak, liquid, melting. A grunt of effort, pleasure, escaped him. He snatched his left hand away, as though it had encountered electricity. His other hand, raised, shook, splashing lilac wax on to his arm, her chest. He tore the candle from its holder and inverted it, wax showering everywhere, the flame fluttering upwards, and drove it hard into her open, wounded eye. She tensed, her limbs flapping like broken wings, as he dug and ground and twisted the dead candle into her eye.

'That's for Oliver,' he panted, and doubled over, clutching himself.

The candle rolled away across the floor.

Her breath, drawn between parched lips, found a note, moaned.

William stood up awkwardly and went to the music centre, stiff-legged. He set the controls to re-wind, lowered the volume. His breathing, harsh and irregular, was louder than the mechanistic shush and shuttle of the tape. He felt the first wetness, stickiness against his belly: slippery, slimy.

The tape clicked off: a sharp crack of sound.

He pressed the play button.

As he reached the door, their voices sifted into the room, quiet, melodious, singing:

Happy birthday to you
Happy birthday to you
Happy birthday, dear Lo-is . . .

William ushered them out of the front door. Nobody spoke. He looked around the hall, at the closed doors, the shining woodwork, the dark green carpet on the rising stairs. He thought it better to leave the light on. Everything was as it should be.

William closed the front door behind him. Vanessa shivered with the cold. Mist, perhaps fog, threatened, made everything soft and hazy, unreal. Real was the damp patch on William's underpants, cloying to his unaccustomed skin.

'Hey,' Andy said and began to leap about the garden, kicking his legs out wildly, crooking and pointing his fingers. 'Trick or treat,' he screeched. 'Trick or treat.'

The others, all of them, laughed. . . .